FLAME OF THE PHOENIX

The Phoenix's Ashes, Book Four
A Circus of Shifters Adventure

By
Rebecca Ethington

Published by Imdalind Press

Production Management by Imdalind Press

ISBN (print) **978-1-949725-21-6**

ISBN (e-book) **978-1-949725-17-9**

Printed in USA

This Edition, February 2019

❀ Created with Vellum

For My Kids
Always.

1

ELLIOT

WALKING DOWN THIS LONG DARK CAVE WAS SO MUCH MORE frightening than it was the first time, and then I had assumed that I was wandering into the den of cave trolls.

I had found the trolls, and they were nothing like I had expected. No bubbly skin, no gross smells, and no clubs. Just a British man and a beautiful little girl who was apparently immune to dragon fire and liked to make things explode 'by just thinking about it'. Seemed legit.

If legit was also terrifying.

Mind numbingly terrifying.

I think I would have preferred the cave trolls with how the once nice-looking Brit was spouting off stories about how he had been my first mate. You know, from my first life, from a couple hundred years ago.

Like I was from a couple hundred years ago. I was still dealing with being in my mid-twenties instead of barely turned eighteen.

The world had clearly gone mad and any hope of me being able to follow his nonsense was becoming less of a possibility. So instead I followed the British troll while staring at him with all the intensity of someone who could shoot daggers out of their eyes.

Who knew, maybe it was another skill that would spark to life if I gave my knife-throwing stare more gusto.

It was worth a shot.

Go, eye daggers, go!

Of course, even if it did work, I might miss him altogether. The cave was dark enough that I couldn't see a damn thing. Jarron could, though, so I clung to him, planning a few other ways to get us out of this in case the eye daggers didn't work.

Like another feather jump, or blasting, or shifting and swallowing him whole.

Getting out of here was happening. Something about this guy was rubbing me the wrong way.

It was like meeting a long-lost friend, and not remembering why you stopped hanging out with them, but you know that it was something bad. Did you rob a store? Was there some kind of graveyard robbery involved? Was a dead cat in the picture? I had no way of knowing, and as much as he smiled and prattled on about happy memories I wasn't about to trust that either.

"I'm not surprised your phoenix brought you back to me," Henry said into the dark, his voice hovering somewhere ahead of us.

"It always finds its way home. To me. Although, this stint was quite longer than usual. I didn't think you could top that time after France, back during the revolution. It was a glorious explosion and caused quite a few issues for their war. Beautiful really, but after three years without you I was starting to grow concerned. This time, after more than a decade, I was beginning to think you had been intercepted and I would have to come retrieve you again," Henry continued on confidently, even though no one was responding to him.

Not that he cared, he was talking about himself like he was some kind of god and expected us to bow down, kiss his feet, and listen to him ramble.

An awkward shiver ran up my spine and Jarron's arm pressed me against him, his heart rate picking up so that his whole chest felt like it was rattling.

"But I never heard anything, even after I was able to bring Lilly here as we had planned. I had thought about moving, many times, but we built this place so long ago, and have so many memories here that it's almost like a homing beacon, for both of us. I hope it becomes that for Lilly as well, she's been through so much she deserves a bit of stability."

It may have been dark as sin, but Jarron was clearly giving me a sideways glance. The intensity of his stare was boring into me, and not because his eyes were little golden flecks in the dark. I didn't know how something that was so beautiful in the light could be so goddamned creepy now, but here I was, clinging to glowy eyed monster as he gave me a look that pretty much screamed exactly what I was thinking.

"It's been hard watching her grow up the way she has." Henry continued, prattling on as we continued our cave floor shuffle. "She reminds me of you so much. She had been waiting for so long to meet you. I am sure you are as excited to meet her."

If I ever got lost in this cave I could follow the breadcrumbs of this pathetic attempt at small talk that he was leaving behind. This guy was dropping every possible inlet into a conversation that he could. He clearly wanted to talk, but for some reason was waiting to be asked to disclose information. Like a child who is hungry but just likes to talk about how pretty the apples are.

Ask for the freaking apple already!

"There is so much you can teach her that I have been unable to. So much of your power is missing from her skills. I am excited to see you work together."

I may want all the answers to the breadcrumbs of curiosities, but I was in no mood to grab onto the lure he was feeding us, especially given that a bright spec of yellow light appeared in the distance.

You know, the one that had gotten us into this mess.

It didn't seem nearly as intriguing as it had before and I would have been quite happy to turn around and walk away. Would have too if it wasn't for super girl behind us, herding us toward whatever trap or cage was in the room ahead.

With the way she was smiling, still playing with a bit of Jarron's fire between her fingers, I wasn't about to mess with her.

I can blow people up with my mind.

"I am so glad you are home, Elliana."

Wasn't going to feed into that bait.

Good thing the guy seemed perfectly content to keep talking to himself.

"About five years ago I had really begun to lose hope that you hadn't been able to regenerate after your last death. I still have nightmares of it from time to time. I don't think I have ever seen you fall so terribly. And especially in a loss. You never lose. Not unless it is on purpose," Henry sighed, his lanky outline bobbing in and out of the speck of light and giving me a general idea of where he was. At least now I had a place to aim the eye daggers. "Neither of us expected him to make an appearance, and the moment he did I knew there was nothing we could do. Watching your wings being torn from your body was heart wrenching. I could only stand there as you fell."

What the fuck? My wings had been torn from my body? We went from revolutionary bombs, to securing children, to raising said children, to some mysterious *he* and now this. Forget leaving breadcrumbs of questions. This guy was leaving freaking boulders!

And one of them had landed right on me.

A massive hundred-ton weight, right on my chest. No wonder I was having trouble breathing, no wonder my spine was aching as if it had been torn in two.

No, as if the wings were ripped right out of it.

I really didn't want to believe anything that this guy was throwing at me, but at the mention of my most recent death, my very alive and very alert Phoenix retreated in a wave of panic that pressed against my heart. I could have sworn my back snapped together, the bones aching with a violent memory that I no longer held.

My Phoenix, however, remembered perfectly.

Shaking my head, I closed my eyes in an effort to expel the painful pressure that was trying to rip apart my bones. Closing my eyes may have been the worst choice, as with one flutter of my eyelids my mind was assaulted with ripples of red, yellow, and a deep azure sky. The colorful feathers of my flame rippled, cutting into the brightest blue sky I had ever seen.

Everything rippled as a different kind of fire wrapped over me. I had seen the spectra of my flame whenever I had flown and dived, but very rarely in the daytime. And never where people could see me, let alone me seeing myself. It wasn't safe, and yet there I was, diving through a beautiful blue sky.

No, not diving. Not soaring. There was nothing beautiful

in these movements. Nothing happy in the fire that was trailing through the sky right before me.

I was falling. Falling like a freaking rock. The flames grew in height as a splash of blood joined the imagery, something big and burning coiling away from me before I snapped my eyes open with a gasp. The memory left and I was back to staring at the cave and at Henry's perfectly outlined silhouette. We were so close to their little cave now that I could nearly see the plaid design on his flannel shirt, which was really not helping his whole "stressed out homemaker who sells paper towels" look.

It was an ugly shirt, and I would have loved to tell him so, but I was still having traumatic flashbacks with every blink, the intense stare that Jarron was giving me making it worse.

"It was quite the fall," Henry mused to himself, the dark chuckle that followed behind out of place against the idea that I had fallen right after my wings had been ripped from my body. You know, unless you were a sadist. And I wasn't ruling that classification out just yet. "I am glad you found your way home."

He turned then, the light framing around him and rippling off the rock until his face was full of so many shadows that he looked as far from human as you could get. Too many dark lines and angles to be alive. Jarron must had seen it too, because he attempted to push me behind him and took one large step closer to Henry.

Protector mode activate!

Which would have been great except that I was now directly in front of the eerie child in a poufy dress, the kid twirling Jarron's fire between her fingers.

Smiling like the creepy ass china doll she was.

"She isn't here to stay." Jarron's firm reprieve would have

been more effective if Lilly's smile didn't stretch, her teeth reflecting nearly as much of the yellow light as her eyes were. It wasn't a good look for her.

All of the warning lights were going off in my head, my phoenix was bristling, and I was sure my skin had begun smoking. Because a threat of explosion was what we needed in this situation.

I had never been so freaked out by a child before. I was one step away from turning this into a messed up horror movie and going all slasher film on her ass. You know, if I had something to 'slasher' with.

I looked away, not really wanting to see more, but Henry was looking just as much of a deranged psychopath as the girl, albeit without the dress.

I doubt putting the guy in a frilly dress would make him look any less creepy. He was smiling and bouncing on his toes as the shadows stretched over him until each swatch of black looked like it was coming from the inside.

And I thought the vampires looked scary with their marble skin.

"You are home, too, young prince." Henry stepped forward and some of those shadows dispersed, leaving him looking a little more human. Well, all except for the knowing glint in his dark as shit eyes.

Pure ice was running over my spine as Jarron and I stood frozen to the spot, the tension that was binding against his muscles nearly identical to my own. Prince. He had said prince. Henry had acted like he didn't even know Jarron's name and now he was calling him prince. I had thought this whole situation smelled bad, well now it was approaching dog fart status.

What the hell did we walk into?

Dog farts and murder, clearly.

Henry had said that he and Lilly had been working against Parris, so logically he should know who Jarron was. But then why play the game before? Why pretend that he had no idea?

Because he's clearly a sadistic cave troll, that's why.

Handsome lumberjack cave troll. Still a cave troll.

"Well, this is fucked," I mumbled and Henry turned, leaving Jarron and I to stare at each other as Henry walked toward the light. Maybe, if we were lucky, he would walk into it and disappear. Doubtful.

Keeping my eyes on the dog fart, I wrapped my hand around Jarron's and continued after the shadowed man, mostly because the little girl who had been herding us was now prodding our backs. I was surprised she didn't zap us like cattle.

"Hurry up! I don't want to miss my show," She whined from behind us, her voice mixed with the perfect combination of cute and malice to make everything freeze further.

Note to self: Next time there is a creepy light in the middle of a creepy cave, don't follow it. Just get out of there.

I could make out the furniture and rough painted walls of their cave now, the light bathing over us as we walked closer to the entrance.

"Lilly." Henry said from ahead, his voice oddly strained as he stepped nearer the light.

With all the confidence and foreboding that had been dripping from him, the fear made him sound as though he was possessed.

The cave troll and Mr. Hyde maybe.

I jerked as Henry's shoulders knit together, my phoenix moving into that same panicked excitement that I had felt before. The emotion made even less sense now. Heat sparked over my chest, my spine burning as if she was going to rip out of me if I allowed her to or not. Except I wasn't sure if it was to rush forward and save creepy-dude from whatever was scaring him, or if it was to grab Jarron and run away.

"Let's go home, Henry." Lilly said before I could decide which path to take, her voice so bored that I was expecting the forced yawn of a snooty pre-teen. I had performed with enough to know the type.

Well, I had performed with Xi, but apparently she was some ageless deity thing, so that hardly counted. I was still going to count it.

With as bored as Lilly sounded, Henry's reaction was the polar opposite. The stitch up his shoulders relaxed, the muscles loosening as he continued forward, leading us right into the brightly lit alcove of their house-cave.

Because all of that was normal. I was ready to run the other way, but china-doll was already prodding us forward. Even though I was giving her a hella good glare, the eye daggers were still not appearing.

Before I could stop it, we were in the house. My house. No. Wipe that thought from my mind.

Not that I could get a good look at the place that was so definitely not my house, I was at risk of being blinded. The walls were painted so white that the fluorescent glow from the overhead bulbs reflected into a wall of white that burned my eyeballs straight back to the other side of my skull. I cringed and buried my face into Jarron's side, grateful when he wrapped his arm around me and blocked what little of the light I was unable to.

It ebbed the pain enough that I was sure my head wasn't going to explode like a fluorescent firework and I was able to take a look at this place.

Under the shadowed parasol of Jarron's armpit, I could make out the couch that split the room into two sections. The huge leather thing sitting in the middle of the floor, facing the television that Lilly was already placing herself in front of. The room buzzed with electricity and the electronic music of her show as she turned it on. All that racket wasn't enough to drown out the faint sound of a lock as Henry shut a pair of wide doors over the entrance to the cave. A tiny smile was playing on the corner of his lips as the lock slipped into place, and he locked us in.

I had figured it was a trap. At least there were no cages or animal restraints or other weird kinky apparatuses involved in this trap. A door I could break down, a lock I could pick.

Well, I thought I could until he lifted a bright white key to his fingertip and pushed it into his finger. The thing moved into his left pointer finger without a drop of blood or hiss of pain. Because that was completely normal and not at all creepy.

I was staring at him with what were possibly the biggest eyes ever and he totally caught me. But he didn't look nervous, or uncomfortable. Instead he smiled, a weird green glimmering in his eyes as he stepped closer.

"Welcome home, Princess."

"You can't call me that either," I snarled, pulling myself away from Jarron, who held on tighter and tried to pull me back from the quickly approaching man.

Henry looked so much different in the light, perhaps not as frazzled, more handsome, more desirable. None of those were allowed, or welcome in my mind. I was sure those last two came more from the swoony bipolar bird that was once again trying to break out of my chest. It was pissing me off all the more.

Now that we were here and trapped inside his murder

room, I expected the facade to peel. I expected that shadowed monster we had seen in the cave to reemerge and the cages and bondage straps to come out. But he was smiling as calm and demurely as he had before.

It was so much worse.

"You let me know when you are ready, Elliana," he whispered, stepping closer until I was between him and Jarron in a warm mate sandwich. I had been in these before and they always led to twistedly wonderful thoughts. But not this time.

This time I was in a position I didn't want him in. Having him so close, and looking at me with those eyes was making that lustful side of phoenix, and my temper, turn up to boiling.

Unsurprisingly, my skin was already smoking. Jarron looked scared. Henry was awed. I was just fucking pissed.

This situation was twenty shades of dog fart. They might as well have smeared it all over the wall.

"You are my wife and I will wait to have you back, as long as is needed." His voice was so low it could have been a bit of fluff in my head, a bit of fluff that fit perfectly with the memory of limbs, sheets and all sorts of things I really wasn't interested in seeing right then.

"Soon."

Of all the goddamned words he could have chosen to say. That was it. I totally punched him. Fist to jaw.

All he did was laugh.

2

KILLIAN

T HE FALCON STARED AT K ILLIAN ALL NIGHT. I TS BEADY LITTLE eyes sinking into his soul as Mattia rambled about a local guidebook he was writing, not so much as touching on the sister that he had mentioned hours before.

No matter how many times Killian tried to pull the old man away from his frivolous mumble about local attractions and back to the old witch, Mattia ignored him. All the while that bird stared at him. Its beady little eyes staring until he fell asleep, lulled there by the irritating grind of Mattia's chuckle and the clink of glass and metal as he prepared one glass of absinthe after another.

How the man was alive with as much of the narcotic he had consumed, Killian didn't know. He didn't care to guess. But it was that thought which followed him into sleep, that and the beady eyes of the bird.

One should never fall asleep while being stared at by a bird and listening to the rambles of an old warlock, strictly speaking it only leads to twisted dreams. Dreams with green fairies that take the shape of girls with beady eyes and bad tempers. The spritely demons glittering green wings cut through his dream, driving him mad as he chased her over caves and through mountains as he shifted between Dragon, man, and a different kind of beast altogether.

He didn't know what monster he had turned into, but the lava that dripped from his broken scales was not promising that he would be the hero in this situation. The tar-like stuff pooled at his feet, causing him to slip from the mountain, to tumble from the sky toward the land millions of miles below.

It was the fall that woke him, and he jerked to sitting with a gasp and a snap, turning right to the ledge above the window and those beady little eyes. But they had gone. There wasn't anything there but the pounding of his panicked heart. The falcon had gone, perhaps escaped out of the open window.

Mattia was asleep on the chair right by the glass, oblivious to the frigid air that was pouring in through the foggy, hand-blown, pane.

"Holy shit, man," Killian grumbled, jumping to his feet. The blanket fell away to reveal his naked ass as he took two big steps to the window, slamming it shut.

Mattia jerked, snorting at the sound. He barely moved beyond that. Surprisingly, the man didn't even hiccup considering that a powerful aroma of alcohol was assaulting the air around him.

He had drowned in the stuff. It was a miracle he was still breathing.

It would probably be better if he wasn't. Mattia had kept Killian from leaving last night, and even with all his talking, Killian hadn't gotten a single word out of him in regards to his *sister*. There was clearly valuable information there, but Killian wasn't going to stick around to find out. Not with a warlock this powerful.

Not with any Warlock.

"Warlocks." Killian spat the word like a curse and shuffled over the frost covered floor to the dying fire in the hearth, reigniting it with one tiny ball of flame. If any mortal had seen him, all they would have seen was a muscular naked man spitting into the fire and igniting it back to a roaring, if not slightly green, flame.

Luckily, there was no one around to see.

The dragon fire burned hotter than a normal wood blaze would, and was already eating through the logs that remained from last night's fire. Adding a few more pieces of the split pine, Killian turned to the still cold room. His fire may help it to heat faster, but he wasn't interested in letting his junk hang free until that happened.

He wasn't interested in hanging around at all until that happened.

He needed to get out of here, and seeing as he was still too injured to shift, or to successfully land a flying leap out of the second story window, he needed clothes so he could walk out of this building like as much of a normal person as he could accomplish.

Mattia was smaller than him, but that didn't mean he couldn't find something to wear that would last the single day's trek up the mountain that it would take for him to heal the rest of the way. After that he could shift.

His broken ribs were already halfway through the healing process, at least from what he could tell. Standing in the radiant heat of the flames was only adding to the way the bones were pulsing as they pulled themselves back together.

Painful, but necessary.

If the fire hadn't gone out he probably would have been

healed by now. The drunken warlock was causing him more than a few problems.

Beside the ribs, and a punctured lung, it felt as though his knee had popped out of joint when he had thrashed around in the forest in his failed landing. Perhaps he had a cracked hip, what with how every step was grinding. He had had worse, and he would heal quickly, but he had no interest in doing it here.

Or naked.

The dresser was small and obviously hand carved, the ornate knots and designs were beautiful and intricate in their texture and shading. The lattice work was beyond the skill of anything he had seen before. That, combined with the deep walnut finish on the hardwood and it was a piece he could see in his home - or what was left of it.

God, his home. They had left Drake and Zoe in a danger that they weren't even aware of. Knowing them, they would rally the Forgotten and form an army to seek out their father. Which, would be sending them right after the vampire who was controlling the King. Feeding right into the nasty little man's plan.

But that was a day ago, or rather, three days from now if the drunken Warlock and his cell phone were to be believed. Ellie hadn't just brought them to the Himalayas, she had brought them back in time and she didn't even know it.

They could perhaps even get back to the cave and stop themselves before all of this happened. He had no idea of how the logistics of all of that worked. But it wouldn't even be an option unless he returned to Ellie.

As quietly as he could, Killian pulled the dresser open, letting the wood sliders grind as he tried to peek inside. He had gone for the first drawer, as it would most commonly contain underwear and any night things. This man was no different than the majority of the population. Perfectly stacked boxers lined the front, what looked to be flannel sleep pants scattered at the back. Those he would fit into. It would be tight, but it would be enough.

Thank god the Warlock didn't have an affinity for lacy underthings, he was sure he would look quite the sight traversing up the mountain in red lace lingerie. And he had thought the idea of scaling down the mountain in his shabby suit had been a bad idea, that would be worse for a variety of reasons.

Grabbing what looked to be the baggiest pair, Killian stepped away from the dresser, and right into a very solid and very foul smelling mass of flesh and sweat soaked clothes.

"Those are my favorites, too," Mattia stumbled over his words, his hand running over Killian's shoulder in invitation as he stepped closer. Killian jumped away, holding the pants against him like a genitalian shield. "I'm sure you will look nice in them. So nice."

Killian's stomach flipped. It wasn't the first time he had been hit on by a man, and while it never really repulsed him, there was something about this time, and this man, that was making his spine tense in dangerous expectation and his fire coat his mouth.

His dragon didn't trust the guy any more than he did.

"I don't want to attract any more attention when I go scaling the mountain." Killian growled, shaking out the pants and quickly stepping inside. He was much bigger than the tiny Mattia and the fabrics barely stretched over his girth. It also helped to accentuate a certain bulge that the warlock was now eyeing. "Humans can't walk around the Himalayas in nothing."

The lust that was consuming the man a minute ago vanished, twisting into something akin to pain as he attempted to step forward, and instead swayed on his feet, teetering into the still open dresser with a bawk.

"You're not leaving." The words were slurred, and Killian had expected a shocked 'are you' to follow, but there was only the statement, the tone was harsh even through the high the man was in.

"I need to get back t--" Killian stopped himself right before he hissed the words 'my mate'.

Even when he had been sober, or mostly sober last night, Mattia hadn't seemed as dangerous as he did now. Darkness was taking over the warlock, black smoke drifting around his hands and up his arms, swallowing any last hint of safety.

"I need to get back," Killian let his dragon growl as he stepped forward, ready to break past the teetering man and bust through the door.

Before he could, the warlock flung his hand to the side, the action sending him off balance for a second time. He stumbled across the room and right back into the chair he had been sleeping in a moment ago with a bang, a thud, and a groan.

Looks like Killian didn't need to push him out of the way after all.

"Drunken fool," Killian grumbled, tying the drawstring of the pants and charging toward the door that was carved and stained with as much care as the dresser.

"She left me," Mattia said from the other side of the room, the strangled sob as broken and defeated as the poor guy looked, crumpled in the chair as he was. "She said I was broken and useless and ran off to the freaking circus."

Killian stopped in place. He had tried all night to get

him to talk about his sister, about Suvi. To reveal why they didn't get along, or his love of black magic. The last of which was more of a survival thing, if he was going to get out of here he needed to know how much of a road block this guy was going to create.

All night, the man had drank and talked about everything but his sister. Now, inches from the door, Killian's hand already extended towards the knob, Mattia started talking.

Killian was a fool in so many ways, and stopping here, steps away from what could be freedom confirmed that. He needed to get back to Elliot, to Jarron, and then on to Rydaim before the cave exploded all over again. But he couldn't stop himself, and his hand dropped to his side, although he did not turn.

"Why did she leave?" The hard rumble of his voice bounced off the door, echoing over the room as Killian turned, careful to keep himself positioned enough between door and wizard that he could escape quickly if needs be.

"She had a job to do she said, but mostly it was me. It was because I told her..." He faded off, and that time he hiccupped, nearly falling forward out of the chair.

"Pathetic." He wasn't getting anything out of this guy.

The man didn't deserve the pity Killian gave him as he turned away, hand wrapping around the cold iron of the knob and turned.

Well, at least he tried to. The knob did nothing. The door did nothing. And the drunken man behind him laughed, the liquid sound of his chuckle burning like ice against Killian's soul.

"I already told you," Mattia said, his voice filled with the same darkness of his laugh, the drunken slur making him more ominous somehow. "You aren't going anywhere."

"Nonsense, you can't keep me here." There was no way that Killian could match the power in Mattia's voice, but he was sure going to try. The boom of his response however, could not stand up to the violent glare that he was now giving him.

Pure black was taking over Mattia's eyes as he pulled himself to standing, the shake in his legs all but gone as he stepped closer. Killian was not one to shy away, but this time he wished there was a way to put more space between himself and the man who was stalking his way over to him. The air in this room dripped with danger. He had to get out. And the window was now a viable option.

Bone injuries be damned, as long as he could get to Ellie... Hell, anywhere would be better than here.

"That won't work either," the dark eyed man said, clearly having followed the line of Killian's desperation. "And don't even think about shifting, you will only hurt yourself more."

"What did you do?" Killian's fear mixed with his anger in a dangerous cocktail that was sending wisps of flame out from behind his teeth, dripping down to the floor where they fizzled out in pathetic little pools of smoke.

So much for burning the building down, looks like the wicked little man had thought of that too. Well, that was only one trick that he had in the many. He could easily kill him with only his hands, his dragon was good for more than burning. It wouldn't take much effort to wring the life out of him. Watch him writhe and cry as his fire ate his soul. He had never done that to a Warlock's soul and he wasn't sure what eating that much magic would do to his dragon. He didn't want to find out, but Ellie was worth the risk.

"Why are you doing this?" Killian diverted the man's focus as he let the fire that was burning inside his heart shift from the green that he was known for, to the black that his father had considered his secret weapon for many years. The fire he had almost hit his brother with, in his rage. The fire that had almost ended Ellie after her attempt to turn him into a eunuch.

"I like you Killian," Mattia said, the darkness fading from him as he stepped forward, the hooded look that Killian knew returning.

"I don't..." How drunk was this man exactly?

"And I plan to use you for a bit of fun," the warlock interrupted, the look in his eyes calming to something less hungry, although he did not slow his advance.

Killian took a step back, finding himself smashed against the ornate door, the cold knob pressing into the bare skin of his back. He shivered at its touch, although he was sure the reaction was more for the twisted little man that now stood before him.

Staring him down.

Not many people could match the height and bulk of a Dragon. Even Drake, who was small for a dragon, appeared to be larger than normal men. This once stunted Italian, however, was looking him right in the eye.

Staring him down.

Killian swallowed.

"And what are you planning on doing?" Killian asked, thankful when his voice didn't shake underneath the bizarre panic that was trying to take over.

"I am already doing it." Mattia's smile stretched wider, his feet dragging him closer.

Killian reacted, pressing his full force against the man. His palms hard on the warlock's shoulders, the rough pressure fully meant to send Mattia shooting through the air.

Mattia barely moved.

"You would think for a prince you would have better sense." The warlock flung his hand casually to the side, the motion sending a plume of smoke from him. The tuft of black spun as it migrated around the room so fast that the light from the fireplace might as well have been extinguished.

The whole world might as well have been extinguished.

Killian and Mattia were swallowed by the dark, the smoke the warlock had created glowing around them, even as black as it was. The room was gone, the world was only Killian and Mattia surrounded by darkness, every part of them illuminated.

Perhaps it was them that were glowing in the dark.

"What are you doing?" Killian's head spun as his words slurred, as the smoke continued to move around them, to press against him. To press into him.

For a moment, it felt as if the smoke was going to swallow him whole. Absorb him into it until he was nothing.

"Qui conturbas animarum hic sedebitis," The slur in Mattia's voice had vanished completely, instead of the drunken warlock the dark magic inside of him had overtaken his features, his eyes completely swallowed with black smoke, his olive skin fading to the shade of chalk, the tips of his fingers dipped in ink.

His voice boomed with each word, the bass rattling against what Killian hoped was still walls and a dresser.

The man extended his hands as smoke rippled from him, curled around him like some kind of pet. A pet that was speeding up.

Faster and faster until it was gone.

It was all gone.

The black.

The fire.

The room was cold, everything numb and smothered with a smoke that Killian could have sworn had been around him. Now it was inside of him, making everything foggy. Making everything ache.

"What are you doing out of bed?" Mattia asked, his hand soft against Killian's chest, his finger tracing over the deep black lines of his tattoo. Of his Phoenix.

His Phoenix...

"Killian?" Mattia asked again, pulling Killian's focus as he stared at him, trying to fight against the fog, to find the phoenix that was somewhere inside of him.

No, on him.

God, what was he doing out of bed? He was clearly tired and needed more sleep.

"Come, before the bed gets cold."

Killian could do nothing but follow him, follow the coils of black smoke that were swallowing him whole.

3

ZOE

I had missed my home. I had missed the Fae. I had missed this underground city.

But this was not my home, and the filthy little girl who had perched herself on the flowered covered pallet, was making that even more clear.

Everything about this place had changed, and she was making it worse.

Fallon.

I should have killed her when she stood with that knife to Drake's throat. Her eyes had looked dangerous, and now I knew why.

Because she was dangerous. She was also bat-shit crazy.

My sympathetic side was really screwing me over now.

There she was, ranting and raving and antagonizing a people that I had spent nearly a hundred years fighting for. People who had no ability to fight and who had no hope in being able to. I had been with them long enough to know that they didn't have magic, and she really needed to stop making promises that she could change that. Lies like that could get her, or any of these people, killed.

Watching her convince them to follow her to their doom was making me wish I could do her in, right then and there. Challenge her to some duel or right to the alpha as it has been done in the wolf packs since the beginning. She was acting like the aggressive, flighty, creatures anyway. Perhaps it was time I treated her as such.

"When we have defeated the dragons, we will do to them the same as they have done to us for the past three hundred years! We will cut their wings from their bodies! We will force them to beg and cry at our feet!" Fallon teetered on the edge of the flower covered pallet, and I envisioned her falling face first into the crowd, smacking her face on the cement.

That was until what she was saying registered, each word stabbing deeper as she looked right to where Drake and I stood, her eyes narrowing.

"All of them."

That's it, if she wants to threaten me with slavery of some kind, then I was going to threaten her with a knocked in jaw. Fucking bitch doesn't get to stroll in here and play that game. She clearly doesn't know what she is up against.

"Stop, Zo," Drake hissed into my ear, his hand firm around my bicep as he pulled me back. Thankfully, he hadn't pushed his silver tongue into those words, if he kept doing that we were going to have a few problems.

Mostly involving a smack upside the head.

All of my muscles were already wound too tightly in agitation for him to be pushing me.

"She's going to get them killed," I snarled from behind clenched teeth, staring down the woman who was now screaming about how they needed a 'savior' with her fist in the air. I supposed she thought she was the one to fill that role.

She didn't look like a savior, she looked like a tyrant.

"Well, she's not doing anything yet. We need to stop her yes, but everyone is too high strung for you to go rushing up there." Damn it, Drake. He was making perfectly logical sense and I couldn't hate him for it.

I did, however, give him a glare that said as much. Damn him even more, he smiled.

"How can they be following this..." I couldn't find a word to finish that sentence that I felt okay saying around my baby brother.

"Wanton whore?" I gave him a look. That was unexpected, and yet decisively perfect.

"Yes."

"Desperation." His tone sounded far too hard and frightened for your everyday desperation. "Which is why we need to get out of here. Before this turns rotten."

The crowd pressed closer to us as they erupted in more cheers, Fallon screaming about taking down those who have betrayed them. It was then, as the breath of the ones who had stepped closest to me whispered over my dirt covered hair, as their fingers tugged at my now filthy and shredded hoodie, that I realized I had been paying attention to the wrong danger.

Fallon was a danger right before me, but as she ranted and raved, she had created a danger all around. One that was now pressing against me, questioning my and Drake's presence here.

Questioning our loyalty.

Well, shit.

My blood was officially boiling, my dragon screaming in my ears as the creature fought to explode out of me. It would be easy, let her break free and destroy all of these fools who were now so ready to attack me. Show them what they were facing.

Except they weren't fools. They were my friends. And they didn't deserve that. As much as they didn't deserve Fallon leading them around like the blind bat she was.

"Come on," Drake hissed as they began to yell again, the silver undertones of his voice pulling at me, although not enough to force me to follow.

I hated that gift as much as he did and normally I would be stubborn enough not to follow based on principle alone. This time I pressed my lips together and followed his lead, refusing to let my focus fall from Fallon until the last possible minute. If only because I was refusing to look at all the Forgotten who I still counted as my friends. I didn't want to see how quickly they had betrayed me. Not when my dragon was so close to the surface, to losing control.

"Maybe move faster," Drake rasped as the screams grew louder, his hand gripping mine as he pulled me toward the back corner of the cave where one of his friends had lived so long ago.

We were a little over half way there when I realized that we were missing a set of steps behind us.

"Where is Callay?"

"She went to go get help. She says she knows someone who could help." He guided me around a shattered little hovel, two of the rooms collapsing in on themselves from our heavy steps as we rushed by.

"That tells me nothing," I snarled as another cheer ripped the air apart. "How do we know she is not working for them?"

I looked back one last time, the screaming volatile crowd slamming against my heart and sending my dragon howling. Thank god their tyrannical leader was screaming loud enough to cover the sound.

"We don't, but seeing as we are pretty much trapped here, I am thinking our best bet is to trust her." There he goes again with his damn sound logic.

I jerked my wrist out of his grip as he slowed to the little indentation in the stone that had once upon a time housed his friend, Gayl. Gayl was long gone, just like her house. We had helped her carve the cavern deeper, to give her more of a house after her aunt had died and left her alone. It was in there that we went, pulling one of the broken pallets from another destroyed hovel behind us, if only to create a bit of security.

"Is this really what we are resorting to?" I asked as we crawled through the low cave, toward the cavern hidden deep inside. "Running away and hiding."

"We didn't run, Zo. We calmly walked away to a place where Fallon and her mob can't find us."

"I hardly see the difference," I growled as my knees slid over the once smooth stone. Now, it was littered with tiny pebbles and debris that cut into my palms and knees like some kind of crude torture device.

As if the cave wasn't enough of one.

Being in such a tight space, inside of a recently collapsed cave was without a doubt the worst possible idea.

I think I may prefer to battle those idiots in the would-be mob than to continue on this journey. We didn't even know if the cavern ahead of us would be open, or if any of this was still safe to travel through.

"They will still follow us, Drake."

He sighed heavily, he knew I was right. The only advantage we had was that it might take Fallon and her flock longer to find us.

Find us in a cave with only one way in, and one way out. We were fools.

"We will have to hope that Callay gets back to fling some magic around then." He turned a corner of the winding cave, the motion taking much of his proclamation with him.

"And where is she again? Ah yes, with a mystery friend we know nothing about." He didn't respond, which I would normally take as a good sign, except he had moved out of eye shot, and my mind was already screaming a warning about collapse.

Both dragon and heart twisted into marathon level panic and I sped up, following Drake around the bend he had vanished behind and into a dark hole.

All the air was sucked from the world as the bottom of the cave gave way, falling into nothing as I tumbled forward with little more than a gasp as my dragon threatened to break free. Which was the very last thing I needed as I slid into a tiny tunnel deep inside a mountain, sliding over smooth stone and down, down into a dark abyss. Well, abyss in that it was dark. The walls were getting tighter, my hips and shoulders bumping into the cold, hard stone as I serpentined through the intestines of the mountain.

Slimy, cold, and leading to some burning pit in the center of the earth more than likely.

I tried to slow myself, but the damp stone grew slicker and more moss covered with each turn, pushing me through the depths faster than was safe. Mortals might call this fun, and I would be apt to join them, if anything about this was fun.

This was terrifying.

"This fucking sucks," I said with a scowl, giving one last attempt to slow myself down before I went through a final turn and was shot out of the tunnel with the force of a missile. A fast moving, I have no idea which was up or down, missile.

"This really fucking sucks," I scowled as gravity found me and my tailbone slammed hard into a cold stone floor. Bringing me to a thankful stop.

After that topsy-turvy ride I not only had no idea where I was, but even if I was alive. For all I knew, I had hit my head too hard on one of those turns and had landed myself in Dragon hell.

And that dull red-brown flame that was glimmering off in the distance was part of that.

Rolling to my hands and knees, I shook my head, trying to ease the raging pressure from landing on my ass before I stood. I seemed to be healing, whatever bone I had cracked in my landing wasn't hurting as much, and my head wasn't quite as spinning. So, not dead.

"Drake," I gasped into the dark, surprised at how raspy and grinding my voice was, but not surprised at the flickering flame that began weaving toward me, bringing a frightening floating head beside it.

I thought I had recognized the color of that fire.

Drake held the dark flame in the palm of his hand. The deep red fire barely illuminated the space around it and gave his face a million shadows of dark and light while leaving his body and most of the cave in darkness. Hence the floating head.

"What in the hell happened?" I asked before he had fully reached me, stubbornly pulling myself to sitting even though my head was still spinning.

"I'm not sure," Drake gasped, his flame flickering from his exhausted breaths. "That drop was there the last time I visited him, but it was neither so long or so..."

"Gross." I provided, trying to wipe the wet off my hands, only to find my jeans equally as muck covered.

"Yeah..."

"So where are we?" I asked, turning in the dark to find anything that I could catch on fire. My fire burned a tad bit brighter than Drake's so I wasn't about to hold it as he was and risk any temporary blindness.

As amazingly creepy as his shadows were, we needed to see more than we needed to build our own haunted house and something about this dark was sucking away my usually strong night vision.

It was almost as if there was nothing but black.

As if there was nothing there.

This better fucking not be dragon hell.

"Screw this," I snapped, stretching my jaw and releasing a string of bright red fire into the dark. My tongue burned with the flame, my mouth coating with ash as the cave illuminated in the blast of my scarlet fire.

The space was much larger than I would have guessed given how far down in the mountain we were. No wonder there had been nothing but black to see, everything was black, and everything was hopelessly far away.

The walls glimmered like charcoal, which twined dangerously in my gut, given that I had ignited the air with my boiling flame. I let out a screech, dropping to the ground in a duck and cover of expectation.

Muscle and bone tightened, ready for the blast as my flame met the coal walls of the cave. The blast never came. Just Drake's low chuckle as the burning glow of my fire rippled over everything.

"You scared of your own fire now, Zo?" Drake wasn't even trying to hide his laugh.

"No, I'm afraid of exploding walls." My voice a snap as I

jumped to my feet, ready to set him straight or rush to extinguish my flames, whichever needed to come first.

Drake was oblivious to both and stood, staring at the walls with slack-jawed shock as the fire in his palm slowly extinguished.

Red reflected in his eyes. Strangled noises popped from his throat in such a way that I would be concerned either he or his dragon where choking. But he was still staring at the walls that were burning with my flame.

It didn't explode, so it should have gone out. Instead, the fire smoldered over the roof of the cave, much the way Ellie's fire had burned in the wood of the coffee table, spreading through it, eating it away.

Except this was no mass-produced coffee table, and this cave was no tiny square. I had noticed its size when the flame had first ripped from my jaw, and the glistening ebony of the walls had screamed danger.

Now, I saw how big it really was.

My flames rippled over the ceiling, illuminating the dark outcropping that I now saw to be a ledge in the wall to an even larger cave. Everything up here was black on black on shadow. But this dank hollow wasn't the only thing that my fire was illuminating, and it wasn't what Drake was staring at.

The flames stretched out from the ledge, casting light into what as first looked to be nothing more than a glistening abyss, but as I stepped beside Drake the abyss sparkled more than endless caverns were supposed to.

"What is that?" I whispered into the dark as I teetered on the ledge, watching the light reflect against hundreds of massive stalagmites.

Stalagmites that were too smooth, and too perfectly

placed. A bit too perfectly created. I had never seen something so unnatural in a natural cavern.

If this had been a natural cavern.

It was carved. Carved from iron, coal, and graphite. Roofs emerged from the misunderstood stalagmites, streets glimmering in the shadows of immaculately carved houses, mansions, and what looked to be a Temple sitting right in the middle.

Or at least what I would assume was the middle.

It was hard to tell in a massive city that was so much bigger than Rydaim.

The city stretched on, the black carved stone reflecting under the ripples of my flame as it continued to spread.

The city was calling to me. Everything about it called to me.

"Would you mind if I...?" I gasped, teetering on the ridge of the ledge we stood on. I didn't even need to say more. Drake already knew what I was talking about.

"One round, then come back to get me."

I couldn't even nod to him in agreement, the beast in my chest was already screaming with need, to take off and fall into the city below. I followed her lead, throwing myself off the precipice and letting the monster take control before I had fallen even half way.

4

ELLIOT

"You have punched me quite a few times, Elliana. But, I do believe that might be the first time that I didn't deserve it."

Henry rubbed his jaw in the middle of the disheveled kitchen, giving me a look that had far too much lust in it considering I had punched him in the face. The bastard looked as though he enjoyed it, which was both disgusting and pissing me off enough that I wanted to do it again.

Which I wouldn't do because he freaking enjoyed it!

"Oh, trust me. You deserved it." Fists clenched against my ash covered thighs, I narrowed my gaze in what I hoped was a threat and not in agony. Pain was pooling over my hand from whatever bone or knuckle I had cracked with the intersection of his jaw.

And I thought punching Dragons was a bad idea, whatever this guy was made of was clearly worse. Luckily, between the heat and the smoke that was drifting off my skin in little dancing ribbons, no one noticed the twist of agony that was lining my forehead.

"You are my wife, Elliana. Calling you what you are is

deserving of nothing but a kiss," Henry continued, pulling himself a step forward, closer to my still balled fist. Interesting choice.

For an idiot. He was an idiot.

I cracked my knuckles loudly. It would be worth breaking a few more fingers to punch him again.

"I don't remember signing any legal papers, so I'm calling bullshit." I took a solid step forward, my Phoenix bristling in what was quickly becoming a bipolar episode. I didn't know what was up with her, my soul was bouncing back and forth between an attack-slash-jump his bones mode that was making me feel like an over hormonal teenager. Thankfully, Jarron wrapped his fingers around my tattered shirt and pulled me back into him.

"Not now Elliot." Jarron's dragon was clearly in control of that snarl.

Okay, maybe I should step back or I would end up with more than a broken hand. Henry's eyes sparked with a weird black light, the same creepy as hell lustful gleam boring in me before he stepped away, smiling in what he was considering a victory.

"Well, my dear," Yet another thing I was not a fan of him calling me, but before I could do more than open my mouth and make a soft squeaking noise of protest he had plowed on. "Why don't you take a look around, see if anything jogs your memory. Legal papers, or otherwise."

Henry stopped next to that same cluttered table I had seen him playing at before, you know, when I was still standing on the other side of the door Henry had locked with his bone-key. Because that was normal.

From this side of the cave, however, the whole set up looked a little less mail-order child's science kit and a little more mad scientist. It was set up on a dining room table that was so covered with scorch marks that it looked like something a teething dragon had gotten a hold of. Well, I assumed anyway.

The burned table was filled with beakers, Bunsen burners, weights, flowers, goo, rocks, and a partially deteriorated head in a jar. The thing was floating in a yellow substance, hovering there with wires and bone shards protruding from the ragged edges of flesh that used to be a neck. Hair and skin fell from the head in weird floating ribbons. Well, ribbons that had come from the surface of hell.

It was official, I would rip his finger off to get us out of here. Who the hell puts a head in a jar? And whose head was that? I had so many questions and no interest in the answers. Seeing as Jarron had turned an odd shade of grey, I clearly wasn't the only one who was avoiding staring at that side of the table.

"Jarron, why don't I show you what I have been working on; perhaps you have new information on our friend Parris that can help in our task." Henry circled the table until he was standing right behind the severed head and giving us nowhere else to look but at the vacant white eyes that were staring straight at us.

My spine coiled, ready to make its own escape and bust out of crazy town. My Phoenix, however, buzzed against my chest in an effort to pull me the other way.

Toward a head that she clearly wanted.

First the cave troll, now the head.

What the fuck was going on? Hot guys, yes, sure that's fine. That whole three mate's thing was starting to feel normal. We should go back to that and away from severed heads in a jar.

I really didn't need to see anymore, my bare feet against

the stone was much safer to look at than a head that I was refusing to believe was familiar.

Severed heads should never be familiar, strictly speaking.

"I'm not going to go on a scavenger hunt for your lies. I already told you I don't trust you, Henry." A nice little trill of energy ran up my spine with the disgust that Jarron was able to put into the guy's name.

Too bad Henry didn't even seem to care. He smiled and ran his hand over the top of the head jar. Because he needed to make himself look creepier.

"Well, then let us learn to trust one another." He was now stroking the jar.

He officially made himself look creepier.

Both stomach and now Phoenix were twisting into uncomfortable rock-filled knots thanks to the way the creep was stroking the glass, his dark eyes still looking right at me.

Jarron's arm wrapped around me and pulled me into him in what was clearly a sign of ownership, which I was going to allow given our current situation. I was stubborn as shit, but instead of pulling away I was letting all of the stubborn spitefulness shine toward creepy cave troll as Jarron pressed his lips to my temple, whispering calmly in my ear.

"Find out everything you can, Ellie. We need to find a way out of here," he whispered in a bright sunny vote of confidence.

Henry grumbled audibly at the display, but he might as well have given a match to a pyromaniac. I turned to Jarron, pressing my lips to his with a quick "promise" before he stepped away and right to the head fondling freak on the other side of the table.

Because what else can you do when you are locked in a

cave with a freaky cave troll? Yes, I was going to call him the cave troll from here on out.

At least the table wasn't covered with blood and the origin of the head could remain a partial mystery.

I practically sprinted away from them, plunging myself into the other half of the large living space on the other side of the couch. I had no interest in jogging my memory, unless it involved finding us a way out of here, which was the absolutely best use of my time.

"Start with what you know," Jarron demanded from behind me, the strength in his voice alone should have been a great comfort, if Henry hadn't laughed with a sound that was just as strong.

Yep, getting out of here needed to be the first priority, which would have been easy if all of the windowless walls weren't made up of rock as deep as the mountain. Thanks to the locked door, the only other way in or out of this room was one heavy door next to the TV. Which was also made of heavy stone, and also very locked.

Even with all the stone, they had done their best to make it look as uncave-ish as possible. The walls had been painted a white that looked a bit too yellow the further you moved from the fluorescent glow of the kitchen. The bright flashes from the weird cartoon on the massive TV was only adding to the disgusting yellow, the bright flickers of light smothered both walls and the little girl who was sitting on a couch that was made to fit far more than the two tiny people who lived here.

Being cave trolls and all, it made sense they would need the space for when they would transform into massive green skinned beasts in the middle of the night. Yes, I knew I was being ridiculous, but if I wanted to get out of here I was going to expect the worst.

After dragon kings, mind reading ice queens, and vampires, I was certain there were a few more terrifying things than "cave trolls" out in this wild world. But these two didn't fit into anything I had seen as of yet, so cave trolls it was.

Cave trolls with a plush area rug that felt like cotton and magic, especially after ass rockets and flinging myself into cold stone. Ridiculously, I thought about laying down and curling up on the thing like a cat in a pile of leaves.

Probably would have too if the kid wasn't staring at me. The flickering lights from the cartoon stretched over her face, turning her eyes into pools of silver dripped with blood. The look got worse with her dark sardonic smile that twisted toward me. Yep, I totally shivered.

"What are you looking for?" The sweet in her voice did not match the haunting smile.

"Just trying to find something about myself." I decided to use Henry's excuse to get me away from Jarron, although I wasn't sure she heard me over the buzzing noise of the TV, seeing as her head cocked to the side like an overly curious animal.

"And you decided to stare at that wall to do it?" The laugh was gone from her voice now. She stood slowly, brushing some invisible lint off her still pristine dress and took two wide steps toward me.

In the dark cave before, she had looked like some macabre china doll. Everything about her frightening. That hadn't left in the brightness of the living room, if anything it was worse. The air rippled around her, everything warming as she stepped beside me and placed her hand against the bare stretch of wall.

The warmth sweltered as her hand glowed in the faintest yellow, her skin shimmering as though it had been covered with the gold that always covered Jarron when he was agitated.

"You can't get out this way," She said with a knowing smile, a nasty little prick of superiority digging into me. Any other time I probably would have insulted the kid, but the image of her happily poking Jarron's flame was still too strong and instead I stepped away.

Of course it took a creepy little kid to help me control my impulsiveness.

"Try the other wall." Her grin stretched as she nodded once toward the opposite wall before bounding back to the couch, and her cartoon.

Well, she sat on the couch. Her cartoon was serving as odd ambient noise as she stared at me, same creepy look in her eyes. There I went, shivering again.

Refusing to look at her, I made my way around the back of the couch, fully aware that her frightening silver eyes were following my every step.

"But have you taken into account his connection with the coven in Northern Russia," Henry hissed as I stepped passed their table in an attempt to escape the kid, their heated conversation fading back into existence as the TV took a break from whatever cartoon explosions had been blasting from the screen for the past few minutes. "It's a strong coven and most people are no longer aware they exist. I have been around long enough to not only know of them, but to have developed a relationship with the head of the clan personally."

"I know of who you speak," Jarron returned, the power in his voice replaced with an irritation that I had only heard a few times before. "We have welcomed them into the court before."

The two men were clearly stuck in some kind of cock

measuring battle, and while my first instinct would be to run in between them and break the mess up, I couldn't move. I was currently trapped, staring at the wall that freaky devil girl had indicated. A wall that was covered in my face.

Well, pictures of my face. Pictures of me in front of the Taj Mahal, standing beside the Berlin Wall as it came down. There was even one of Henry and I dressed as pioneers in some studio that made souvenir portraits. At least that's what I hoped it was, the picture looked too cracked and low-quality to be from some gaudy theme park.

Not that it being recent would help the situation. If it was recent, I would remember it. I would remember all of this, but I remembered none of these images of me with a smile plastered on my face, especially some creepy old timey picture that may or may not be from the 1800s.

The images were everywhere, each one surrounding a large painting as though the old antiquated thing was the center of some kind of shrine. Which is exactly what I was sure it was.

A shrine to me. To my Phoenix.

I had never seen my Phoenix before, at least not with this clarity. Seeing the reds, golds, and blacks reflected in mountain lakes or the sides of window covered high rises had given me some idea of what I looked like, but those were distorted and discolored.

They were nothing like this.

This was fire sparking against pain and memory and ripping it to life; this was almost real. Swooping feathers cut through blue sky, glitter and ash trailing behind like ribbons and starlight. Brilliant emerald eyes glimmered so perfectly it looked as though I could reach up and pluck the stone from the paint. The beak of my bird, my beak, was open, golden flame shooting into the sky as the wings spread behind. I could almost feel the air, smell the smoke.

I could almost remember being there.

This was beautiful. Even my Phoenix knew it, the powerful bird was ruffling those same burning feathers inside of me, as if she was seeing herself for the first time, too.

"I really am badass." My whispered awe was met by a giggle and I nearly jumped, rounding to the silver haired child who had appeared beside me like an apparition.

The frilly red dress of minutes before was gone, replaced by a gauzy number you might see the flower girl wear at a wedding.

The thing was all lace, equally as frilly as the last one, and had little jewels embedded along the waistline. The bright white dress and the silvery glimmer in her hair and eyes made her appear as if she was dead already, just some haunted child that liked to follow me around.

"It is beautiful isn't it?" Her voice was strangely deep, her focus digging into me instead of the picture.

Could she look anywhere else but at me? Her laser pointed focus was really wiggin' me out. She seriously better not have x-ray vision or some shit. I mean, not that this shirt was making any effort to hide myself, but still, this level of focus from a kid was not natural.

Unless she was like Xi, whatever Xi was.

"Yep. I look as though I am about ready to jump off the wall and burn everyone," I tried to keep my voice casual, well, as casual as you could when all you wanted to do was threaten children, steal bone keys and get out of Dodge.

"And who would you burn, given the chance?" This comment did not come from the kid, although she was still looking right at me. This one came from the deep voice of a British man, and directly behind me.

The kid may have been freaking me out, but she was clearly the pre-show to a much scarier feature presentation.

Exes always are.

"I can think of a few people."

Speaking of x-ray vision, I folded my arms over my chest, careful to cover as much as I could and side-stepped creepy cave troll number two.

"She won't burn," Henry's voice was covered with an eager malice as he stepped closer, Lilly giggling from right behind me. Creepy cave troll sandwich. "But I am sure you have figured that out by now."

His smile was so familiar that I barely registered Jarron pulling me away from the Brit and right into his arms. The dark of his embrace swallowed me, and I pushed into it pinching my eyes shut.

I expected dark, I expected a brief moment of calm and maybe an exhale. Instead, my mind was filled with a nearly identical smile of the one I had been pulled from, and an even more frightening version of Henry.

A Henry wearing a top hat and tails. A Henry that I had seen before, even if I didn't remember it.

"You know this is a mistake." The memory of him hissed into memory, his face stretching in impossible ways. *"You know there is only one path and I will be the one laughing when he rips your wings from your body."*

The same weird gleam was in his eyes as I forced my eyes open and back into reality. I already knew I shouldn't trust him, but I was starting to think there were a few more reasons why.

Reasons that were ready to burst their way out of me.

"I wasn't planning on burning either of you." There

wasn't a trace of a shake in my voice anymore, no matter how scared I was. "I can, however, burn vampires, and Parris is first on my list."

It was only a partial lie, because I was still going to turn Parris to char. But with the way things were going, creepy mate number one and his equal as frightening side-kick were going to be the first to go.

5

———

CALLAY

THIS WAS GOING TO BE FUCKING GREAT.

I hadn't even taken one step into the hut village of The Forgotten where I had left Zoe and Drake and it was clear that one of two things were about to be true.

One: Zoe and Drake would be tied to some kind of pyre while Fallon led The Forgotten in a foolish coup to the surface.

Two: They would already be dead.

I was praying that what I would actually find was somewhere in the middle and those two were hiding in the wreckage of the underground hut village where I could still check on them before going all stalker on fucking Fallon.

Judging by the screaming and chanting that was echoing through the tunnels, however, I wasn't holding out much hope.

I was gone a few minutes and that girl had already pulled those tattered Forgotten into full on mob status. And I thought Zoe was the only one to have that skill.

I had a right to be worried.

Something was wrong with that girl. And freakin' Xi and

her tirade about demons and creating monsters was not doing me any favors. The crowd was screaming again and I picked up the pace, running to their cave. Thank god for sneakers, even if mine were still full of freezing cold vampire ash, maybe the mush would help to disguise my arrival.

Not that I couldn't bust in there with fire and light, fly through them all like a badass Fae, save the Dragons, and get us out of here. Which I could. But that was looking like it might be too dangerous. Their chants were starting to make sense now and me and my uncut forearms were clearly listed as one of the things that were 'going down'. I didn't want to know how a bunch of magicless Fae were planning on taking any sort of magic down, but I wasn't about to ask.

Xi had said to keep an eye on Fallon and to stop her from doing something stupid. That eliminated the bustin' in scene that was unfolding in my mind, even if Xi hadn't forbidden me from using the full breadth of my magic.

Stupid Xi. Can't use my magic. Can't team up with the power-dragons. I just get to babysit some creepy ass revolutionary.

Which was a shame because Fallon and her ugly shed magic really needed an eye opener.

I had a feeling that to stay close I was going to have to fit in. As if I hadn't done enough of that. I got to spend a couple hundred years pretending to be a slave to some super-hot dragons that I may or may not have lusted after a few times. Why not flip the switch and pretend to be a magicless Fae that lives in an underground city with a whole bunch of other magicless and now murderous Fae?

Okay, so that wasn't going to work, which means that I needed to fit in another way. Like infiltrating from the inside. Lay plans, build an army, get the murderous leader to trust me.

Great. I had to become fucking Fallon's best friend.

Yeah, friends with the servant of a creature that was created by the same masochistic unicorn that I was. Except he was all evil and crap. Light and dark battling it out. Seemed familiar, but more in that I was sure the blasted unicorn had said something about things being equal at some point in time. Light and dark, good or bad, or something.

Who knew? All I knew was that sucking up to Fallon was going to fucking suck. Just like her magic fucking sucked. Ugly shed magic. I was going to call her that from now on.

Not that she would hear it, not with the way she was screaming. She was already on a roll.

"When we have defeated the dragons, we will do to them the same as they have done to us for the past three hundred years! We will cut their wings from their bodies! We will force them to beg and cry at our feet!"

She was raging like a mad man, the crowd cheering after her and drowning out whatever she had said after. I took one peek around the dust filled entrance of the cave and nearly turned back. The bitch was standing on a piece of an old building, balancing on a pallet and screaming about cutting wings from dragons' bodies like it was easy, or even possible. All the naive Forgotten were eating it all up. Forget Fallon being the leader of a revolution, she was clearly trying to turn them into a cult.

Great. Revolution I could handle. I had dealt with that for years, but if I had to start wearing white robes or something that blasted Unicorn was on her own. I would face the repercussions of breaking my contract with her.

"We will make them bleed as we cut their dragons from their bodies and force them to watch as the creatures writhe in misery," the revolutionary cult leader yelled, her declaration followed by more cheers of agreement and excitement.

I unabashedly rolled my eyes.

"That's not even possible you loon. Don't you know anything about dragons?" I mumbled to myself as I plunged into the grungy air of the cavern, skirting around the edge of the cave and concealing myself as much as possible with the broken down houses. "They don't live inside of them like parasites. Not like whatever is living inside of you to cause your magic to rot like that."

Thankfully the crowd chose that moment to yell at something that Fallon had said and covered up my mumbling giggles. The image of her little magic parasite squalling around on the floor was too good. Maybe I could squish it with my shoe.

Would sure make this whole thing easier.

"See, Xi, no magic involved." I carefully moved my way through what was left of someone's home, one of the walls having been blown out by the attack the vampires had staged before we even got here.

These poor people. First vampires. Then a cave-in. And now... this...

"When we are done they will cower before us like they were meant to do! They will serve our kind as we should be served!" Woah, that was a bit loaded for your general cult recruitment process.

I tucked myself behind a tilted slab of wood and peeked around the edge to double check that she wasn't passing out robes, or drugs, or whatever they do in cults. Nothing but fist pumping, thankfully. Well, that and the ugly sparks of her magic that dripped over her hands before plopping to the ground like little glitter slugs.

Sick.

Time to move before she infects anyone else with that nonsense.

If I rushed into the back of the crowd and worked my way forward I should be able to hear their banter, hear how much they are believing and what not. She'll recognize me, I'll cheer about how right she is, how *amazing* her magic is, then I'll offer to braid her hair and we can rule the cult together. While I am systematically undermining her.

It'll be just like a fucking mortal high school.

There I went again, rolling my eyes, although this time it served more of a purpose than making me look like the high schooler I was gearing up to be. If I hadn't looked away, I would have missed them.

Everything about them was brown, from their hair, to their clothes, to the bits of ash that were clinging to their backs, but it was clearly them. Zoe and Drake, dodging behind a slab of wood and into what appeared to be a solid stone wall.

"Huh?" I tilted my head as if it would give me a better angle, staring at the spot and waiting for them to reemerge.

Zoe was not really the type to run away, especially from a bug in her side like Fallon. Drake must have used his silver tongue on her to get her to jump on board with that plan. Which was good. They were safe, out of the way, and not apt to start a counter revolution that would make my task harder.

Xi said to trust them, and if trusting them means letting them hide in between a slab of wood and cave wall for the next little bit I was fine with that.

Operation 'Best Friends Forever Before I Double Cross You, Bitch' was a go.

BFFBDCYB for short. It needed more swears, but it was already a mouthful.

I took one last glance at the pallet to make sure they weren't going to hatch out of it like newborn dragons before plunging myself into the herd of sheep that were already following this girl around like she was a god.

Shed magic.

"It is our birthright to hold magic in our veins and once we have taken the wings of the dragons, once we have pulled the creatures from their bodies to leave them writhing and gasping, we shall force them to return that power to us!"

She yelled again, the crowd cheered, and everyone around me nodded in excited agreement. Sheep. I really would have thought that at least one of them would have realized it didn't work that way, but I guess not. They were called The Forgotten for a reason.

They really knew nothing.

"Once we hold our magic in our hands again we will show them what power is," She ignited the flame in her hand again, as if for reference, but the flame did little more than kick and splutter, like someone was repeatedly spitting on her palm and big old fire loogies were dripping out of it.

"We will show them what strength is. We will show them what it means to be forgotten!"

I may have gone deaf in my left ear with the level of the scream that was forced into it. The dirt covered Fae to my left yelled alongside the child she held, the two of them extraordinary loud voices in the sea of Forgotten that were so far past the intervention stage that they would probably all have to be committed.

Awesome.

So phase one of plan BFFBDCYB was a bust, which left the actual best friends part. I wasn't sure if I knew how to braid hair, but I would be glad to accidentally knot hers and then laugh about it while drinking wine or something.

Or chocolate milk. Pretty sure they don't drink wine in high school. Or they aren't supposed to. Doesn't matter. Let's get back to knotting ugly shed magic's hair.

"We will show them what the Forgotten can do!"

I had almost reached the front of the crowd and the ringing in my left ear was turning into a migraine thanks to the yelling. Something that I was now joining in on. Not because the cult had successfully reined me in, but because a particularly large man was staring me down. I gave him a smile before yelling and pumping my fist along with the rest of them and muscling my way past the final line of Fallon's worshipers and to my new BFFBDCYB herself.

She saw me immediately, her eyes widening before darting away, and then back to me. I had no clue what she was looking for, Drake and Zoe probably, but the second she turned back I waved and smiled like how I assumed you did when you were seeing your BFFBDCYB for the first time.

She looked like I had slapped her. Perfect. I would have to make sure to actually do that before all of this was over.

Unfortunately, she recovered quickly from her virtual slapping and stepped back toward the crowd, the pallet that she stood on teetering dangerously underneath her. It would have been a perfect chance to upend the slab of former wall and send her flailing into the crowd like a rag doll, but they would probably catch her and spoil my joy.

Fucking sheep.

Another thing on the list.

"We must start by sending one of our own into the belly of the beast. One who stands with us and fights for our purpose, but is trusted by the foolish dragons and can infiltrate them with ease." Damn it. I already knew where this was heading. It was going to be much harder to keep my eyes on her than I thought. "There is an uncut slave who stands among us, who served the princes that have deceived you. She was brought here by the princess who swore to help all of us. The royal bitch who has mysteriously vanished in our time of need not once, but twice."

Our? Bitch? Shed magic had some serious balls on her if she thought she was part of this club.

"There is only one among us who can seek entrance to Rydaim, who can stand before the king and help us infiltrate the crown. What say you Callay, will you stand with us? Will you help us put your master's head on a spike?"

First of all, I only have one master, and I'm not dumb enough to try to put her head anywhere but on some gossamer pillow, still attached to her neck. And second, your head would look better on a pyre.

Best to bite my tongue and restrain the eye roll. She held her hand out to me, little sparks of her magic still falling from her fingertips. Little sparks that wouldn't take much for me to send right back into her. Nothing too painful, just little bits of fire that would fry her nervous system. Brain and all. Easy.

I still owed her a bitch slap, though, so I restrained my magic and grabbed her hand, letting her pull me onto the former wall, the pallet rocking and pulling me into her.

Like the best friends we were. I smiled, something that she quickly returned, the two of us standing there with the biggest shit eating grins that we could muster. Neither of them looking real.

Not that I should be surprised.

I should have called it Best Friends Until You're Doubled Crossed, You Bitch'. BFUYDCYB.

It had a better ring to it.

"What say you Callay? Will you stand by my side? Will you support me in everything I do?" She spoke low and menacingly, making it very clear that she could either read my mind, or my plan wasn't that unique to begin with. The smile dripped from my face like pudding down the shower door. Not that I know what that looks like. But it sure felt like she had stolen my pudding.

I was really looking forward to the fucking pudding, too.

I had clearly underestimated the brains on this girl.

"Will you stand with us Callay?" She held me against her, hand around my waist like the bitching best friends we were and yelled to the crowd.

So much for any hair braiding or knotting or whatever, shed magic had trapped me. All I could do was smile, nod, cheer, and pump my fist in the air like the cult member that I clearly was.

She was smiling with all the joy of a pudding thief as I turned to her, wiggling in her arms and tugging at the tips of her ugly brown hair. Fucking shed magic.

"I will! But only if Fallon returns to Rydaim with me. I can show her the inner workings of the city, of the capital, and of the king. I can reveal to her all that she needs to know to help us defeat the bastards!" God, even saying that word was like acid on my tongue. Acid that I was clearly going to spit right back on her. "We need a leader with powerful magic, who understands the world above, and the world of the royals. I can show her this, and I can use the magic that I retained to save her, to save all of you!"

Their cheers didn't follow. They looked between me and Fallon as her dumb face fell with every word I spoke and she realized how much her little power play had backfired. The shock and horror in her eyes deepened as I extended out my hand, the palm lifted to the ceiling as I let the full breadth of my magic free, the brilliant white light swirling through the cave in a rush of sparkling wind.

Broken pallets lifted into the air, fabric mended, makeshift furniture fit back together like pieces of a jigsaw as the entire village returned to its former glory. Well, glory-ish. It was still a mess. Fallon's once enraptured crowd watched with sagging jaws and wide eyes. Real magic. Not fucking shed magic. And sure as hell not the lame-ass powers of all the Fae that were enslaved in the city.

Real fucking powerful shit that only I could do. That none of these guys had ever seen. I was sure even Zoe would shit a brick. It would probably be solid gold. But still, a brick.

Game. Set. Match.

Xi was going to be so fucking pissed, but right then I didn't even care.

I had so totally just bitch slapped my new best friend.

6

JARRON

JARRON HAD BEEN AROUND ENOUGH OF THE SUPERNATURAL world that he had felt fairly confident in his abilities to classify and define the beasts of his world. Fae. Vampires. The Merfolk. Even the more elusive shifters of his kind; wolves, panthers and everything in between.

He thought he had known them all.

Then Ellie came into his life, and Ellie was so unlike everything he had ever seen that at the time he had no hope of knowing what she was. But their two captors were different, he wasn't sure what they were.

But he had an idea of what they were. And the idea wasn't good.

Lilly reeked of Fae, the way the air melded and heated around her, the silver shimmer in her eyes. It was similar to all of the Fae he had known and that he had helped in his life. She could have been a clone of one Fae in particular however, one he knew.

Her age was right, her coloring was right, even the way she focused on pristine clothing reeked of Callay and the child that had been torn from her.

Callay and Parris' daughter.

Jarron wasn't going to jump to conclusions, and not just because the eerie distortions of the girl was giving him the heebie jeebies. But because someone had turned this child into a weapon, and he really didn't want to be correct about what the other of their captors was.

"I assure you she can take a shower on her own." Henry's voice snarled in Jarron's stomach, ramping up his fear as he stepped away from the harrowing smile of the man and toward the heavy stone door that Lilly had dragged Ellie through a minute before.

The only other door in this room, well besides the one that was locked with a bone key.

"She is quite capable."

Capable of what exactly? Nothing good. Like hell if he was going to leave his mate alone in this underground prison with either of these two. His dragon was screaming with a need to attack and lunge after the man, rip him limb from limb and get them both out of here, but he had to be careful, and that meant treading wisely.

Luckily, he was the golden prince. Charm was something he was not lacking in.

"This I know," Jarron said, leaning over the table scattered with supplies and keeping himself as far away from that damn head as possible. "As you would like to protect her, that is my place right now. She has had quite a scare and needs support as she comes to accept you and allow you back into her life."

Each word coated his tongue in bile and ash, courtesy of his equally frustrated Dragon. Playing into this man's hands was frustrating. Especially seeing as he didn't seem to care. Henry continued to fiddle with a Bunsen burner and a beaker filled with fluid he had extracted from the head-in-a-jar that was clearly his pride and joy.

"She will be fine without you, Jarron." Henry gave him a side glance, his knowing smile twisting nefariously before he went back to his science experiment. "I can promise you that. She has been showering for years without you. I have seen that capable being shower for many years. More than you can ever hope to."

"Then you can understand why I would want to join her. Show her what she's missing before she runs back to you."

Henry's smile faltered, but not in the defeat that Jarron had hoped for. His jealousy spiked, followed closely by a hideous anger that darkened his face in violent angles.

What Jarron wouldn't give for even a slice of his brother's silver tongue right then.

Although, if he was right about what Henry was, it wouldn't matter anyway.

"Well, then you better hurry before your last opportunity passes you by." Henry's smile twitched, pulling his eyes into dangerous little slivers as the silent threat traveled between them.

Jarron didn't dare say anything as the man went back to his work with the head, whatever that work was Jarron had not found out. He moved as fast as he dared out of the large living space and through the stone door that Lilly had led Ellie through.

There was more to his request to leave Henry and his frightening experiments. Showering with Ellie would never be unwanted, but seeing as this hall was the only exit from the main living space, it was their only chance at finding escape. Knowing what was on the other side was vital.

He hadn't expected a flashing neon exit sign to be on the other side of the door, but he also hadn't expected an endless hallway with identical doors carved into the stone every few feet. Great. Their host liked mind games. Not that he was surprised.

Any form of logic was surely useless given what little he had seen of the two, so rather than trying to deduce which door to follow, he simply opened doors. Going down the hall as if it was a conveyor belt, door after door was locked. Door after door, knobs didn't turn. The bolts didn't even jiggle.

Eleven doors later, he realized that they weren't even doors at all.

So, it wasn't a maze, just a facade. Even better. With facades he could find holes.

Find the door that opens, find the hole.

Moving faster, Jarron raced through the conveyor of doors, jerking at knobs until he found one that jiggled.

Unfortunately, when he did, it was because it was opening and a sheath of silver hair was swinging towards him.

Oh look, a hole.

"Hi Lilly," Jarron said with the kindest voice he could muster. "How are you doing?"

Winning smile, kind eyes and a little bit of his golden prince style, and Lilly was still staring at him like she was ready to kill him.

He hadn't had much luck with children in the past, so of course that trend would continue with the only person alive who was immune to his greatest, and pretty much only, weapon.

"If you are looking for information I am not going to give you any." Her look was growing harder, her eyes little sparks of anger as she folded her arms over her chest.

"Information?"

"It's clear you and the Phoenix are trying to find some escape out of here."

"Oh, is that so?" Jarron attempted to put as much coy in his voice as he could, casually leaning against the stone wall as he looked down at the little girl. A move that he realized too late was not truly the best choice seeing as he was still bare chested after their arrival from Rydaim. He didn't need Lilly's questioning stare to point out his faux-pas. At least she no longer looked as though she was going to eat him for breakfast.

Her cheeks had begun to color as Jarron became concerned with his lack of shirt. He was now trying to fold his arms so as to cover most of his nudity, something that wasn't quite working given the proportion of his arms to his bare chest.

In the end he crossed his arms and gripped his neck, building himself a skin turtleneck, even he was aware he looked ridiculous.

"I'm not looking for a way out." He sounded more uncomfortable than casual now, and even his dragon was rumbling laughter in his chest. He deserved it. "I was actually curious about you. How old are you? You weren't even scared of my fire back there."

Lilly tweaked a brow at him, narrowing her eyes in an attempt to figure out his game. It was a fool's game, but Jarron wasn't going to give up that easy.

"Fire doesn't burn me."

"I noticed that," Jarron forced a smile, lowering himself to stare at the girl eye to eye. She didn't seem so vile then, looks like some of his skill wasn't completely useless. "But most kids your age would be scared of fire..."

"Most kids my age are in primary school and poking slugs with sticks," she interrupted with a scoff, popping her hip and sending the frills of her white dress bouncing. "I could swell those slugs until they exploded in their faces. It would be fun to watch them scream."

Just like that the darkness was back. He had to get this back on track before she closed up again and he wasn't able to get anything from her.

"Poking slugs?" He was careful to overemphasize the question. "Surely you are older than the five year olds that do that."

"Five?" Her voice was a shriek and nearly as irate. "I am much older than five. I'm seven."

And the pride was back, for a moment she even looked like a child. Her chin stuck out, her eyes shining. Jarron's heart, however, fell.

Assuming that she had been told the correct age when she had arrived here, it matched up perfectly. He really didn't want to think that this little monster was what had become of Callay's child.

"Well, your daddy seems very proud of you..."

"He's not my father," she snapped, cutting him off, the darkness in her voice so sour that he could feel it drain the warmth from the air around him. "He stole me from my father and the bitch that made the mistake of creating me."

"I'm sorry?"

"That bitch who created me," she said each word slowly, as if that would somehow give more explanation to what was being said. Instead, the words sliced deeper into Jarron, widening the already gaping hole in his chest. "She wasn't fit to be the mother of someone as powerful as I, so he took me away. He brought me somewhere they couldn't find me, so that he could raise me the way that I should be. So that I could become strong."

It was clear that she believed every word, even with the

malice and hatred that dripped from them. Her eyes grew darker until the silver almost appeared as dark as the walls in the endless underground tunnel, little sparks of fire or blood dripping from their depths.

"Well, he has done a wonderful job." Jarron wasn't about to argue with her. The child was so much more powerful than he expected.

Then he or Killian had assumed when they learned what had been done to Callay.

It would be a miracle if they were able to escape.

"He has, which is why you should stop thinking I will give you information, or whatever it is you want from me. You can't escape. She belongs here, that means you belong here too."

Her smile stretched and Jarron fought the need to step back. She may be a child, but she was a haunting child who clearly had no qualms delivering quick slug fueled deaths.

He stepped back anyway.

"I don't think either of us want to escape." His lie was extinguished by a knowing grin from the girl.

"Good. Then you might as well make yourself comfortable. This room is hers, that one is yours," her smile slipped as she stared at the doors with a curl of disgust in her lips. "Separate rooms. I would keep it that way unless you want to wake the dragon."

It was clear she was trying to threaten him, but he couldn't keep the smile off his face at the ridiculousness of the saying.

"You do realize that I am a Dragon, don't you?"

"I'm not stupid. I saw your pathetic fire," she snarled, her eyes flashing with that same crimson spark. "But you are nothing but a marionette with broken strings compared to what he is."

Noted.

"And what is he?" he asked, knowing full well that the girl was not going to give him a straight answer. The way her hair had begun to shimmer and drift in an invisible wind guaranteed it.

Just like her mother's.

"He is something that you cannot beat, so you shouldn't even try."

"And what about Elliot?"

"Elliana is everything. And soon even you will bow before her."

7

ELLIOT

THE WATER WAS STILL RUNNING, FILLING THE TILE AND STONE room with a layer of steam so thick that I couldn't see anything. Not even the sink, and I was sitting on the toilet. I mean, I wasn't sitting *sitting* on the toilet. I was more like huddled up on the toilet in one of the big fluffy towels, legs tucked in, chin on knees, staring in the direction of what I thought was the door.

Of course, I could be staring at the sink for all I knew thanks to all the steam. Although I was sure that one was right beside me.

I had been ushered to my new room and en-suite to "freshen up" and I had. Well, as much as I could before I started to feel like I was losing my mind. The ash was gone, the shirt had found its way into the garbage can, and I was 'clean' as far as anyone was concerned.

I wasn't interested in heading back into the claustrophobic living space, however. Especially considering that I had essentially turned into a delusional crazy-woman.

Every time I blinked I was assaulted by new memories. Or hallucinations. I was going with hallucinations. I really wasn't ready to accept them as memories quite yet considering each one was getting more weird and twisted.

I was starting to feel like I was trapped in a nightmare, well a nightmare that only took place when you blinked. Hence the steam. With wet air I shouldn't have to blink as much. It was a ridiculous thought, but it was working. Except that thinking about it was bringing about a need to blink. Like when someone mentions lice and you automatically start scratching your head.

Great, now I was scratching my head. And blinking.

The moment my eyes drifted closed both the white of the steam and the black of my subconscious was wiped out by a flash of red, a mirror, and Henry screaming some profanity at me while brandishing a knife. Fear drowned me alongside the memory, every muscle so tense that I was one second away from screaming.

I pried my eyes open before that happened, thankful when it was just white steam ahead of me. White steam and a shadowed silhouette, snaking its way toward me.

"Holy shit," I hissed, holding the towel tighter around me and backing myself against the toilet until I was hovering on top of it like a cat ready to pounce. I was one shaky inhale away from leaping when the shadowed stalker began to sparkle in a faint glow of gold.

"Hey, Darling," Jarron whispered as he pushed through the last of the steam. He was smiling broadly, as if that would help me to calm down. Too late for that, between murderous memories of Mr. Psycho Cave Troll and being stalked by a shadow my heart was going to either beat out of my chest or explode. With how my Phoenix was bristling in agitation, I was putting my money on explode.

"You freaked me the fuck out, Jarron," I returned,

keeping my voice low as I clutched the towel to me. Not that I didn't have anything that Jarron hadn't seen.

He wasn't even looking at me anyway, he was looking through the steam as if he expected someone else to be stalking in its white smoky midst. The way he moved, the way he was peering into the smoke was only adding to the icy dread that I shouldn't be feeling in the warm bathroom. So, of course I chose right then to blink and was instantly assaulted with a vision of myself in the mirror I had seen before, this time holding a vial in my hands.

The small glass vial was similar to the one that Killian had given me, even from where I stood in front of the memory I could see the same swirling opalescence move through it. I could feel the same pull I had felt with the other one. It was familiar, everything about it was familiar.

Well, except that I was wearing an outfit that looked like it belonged in a disco museum, staring at myself in a mirror that looked about a hundred years old. Killian, Zoe, Drake, they were nowhere to be found.

Just me and a vial as I slowly lifted it to my lips, hungry for whatever it held inside.

"It's a spell," I spoke aloud, eyes popping open to Jarron who was staring at me, completely clueless to the fact that anything had happened.

"What's a spell?" He was lost and I didn't blame him, he was still glancing at the smoke as if I was answering the question to someone else.

"I mean, we're alone." I quickly recovered, not quite ready to detail my insanity just yet. "Well, unless something followed you in."

I was hesitant to refer to either Henry of Lilly as someone, and not even because of the whole cave troll thing. All of these flashes of memory, they weren't adding up.

Something was very wrong about that guy. And not in a cave troll way.

"I don't think anyone followed me in." Jarron's response was more dragon than man. "Which is good, because we need to find a way out."

I could only nod, "Tell me something I don't know. But good luck finding it. There is nothing in that living room, and I am sure this whole endless hall of doors is a maze, at least with what Lilly said."

"What did she say?" His brow furrowed into a dangerous scowl, his knees hitting against the toilet bowl as he leaned towards where I still sat on top of the tank.

His skin was glistening with sweat and steam, the ash and blood that covered him dripping over his skin, over the bruise that was forming near his eyes, over the dozens of cuts and still healing gashes that were lining his torso.

We were surrounded by steam, just like when we had met. Then it had been me covered in ash and neither of us looked as though we had come through the losing side of a war. Jarron's eyes burned as he waited for a response, the gold nearly swallowing the black abyss of thought that occupied his face.

"She said that the hallways were a maze," I said with a smug smile, "She also said more about endless walking and never escaping. You know, normal bad guy stuff. She creeps me out."

"Don't worry, you aren't alone in that," Jarron sighed, sinking to sit on the toilet below where I was perched on the tank so that his back was pressing against my thigh. The subtle contact made me want to fold into him, to curl against his warmth and the smell of pine like some kind of cat.

Meow.

"I met her outside. I'm glad I found you. We have more problems than smug little girls..."

"I know," I whispered as I blinked, my mind filling with a flash of another white expanse, and another shadowed shape stepping toward me.

This one wasn't steam. It was fog, and that shadow smiled at me before I pushed it away. My mind filled with the memory of a scream as creepy ass Henry stumbled back, off what I was sure was a cliff.

Why were my crazy memories full of so much death and murder? This wasn't really boding well.

I shook my head in an attempt to banish the image and scream. But it lingered as I stared at Jarron, at his wide fearful eyes, sure that that time he had seen.

Well, maybe not the memory, I didn't think I was that powerful. But for all I know my eyes rolled back and I started speaking in Latin.

"Are you okay?" Yep, he totally saw something.

"I'm okay, whoever I just threw off a cliff may not be so lucky."

"What?" He quirked an eyebrow. "Since when have you been throwing people off cliffs?"

Well, I had been throwing myself off cliffs long before he came along, but I wasn't going to get into that.

"Every time I close my eyes I keep having some kind of memory flashes. They started after I saw Henry for the first time and have gotten worse since then. Not all of them are good, and not because of blood and stuff."

There had been plenty of that, but it wasn't just blood and knives that were filling my mind. It was plotting and mayhem and things that I was still going to stubbornly deny that I had seen.

"I am not the bad guy." I said it like it was a mantra that would banish the bad that was trying to seep into my soul. I wasn't sure it worked. I couldn't get the scream out of my head from when I pushed Henry off the cliff, or my laugh from when I had pestered a child in some warehouse, or what I was sure was some kind of experiment room.

That was the one that was gluing itself to my soul like a parasite. Didn't help that the whole set up was eerily similar to the micro lab Henry had in the kitchen, right down to the head in a jar. Except this head was a different head, not that it helped.

More was better in everything *but* heads in jars.

I pushed my focus into wiping away the gunk that was dripping from Jarron's face, my motions rough and agitated as I tried to wipe what was probably a bruise off his neck.

"Elliot," Jarron whispered, his hand wrapping around my wrist as he stopped me, his thumb dragging over the skin.

His fingers were warm, his hand was soft. I was frozen underneath his touch as his fingers dragged over my skin, the liquid pools of blood and ash dripping from his chin to congregate against out intertwined hands.

The swirls of red and black looked like gnarled gems against our skin, the colors as tangled as my mind right then. I wished I could wipe these memories away as easily I could a bit of blood. At the very least, I wished the memories were as graceful as the color that was dripping onto our skin, dancing over our hands.

"You are not the bad guy," he whispered, his finger soft against my chin as he pulled my focus to him. "Trust me. I have been on the bad guy's side before. I've *been* the bad guy. And you don't even come close."

"Some of the things I am seeing are things that the good guys don't do." I was firm, or at least I tried to be. But like a fool I chose right then to blink and was granted the vision of Henry again, the knife swinging between us, except this time he wasn't the one who was holding it. I was. And the thing was covered with blood so dark it looked black.

"Fucking black blood." I gasped as I shifted away from the dark blood that lingered between memory and the smooth reality of Jarron's cheekbones. Pressing my back against the slick wall of the bathroom, I took a few deep breaths before my senses caught up to me. Damn it all, this memory Ferris wheel I was on was really causing a whole lot of problems.

"What did you see, Ellie?"

Pain shot up my arm as the pressure of his hand around my wrist increased and I smacked him away, giving him a glare that might as well have been received by a brick wall with how his brow had furrowed.

"Fucking cave troll." I was so freaked out right now I wasn't even going to give the guy a name.

I tucked the towel closer to me as I nursed feeling back into my hand, the skin had gone red so fast I wouldn't be surprised if his dragon was thinking about eating me, the smoke that was drifting from between his teeth was a frightening grey color against the white steam that was slowly starting to dissipate.

The water was still running. I guess the hot water had run out. I hope no one else wanted to take a shower, like the blood covered boy beside me for example. He already looked pissed, but I had a feeling that was for other reasons.

"What did you see?" Jarron repeated, hissing through his teeth and sending more tendrils of dark grey smoke to dance with the steam.

"Henry, with cuts all over his face..."

"And black blood." Jarron cut me off. "His blood."

"Probably. I was the one with the knife." I sounded way too nonchalant for what I had said.

"I was right." Jarron left the toilet, stepping toward the shower.

"Right about what?" My question bounced against stone and tile, echoing until it was twice as loud as I was sure I said it. Either that or I was stress yelling.

Jarron's face twisted into panic as he dropped his pants and stepped into the shower, giving me a perfect view of the muscular roundness of his ass as it flexed and disappeared behind a curtain.

He clearly wanted me to join him in with how he was now waving me down, leaving the curtain open enough for me to slide through.

Because hopping into the shower right this second was clearly the best option for us.

How had this conversation gone from a freaky hissed discussion about black blood to an invitation to what I could only assume was shower sex? My muscles still too tense and uncomfortable for that to happen. Even standing and walking toward him was lodging that knot deeper into my gut.

"I'm not going in there," I hissed from the other side of the curtain. I refused to look in and I refused to drop the fluffy towel. Images of his body pressed against mine were trying to sneak in already. I snapped my eyes shut in a need to banish the fantasy, and was instead assaulted by the same knife, and the same streaks of black blood as Henry laughed and began to change, his face elongating....

Yeah, I totally screamed. The sound rumbled off the stone and tile as Jarron grabbed me, his still dirty hand wrapping around my mouth as he stifled the scream and dragged me into the shower anyway. He held me against him, the lukewarm water falling over us like a rainstorm, the soaked towel clinging to each of my curves like the little black dress that Killian had bought for me once upon a time.

That memory hurt as much as all the others.

"Shhh," Jarron hissed in my ear, still holding me against him, even though his hand had thankfully fallen from my mouth. "The last thing we need is those two barging their way in here."

"Would they do that?" It was a dumb question and I knew it. I was actually surprised I had been able to shake Lilly in the first place. She really hadn't been interested in leaving.

Which was a shame because I had been *really* interested in showering in front of a kid. I won that one and shuttled her ass out of here.

"Tell me what you saw," Jarron whispered, still holding me against him. The water fell over us so that I could barely hear him. That, I realized, was exactly the point.

I hesitated, keeping my eyes wide even though droplets were pouring over my face, dripping over my forehead and off my nose like you see in all those romance movies. Jarron's was doing the same, but, you know, with blood and ash.

And the romance was gone.

"First, I saw him with a knife. I think he had stabbed someone. I felt pain and the knife was covered with blood. Then I saw me with the knife. His face was cut, he was bleeding and the knife was covered in blood. But it was black."

"Did you see any more than that?" His hands had been

gentle against my back until that point, his fingers soft as they pressed against the towel. Suddenly they were pushing into both towel and back like tiny little pricks of pressure and I cringed.

"No."

"Can you try?"

His voice was so dark that I wasn't about to fight him. Although I did give him a fiery look before I closed my eyes.

This time, however, there was no more blood, just a lot of steam and other hands. Hands belonging to another person, hands that were traveling over my body in uncomfortably similar ways.

Gasping, I forced my eyes open and stepped back into the tile sides of the shower, cringing against the cold.

"What the fuck?" I really didn't need to be seeing that again. Not that Henry looked bad, but I didn't want him. And I certainly didn't want my mind full of the abs and hands that didn't belong to the man in front of me.

"Elliot? What did you see?"

"Something I have no intention of seeing ever again." I answered him, grateful there was a little bit of space between us with how my heart was thundering against my ribs.

The only downside of having stepped away was that I could now see him, in all of his beautiful Jarron glory. I swallowed, willing my eyes to stay open and not tarnish this vision with something, or rather someone, else. Something that was even more important with how I was still reacting to Henry's existence. There was definitely something about that guy that I was missing, and the bipolar lust my Phoenix was experiencing was making it worse.

Half the time I was sure my Phoenix wanted to jump into his arms, the other half I was pretty sure that both of us wanted to rip his head off and find escape away from him and the creepy kid.

"What's going on? I mean, besides us being trapped by some creepy cave troll and his daughter?"

"He's not a cave troll," Jarron's voice was as hard as the gold in his eyes. "As far as I know those don't even exist, but what he is, is far worse."

I waited for him to continue, cold water hitting against my skin as the last of the steam faded away. We were officially exposed and who knew what was on the other side of the opaque shower curtain. I pressed myself against the tile, feeling the slick stones begin to heat under the agitated boil of my skin.

"Well, that sounds promising," I mumbled when he didn't say anything. Jarron checked behind him, peering at the curtain as if he could see through it. Well, at least I wasn't the only one who was feeling vulnerable.

Which really wasn't helping.

"No matter what you do, do not speak his name aloud." Jarron hissed the sound only slightly louder than the water as he stepped back into the stream, pressing himself closer to me. "In fact, you might even do better not to think his name. I do not know how deep his power can penetrate."

I had never seen Jarron look so stern. So scared. Even when he sat tied up and ready for death at the fountain in Rydaim this level of haunting agitation did not color his eyes.

"You're scaring the shit out of me, Jarron." Even my voice was shaking, the nervous energy having grown so much that water was now evaporating the second it hit against my skin with a faint pop and a sizzle. "Why can't I say his name? Not that I would want to, but don't you think that is extreme?"

Jarron shook his head, although his eyes never left mine.

"You don't want to welcome a demon into where he doesn't belong. Lock his name away..."

"A demon?" I interrupted before he could continue with his instructional 'how to avoid a demon' video.

I wasn't quite ready for that yet. I was still stuck on the first disk of this instructional series. 'Surprise! Demons exist and you used to be mated to one!'

I was sure I was going to be sick.

"Yes, but I wouldn't go around advertising that we have figured out that bit. Not that they are doing a very good job with hiding it. The guy smells like what happens when rot begins to decay." He wrinkled his nose. I wasn't about to ask how he had smelled them, I had dealt with that enough with Zoe. Must be a dragon thing, identifying supernatural creatures by smell.

My powers had been unlocked, but I wasn't smelling anything besides damp cave rock, which wasn't exactly pleasing in its own right.

"So, is Lilly...?" It was weird that I was hopeful that the answer would be yes. It would definitely explain some of the creepy as hell vibes that the little girl was putting out. But Jarron was already shaking his head no.

"She is something else entirely. I have an idea, but I need to find proof first. Either way, she appears to be one of Parris's creations, not that that makes her existence any less troublesome for us."

"Vague some?" I prodded, but he shook his head, clearly he wasn't ready to elaborate. "Okay, fine. So how do we defeat a demon?"

"You don't." He was sure and I was going to throat punch him, but in a non-violent, loving way of course. Instead, I settled for shrieking.

"What do you mean we can't!"

"Shhh!" Jarron hissed, smashing his palm against my mouth and giving the other side of the shower curtain a solid glare. "You are seriously going to get us killed."

"It seems we are already on the fast track to that." I grumbled, earning myself another exasperated look.

"We need to get out of here, Elliot." Jarron said, still peering at the shower curtain as though it had offended him. "We need to escape, and we need to take the kid with us."

"Are you sure that's a good idea? Even if we can find a way out, I am pretty sure the haunted marionette would either rat us out or make us explode before we see daylight again."

"Let me worry about the kid. I need you to worry about finding us an escape."

I folded my arms over my chest, hoisting my towel up. "And how do you expect me to do that?"

Jarron turned back to me, that playful smile twitching around the corner of his lips as his eyes sparked with gold.

"You got us out of Rydaim. You clearly got away from him once before," Jarron whispered, pushing some of the long strands of my hair behind my ear, the tips of his fingers lingering on my temple. "Channel the power inside of you, Elliot. I know you can get us all out of here."

I knew what he was asking. While I wasn't exactly against it, there was something else inside of me that was going absolutely crazy at the idea.

This time, I knew what my phoenix was thinking. I knew what she was trying to do. Because I felt it too.

It wasn't the first time I regretted drinking the Kool-Aid. But I had a feeling any power I was about to harness wasn't going to do what Jarron wanted it to.

Go, scary ass cannon go!

8

KILLIAN

WIND WHIPPED THROUGH KILLIAN'S HAIR, PULLING THE strands over his face and adding curled lines of chestnut to the endless blue sky. The color bathed the world, it covered everything and even though he could not see the sun, he turned his face up to the warmth of the sky. The only place that wasn't drenched in azure was the tall white and brown spires of the mountains that stretched up like spiny fingers. As if the mountains wanted nothing more than to reach it.

Killian wanted that. He wanted to reach the blue, the clouds. He wanted the icy wind that tugged at his hair and clothes to be everywhere, he wanted to taste the sky. He wanted to dance beside the mountains and cut through the boiling grey clouds like some kind of winged snake.

Something inside of him wanted that, but he didn't know what it was. He didn't know how something like that would even be possible. It was a dream. A dream that buzzed in his head, swirling with the black fog that was always filling his mind.

Always. Although how long *always* was, was a mystery. Perhaps as long as the dream to dance in the blue sky had been with him. Not dance. Soar. There was too much bulk on Killian for him to look like anything other than a boulder when dancing.

Black smoke drifted through his mind again, wiping away the dream and leaving him standing, his face turned up to the sky as the wind rushed in all directions, pulling at the hem of the thin cotton pants he wore. The thin fabric tugged against the wind, letting the cold in as though nothing was there, but Killian barely shivered, he barely felt it, even though everyone around him was clad in layers of leather and fur.

They looked like bits of animals sewn together, swathes of fur huddled as the wind blew in another gust, the babble of his master carried on its back. The little man was steps away, haggling with an angry man who was saying something about how he was being robbed, or that was what Killian's mind was telling him they were saying. The language sounded familiar, even though he was sure he had never heard it.

His master snapped back in a threat that was as clear, the tone of it zapped the last pull of the sky out of Killian's heart, his spine zipping up in expectation. He had a job to do here. Guard him, that's what his master had said.

Hopefully the shopkeeper would think better of his foolish words. Killian had a feeling that if the little man didn't give his master his way it would not end well.

And that he would be the one to end it.

The wind blew colder, bits of ice hitting against Killian's cheek and filling his head with the scent of pine and snow as a storm grew closer. Snow was only a few minutes away now, they needed to get back to the inn before the winds picked up too much.

Killian shook his head. Why did he know that about the

snow? There must be a reason, but like the sky, like the heavy weight that was always screaming in his chest, he couldn't figure out why. Hair whipped over his face, his vision filled with curls that looked more like smoke, smoke that obscured his vision and made his head spin. The broken colors twisted over his master as he walked back from the seller's tent, the shopkeeper grumpily packing up his wares in expectation of a storm.

Mattia was smiling, clutching what looked like nothing more than a square of fabric to his chest. The tattered thing didn't look like something to be proud of or something to have gotten so upset over, but Mattia was happy. Good, seeing as the sky was ready to open up.

Churning clouds were multiplying around the tops of the mountains. They circled and boiled as though some old witch was stirring the sky, preparing to swallow the entire village with her spell. This far up in the mountains the only thing they could do was take shelter.

Again, another thing he didn't know why he knew. Before he could think on it, the black smoke clouded his mind, swelling over a memory of what looked like Mattia swaying by the fire.

"Come, come, darling," Mattia said as he reached Killian. The man's voice pulled through the black fog as his hand wrapping around Killian's hip, pulling him toward the tiny wooden structure that sat in the center of the little village. The heavily shuttered two story structure was the only space to rent a room, and the only safety from the snow that ravaged these mountains.

Killian hesitated, Mattia's urgent fingers slipping from his hip as he hurried past him. He didn't even notice that Killian hadn't moved.

Killian hadn't turned from the fast moving clouds that

were consuming the blue, the pillows of white dancing without him.

Without him.

He needed to be there with them. Perhaps if he jumped high enough he could grab hold and push himself up the rest of the way. The idea was ridiculous, but the warming burn in his chest didn't seem to think so, the heat that was radiating from his heart wanted that. He took a step forward, preparing to jump.

"Killian!" Mattia had come back. His voice was a slither of ice against Killian's neck, it was a fog of black that moved through him and swallowed the clouds, swallowed the desire to be among them.

He was clearly losing it. No one could dance among clouds. No one could grab hold of them. And clouds certainly didn't want you to mingle with them in such a way. His master had warned him before they left that there would be magic in the air. He clearly should have done a better job of heeding the warning.

"Come Killian," Mattia commanded, his voice pulling Killian on a string, the two of them weaving through the villagers as they brought in livestock and wares and everything else ahead of the storm.

The door to the inn was a heavy slab of oak, the hinges groaning loudly as they pushed open. The warm air inside the wood structure mixed with the cold in a tornado that pushed and pulled against the door and rattled the single window that was inset in the wall opposite the fire. The window was already bolted and shingled from the outside, but it screamed as though it was trying to escape. Warning them all that it was no longer safe.

The window's screams were drowned by the shouts of the occupants as papers and fabric were sent flying, extinguishing the fire with a puff of giant's breath. The panicked babble swelled with anger as Mattia calmly walked into the inn, striding past the dead fire and the ripped and aged chairs toward the staircase, leaving the door open behind him.

At least five men rushed to the door in their attempt to shut the thing, but even with five of them it didn't budge. The wind pushed against it as though it had been welcomed for dinner, barging its way in and holding the door open for the specks of snow that had begun to fall. Mattia continued to the staircase, still holding the square of fabric in one hand, and Killian's tether with the other.

Although that one might be in his head.

Killian could feel the pull after his master, even if he didn't see a rope.

He fought against the invisible line, pushing the door closed with little effort as it slid back into place. All of the locals stood a foot below him and they all looked up at him in awe, mumbling what he was sure were thanks before they bolted the door shut with large slabs of wood.

Looks like they were the last ones in, or the storm was bad enough that they wouldn't take the chance to open the entry again. Either way, they should all be glad that they were on this side, the storm that was coming would swallow the inn. Hopefully they had enough food to last that.

Hopefully they knew that, because Killian wasn't sure how he did.

"Come get me if it happens again," Killian said, his voice weirdly echoing in his head. The shorter men looked at him funny, heads cocked to the side as they tried to understand him.

Perhaps they didn't speak English, or perhaps his voice was as echoing to them as it was to him. He didn't remember everything sounding so garbled before. He remembered sounding much more powerful than that. Much stronger.

As strong as the door.

No, stronger.

Maybe he was stronger. Before the thought could fully form, Mattia called down to him, his voice echoing over the stairs as that line he felt between them yanked him forward and sent him stumbling up the stairs.

"I wish you would stay closer, darling," Mattia said as Killian reached him, juggling his precious cloth and the keys as he worked to open the door. "I hate having you under my full control. But no worries, we will get there soon enough. It was the same with my dear falcon in the beginning, I couldn't trust her anywhere but by my side. She came to love me in the end. Oh how I miss her. Her warmth against me... you will have to do in the meantime and when she returns I will introduce you to her the proper way. Then all of our warmth can lie together."

He was rambling as he pulled Killian into the room, nothing of what he was saying making any form of sense. There was a falcon, Killian could remember the beady eyes staring at him, but he had been sure that was a dream and not something from this reality. The way his master was speaking made him wonder if this was all a dream.

"I know you will love her the way I do." Mattia turned to him, his accent dragging through his consonants as his eyes darkened, as he stepped closer with a weird hunger in his eyes, the square of cloth still held between them. "The way that I am learning to love you."

Killian's stomach flipped, his muscles tightening as that same warmth in his chest tried to break free. He wasn't sure what he was feeling, but the emotions didn't match the weird look that was glinting in Mattia's eyes as he stepped closer to him, his hand grazing over his waist as he reached back and pushed the door shut.

It shut and locked with a snap that made Killian jump, the room exploding in light as the fire and the two lanterns burst to life.

"Now, come Killian, let me teach you about your master," Mattia's eyes were hooded before he stepped away, his hand sliding through the air and bringing a table and two chairs to the center. A pot of water and a bottle of green fluid came next, followed by a spoon, cubes of sugar, and a little brown jar that looked as old as much of the furniture.

It was like a tea party for two, but not one where little girls would act out fantasies. Well, unless those fantasies were dark and twisted.

"Sit." Mattia said, tapping the chair on the opposite side of the table before he sat down himself, setting the grey gingham in the center. He smoothed it out like one would a tablecloth. Odd, considering that the thing was little larger than the palm of Killian's hand.

There was nothing pulling Killian toward the table but the directions of his master, and in that moment that was not nearly enough to keep him from the bed and the sleep that the darkness in his head was screaming for.

Master or not, he wasn't quite sure why he needed to listen to him. He was tired and the warmth inside of him was tired. He needed to sleep. Sleep and to heal, although he wasn't quite sure why the second part of that existed in his mind.

He was headed to the bed when Mattia pulled back a corner of the fabric unfolding the square until it was twice the size, revealing a bit of black sparkle in the center, like stars scraped from the night sky. The tiny specks of pitch were darker than the ash that sat in the hearth and yet brighter than the light that burned in the lamp Mattia had set on the table. They sat in their dark glow, large enough to consume his whole soul while small enough to sit atop the point of a needle.

It was everything and was nothing. It was the whole world and it was nothing at all. And it was pulling him right to the chair.

The feet of the old wooden seat ground against the floor as he haphazardly pulled it out in his haste to get closer, his knee bumping against the side of the table and sending the bits of black rolling over the surface of the cloth like fish in a rollicking sea. The specks glimmered in the lamplight as they jumped and danced.

"Be careful you big moron!" Mattia swung into a rage as Killian sat down opposite the table. The little man's hands spread over the table, cupping around the black protectively as he dragged whatever had escaped back to the center. Coaxing them back as though they were alive.

"This is the last of this kind of magic on earth. The things I have done to hide it, to regain it. If we were to lose even a speck... you cannot understand the magic that would be unleashed."

Mattia fluttered around the table as he mumbled so low Killian wasn't even sure if he was talking to him. The man seemed far more agitated than a bump to a table would dictate. Cursing in multiple languages, speaking to them as one does a child as he continued to gather and fidget. His focus never left the specks of black.

Killian couldn't be sure, but that didn't seem normal. Best not to disturb the man. Killian sat back carefully, keeping his knees tucked away from the table and his immense bulk hovering on the tiny chair. It was an uncomfortable position, one that required a little bit of gymnastics to accomplish, but he forced himself into it, if only to be closer to the fine specks of dust that Mattia was finally moving away from.

It took too much willpower to keep himself bound against the back of the chair and not leaning toward the things. The glittering bits were calling to him, begging him to whisk them away and... and... he didn't know what, but he was sure he wanted them, he was sure he could hear them whisper in the back of his mind.

"What is it?" Killian finally asked when Mattia had stopped muttering and he could get a word in. Mattia however, jerked his head up, his eyes hard little specks that reminded Killian of the falcon from his dream. He nearly jumped away, but his bumbling knees were capable of sending the table flying and he cowered against his chair instead. Anything to keep the bits of everything safe.

Luckily, the wicked gleam left his eyes and Mattia leaned closer, over the table and the fine black powder as his smile spread between them.

"Have I told you about my sister?" Mattia whispered it like it was some kind of secret, as though he was worried about the answer.

Killian didn't know why he would be, nothing about a sister of any kind was ringing a bell. There had been a mention of someone, an interest of something. But he couldn't remember any more than that. Everything was too muddled, too full of black smoke. Smoke that drifted through him with the same color of the ash, the same glittering black.

"Suvi," Mattia clarified, as if that would help. But his mind was still nothing but black smoke and he shook his head.

Mattia's smile stretched and he sat back in his chair, his focus still drifting between the folds of the cloth and Killian until he shifted, the chair creaking beneath him.

"Is that what this is? Your sister?" Killian asked, the greedy rumble of his voice lined with a childlike wonder that didn't quite match. Something wasn't adding up, it arced against Killian's heart, that warmth returning. Although this time he was sure the heat was because of the glittering ash. He wanted to touch it, to find out. He reached forward, but didn't get any closer before Mattia batted his hand away, giving him a dangerous look.

"You are more stupid than I would have thought." Mattia sighed. "Perhaps you will not be of use to me as I had hoped. Let's find out shall we."

Nothing of what the man was saying made sense, but the wretched darkness had returned to his eyes, his lips twisting together in a sneer before he pushed the tip of his finger toward the sparks on the cloth.

He was going to touch it, to feel the light that was emanating from them. Killian would have been jealous, but his master's finger never made contact with the tiny bits, they all scattered away from his skin, shaking their way to the edge of the fabric as if they were scared of him.

Wind howled outside, choosing that moment to pound against the shuttered window and sneak through the flue of the hearth, filling the room with smoke and glowing embers of ash and soot swept up from the fire. Papers, blankets, and even an old satchel beside them rattled as the wind spun through the room as though the storm was trying to find its way inside.

Warm and cold washed through Killian's muscles, something in the wind trying to pull him to his feet, even as the specks of black planted him in his chair. He was stuck, watching the world shutter, watching the tiny things hit against the edge of the cloth, shivering as if they were cold, as if they were trying to escape.

As if they were alive.

The wind picked up more, the chill from the wind dripping in the air as ice coated the inside of the room.

"This is not my sister," Mattia said, not so much as jerking away from the howling wind, away from the bits of snow that had trailed down the chimney and were now pressing against the inside of the glass panes, forming tiny little drifts against the spiderwebs of ice that were coating the surface. "But my sister is the key to everything. I don't know how much you know about magic, but I will tell you this. There are two sides to every cause. Good and bad. Light and dark. Demon and angel. And in the center is something that is worse than both, something that carries power, fear and hope on their back like a mule. It creates the battles that rule the world and plays with its creations like mice against a maze."

Killian sat in confusion as ice caked against the walls, the room growing dark as the last of the fire extinguished and took any hope of warmth with it. Even the warmth in his heart was gone.

It was only the two of them sitting by a table of absinthe, a flame, and the specks that held the entire world. Mattia wasn't making any sense, and what these things were was making even less. His master was chasing the specks around the cloth now, his too long nail scraping against the coarse cotton with a noise so fine that Killian shouldn't have been able to hear it. It shouldn't have ground against his bones the way it did.

"My sister and I are on either side of that line. One traveling along the line of light, the other along the dark.

She is proud to be light. As I am proud to swallow the dark of the world," Mattia finally continued, the motion of his finger coming to a halt, although the rest of the room did not calm. The ice was growing so thick now that the rustic wood paneling of the walls below was swallowed. They were in a room of ice, sitting amongst the snow. Even when they were outside in the brisk wind Killian hadn't shivered, but now everything was freezing against his bones.

"So it is dark magic?" Killian's teeth chattered together with the question, the thick coils of his arms wrapping one over the other as he tried to keep any remaining warmth inside. But it was all slipping away. Sliding to the floor with the rest of the ice.

He didn't know how to make it stop. The fire was still burning in the hearth.

"It is what is in the middle. It is what creates the world." Mattia had stopped chasing the specks altogether now, and was now pouring himself a glass of the absinthe, carefully placing the spoon and sugar in a stack. He didn't even shiver as he scrapped ice from the corner of the table and added it to the glass, his hair didn't even move against the wind.

"Touch the cloth, Killian." Mattia wasn't even looking at him, he was hungrily preparing his drink, his tongue pressing into the side of his cheek in a pucker of anticipation.

The wind had picked up, the ice growing so deep that it weaved against Killian's hair, the chill snaking against his spine as it built underneath the cotton of his clothing. He didn't know what was going on, or why Mattia didn't care that he was moments from freezing to death.

"Touch them." At Mattia's command, the warmth in Killian's chest grew, the heat spreading over him and cracking the ice, pulling him toward the tiny black specks.

Something told him to be afraid, to take the cloth and run. Instead, he leaned forward and placed his finger in the center of the cloth, his eyes widening as all of those little black specs skittered toward his touch.

The bits of black danced around the tip of his finger, spinning and rippling as though he had dipped his finger in a pool of water. Water that was clinging to him. Each little speck glittered as it trailed over his skin, the mass of glittering black stretching over his knuckle and his hand as though they were going to consume it. It was frightening to see, to see his hand turn to the depth of a starry sky.

As scary as it was, however, he felt nothing. Nothing more than a whisper of touch, and a vastness that was consuming him from the inside out. Everything in his mind, in the world, was open. As though he could see through the universe. Right to the woman with the red hair. Mattia's sister maybe? Or perhaps what was in the middle. The answer was on the tip of his tongue, but before he could pull the name out of the expanse, Mattia's raspy voice and aggressive touch pulled him back.

"Wonderful," Mattia said, taking a sip of his drink before grabbing at Killian's finger, letting the pads of his fingers drag down the skin and chase away every last one of the glittering black specs, the ebony skittering away from the warlock's touch. "It looks like you are good for something, darling. She knows you are here."

Killian jerked up in question, ready to ask, but was instantly pushed away in confusion. The ice had gone. The chill from the room had gone. The fire was roaring in the hearth. Everything was as it was before, as if he had imagined it all. Killian's jaw hung open like a fool, his eyes wide as he looked around him like a child who was seeing snow for the first time.

"She has taken it away," Mattia said, as if that answered anything.

The tiny specs of black made even less sense now than they did before, and Mattia's announcement only added to that. The pull to learn more about them however, had vanished, taken into the vast abyss that Killian still felt pull somewhere inside of him. Like a drug he could never get enough of.

"Don't get lost in the fog, darling," Mattia whispered, setting his glass down to wrap his hands around Killian's vast palm. He must have noticed him trying to sneak his fingers closer. Luckily for Killian, he did not look upset this time, his lips were softer, his eyes glazed over. Mattia either understood what Killian was going through, or he was drunk.

Killian would fancy a guess that the absinthe was hitting him.

"I have been there. I have felt the world as you have. I felt her soul and sold mine for a piece of it. If I would have known what I was selling, however, I would have killed her instead. I will kill her someday. I got this much already." His words didn't slur, but the longer he spoke the more the darkness in his eyes faded away, until he looked like the man he had met the other day, when he had fallen from the sky.

Killian jerked, warmth racing through him as the thought hit him, the utterly ridiculous thought. No one can fall from the sky. They would have to come from the sky, they would have had to fall from the clouds.

The clouds.

He had wanted the clouds. He had wanted to jump up to them.

The thoughts buzzed inside of him, swirling with the

black as they had before. Except this time it wasn't as much smoke as it was the empty nothing of the universe that had pulled into him. The beads of black began to race again, even though no one was touching them. They were drifting over the cloth on their own, pulling themselves closer to Killian. Trying to reach him.

"Don't touch them again, Killian, or they will take you where you don't want to go." Mattia dropped Killian's hand, and he almost lunged across the table to grab the cloth and the specks and carry them out of here, away from the warlock across from him.

Mattia was already folding the cloth, however, stowing them away with one hand and drinking the green poison with the other.

"But master," Killian pleaded, the title bringing a smile to Mattia's lips. "They are wanting me."

"They will come to you soon, but not today. Not until I have taught you what you need to do to protect yourself. These are not for you. Not yet."

Now his words were slurring, perhaps he could get his answer.

"What are they?" Killian asked, his voice deeper than he thought it could go.

Mattia didn't even hesitate.

"It's the last of the ash from the soul of the earth. The last fragments of the horn I stole from the heart of the earth. The Unicorn. That's why I need you. You are going to kill her for me and collect the pieces, then you can have all that you want. It can be yours Killian. But I? I need her soul. She will come to you, Prince Killian. And then the world will be mine."

Prince?

The black buzzed again, the universe swallowing the

smoke and pulling him right into a city, right to that same red headed woman. She smiled at him and little bits of reality peeked through. Yes! He was a Prince! He was a prince, but before he could grasp any more of the thought it was gone, swathed in black as Mattia snapped his fingers and Killian slid sideways off his chair, falling face first to the floor.

"Not yet, though. You aren't ready yet. *Killy.*"

That was familiar too, although he couldn't recall why. He lay there, trying to hold onto his life as the sieve of his memory spread over the floor, watching the wet of heartbreak pool over his cheek, and staring at a speck of black that had rolled under the bed.

9

ELLIOT

Finding your way out of a scary underground cave that is haunted by a demon that you used to be mated to was harder than it should be. Especially when you were locked in a bedroom that was part of a maze of doors that quite literally stretched on forever. Add to that my inability to blink without being assaulted by what was becoming a string of murders and I was starting to think that Jarron had put his trust in the wrong person, and not because finding an escape out of here was going to be impossible.

Yes, it was probably pessimistic, I couldn't be the villain after all, we already had too many of them. Plus, Jarron had promised that the doors were facades, but it's not like I could check. Because as I said, I was locked in my own personal underground bunker. Jarron had been shuffled out shortly after our shower, Lilly mumbling about how she was going to show him his room. Before I could follow, the door slammed shut in my face and I was left in the bedroom only seconds after leaving my slightly steamy bathroom. I hadn't even had a chance to inspect the bedroom, and now I was considering hunkering down in the bathroom for the remainder of this trip.

Past me must have been a very vain creature.

I had thought the painting in the living room was beautiful, but the painting that pretty much made up my headboard was equivalent to those oversized gaudy pictures that old ladies have done of themselves.

All I was missing was an overly groomed dog with a pink bow.

The painting wasn't the worst of it, the room was littered with slightly dusty images of 'my first mate' and I, a weird selection of trinkets, and clothes that were way too pink for someone with hair as red as mine. For being so vain, past me also had no style sense.

After going through a few drawers of the overly large and far too intricately carved dresser, I finally found a long cottony jumper that I was sure at one point had been considered underwear and decided to wear that. It was soft, not too see-through, and covered more of me than any underwear I had ever known. Like an old timey bathing suit or what hookers would wear in the 1600s. Because I clearly knew about that.

Which I didn't, even though I had been slapped with an image of a red windmill and French can-can dancers. Nope, not going to accept anything about that. We had been in Paris on tour a few years ago and we all went to see the show. Well, they went and I snuck after them like the under aged troublemaker I was.

I knew what went on in there now, and what used to go on in there a hundred years or so ago.

"Must. Keep. Eyes. Open." Saying it aloud would have been far more effective if I didn't force my eyes open to a framed picture of 'that guy' and I, this one looked to be of us on a beach. Didn't matter. Didn't care. I slammed the photo down and tried to lock away both image and the guy's name.

A demon. I had been mated to a demon. Which also meant I had been in love with a demon. My Phoenix rustled and cooed at that thought, my heart beating like the thing was a micro-furnace inside of me. I was so not okay with this. Not the demon. Not the being in love with a demon. Not my masochistic Phoenix being in love with a demon. I always thought I had a bad side, but this was extreme.

I slammed down another picture with even more force, the sound of shattering glass like music to my ears and turned to the rest of the room, and the pictures of He...that guy and me.

A blink gave me another flash of his smiling face, a rush of warmth from his hand wrapped around mine and I cringed, which is really hard to do with your eyes open. Like sneezing with your eyes open, I was sure I looked like I was about to cry.

"Okay, step one, get the hell out of here," I mumbled to myself, taking stock of the rest of the room. Beside the massive rich-lady mural the room was boring. A dresser, a bed, a million pictures, and a few looming shapes covered with sheets. And rock. Rock was everywhere. What I wouldn't give for a window right now. For sunlight. And air that didn't smell like damp gym socks.

Oh, and escape. Definitely for escape.

Back to business.

Seeing as I didn't want to be caught fondling rock in an attempt to find a handle or lever or something that would open up a mysterious cavern to safety, and I didn't know when the demon cave trolls were going to be making an appearance, it was best to start with the sheet blobs. The two looming shapes were creepy anyway.

Big one first, little one second. The big one was about twice as tall as me and bulky like a wardrobe or something. A wardrobe with a secret path that would get us out of here.

Hey, a girl can hope.

Dust plumed into the air like a peacock fart, falling over me in glittering specks that I was sure looked pretty. Well, prettier than whatever I had unveiled.

"What the fuck?" I didn't even try to keep my voice down.

I was right, it was a wardrobe. A wardrobe that was tall and dark and beautiful. It was covered with carvings of birds and deer and cute little rabbits that nearly made up for what was carved into the rest of it.

Me.

It was mother-fucking me. A fully naked me, with pointy nipples and a full... umm.... let's just say I matched the forestry undergrowth I stood in. Nudist colony me was staring into space with a serene smile as if I was happy to be a towering wood giant with bushes and pointy nipples.

"Oh fuck no," I snarled, heat rising through chest and skin. I would have burned the ridiculous thing down to the ground right then, show those pointy nipples who was boss.

But Narnia.

Trying not to make eye contact with my drugged out grin I threw the doors to the wardrobe open and prepared myself to face more dust and of course a whole line of equally dusty fur coats. If I was vain enough to have someone carve my naked ass into wood and paint my feathery persona into equally as gaudy headboards then I was sure to be hoarding fur coats and secret passageways right back to Rydaim.

But there were no fur coats. There were instead, suits. And no, not women's power suits from the 80s but men's suits from what looked like a cake walk through history.

There were probably ten of them, a caped number that looked like something out of a medieval painting. A grey suit with tails that I had a feeling went with the top hat in the bottom of the wardrobe. And a black jacket that was covered with intricate gold lace, that one was clearly French.

They were all perfectly pressed, hung, and preserved. It was as if someone had traveled through time and placed them all here for safe keeping. Or they would, if they all didn't have one absolutely terrifying thing in common.

Each and every one was stained. The suit jackets, the white shirts, the capes, even the hat was speckled with a wide spread stain of the darkest red. Like someone had come up behind each of the men who had worn these outfits and spilled red wine over their necks.

Except I wasn't as dumb as the vapid beauty carved into the wardrobe. I sure as shit knew that the stains weren't red wine.

"What. The. Fuck?"

Okay, maybe I should have burned the thing down. It was the most morbid trophy case I had ever seen, although what they were...

I blinked.

I fucking blinked and was met with what was the worst moment in probably all of history. Forget me throwing men off cliffs. It was me kissing the man in a top hat, beside a river. The twinkling of fire-burning street lamps next to the bridge looked like a line of stars to heaven. It was my lips against his, his hands pressing against the beaded waistline of my gown. It was the taste of sweat as our tongues connected and the bristling power of my phoenix screaming so strong that I was sure it was happening both in memory and in this freaky as hell room.

I pulled my eyes open, not wanting to see anymore, but

my brain wasn't quite done playing with me. One more flash, this time in a darkened alley as the demon laughed and the same guy's head fell to the ground.

His head. Falling to the fucking ground.

Oh my God.

"Head in a jar." The world had turned as cold and blood soaked as the colors on these poor fellows. I was still being haunted by the creepy thing in the kitchen, and I had seen another in a flash of memory in the shower. Heads in jars and now blood soaked necklines.

My phoenix was screaming. The heat that was running through my veins could never be enough to extinguish the ice that had covered me. The world had frozen over.

I should have never opened the door. I should have never followed the light. I should have never brought us here.

Screw secret passages. I stumbled away from the wardrobe, my skin prickling as the pain of my phoenix was ripping through the air in a string of fire. Heat swelled in the air as the fire swirled, my breath coming in heaves as fire whipped against the wardrobe sending the whole thing rocking and the doors slamming shut with a bang.

The sound was like cannon fire and I jumped, falling back on the dust covered bed as I tried to put distance between me and the haunted suits and the vapid nude that was on the doors to the wardrobe of horrors.

Except she wasn't a vapid nude anymore. Her face was angry and even without pupils, without color, without life, I was sure that she was staring at me.

She? What the fuck was wrong with me? It was a carving, not a thing, and yet her eyes were digging into mine.

"Oh fuck," I cringed, foolishly closing my eyes only to be

assaulted by a flash of Henry in the alley, holding the head up.

This room was nothing short of a house of horrors. I jumped up, ready to burn the thing to the ground when the air boomed with the knock on the door, three forceful fists hitting against stone or wood or whatever was holding me prisoner.

I whipped toward the sound, hands already smoking in preparation to destroy the haunted wardrobe; trying to convince myself that I was imagining that the carving wasn't staring at the door too. That she wasn't scared.

The two of us, staring with looks of panic at the knocking. Before I could decide if I needed to call out or just ignore it, the knocks came again. Louder, more forceful, and removing any options I had.

Smoke continued to drift from my fingers as I stepped toward the door, wishing the darn thing had a peephole or something. The last thing I needed was to swing the thing open and come face to face with a demon I had seen beheading a guy I think my Phoenix had a thing for. My chest bristled at that, claws pulling at my flesh in an agony I wasn't sure I understood. Well, except that she clearly had a soft spot for top-hat man.

I needed to figure this out.

"Please be Jarron," I mumbled with all the force of a mantra before pressing my ear against the cold, hard door. Because that was going to help me see who was on the other side.

"Who is it?" I asked, but there was only another knock, this one rattled the stone against my head.

Okay, fine, be that way. Not that I could open the door anyway, teeny demon had locked me in. So, of course that would mean that this time the doorknob would turn as though it was made of butter. Damn it all.

I opened the door, as much as I dared, peering through the crack as I continued my mantra.

It wasn't Jarron.

Of course, it was the demon. His face was already spreading into what I assume he thought was a pleasant smile. It was pleasantly reacting like ice and acid against my spine.

"Hello darling." Forget burning the wardrobe, I could burn this guy instead.

"I told you that you aren't allowed to call me that." I curled my hand around the ridge of the door, showcasing my still smoking fingers in warning. The guy didn't even flinch. No, he smiled. He smiled the same as he did before he lobbed that guy's head off.

Damn it.

"Well, what would you like me to call you then, princess?" His voice was low and deep and pulled at me in ways that I never wanted to feel with anyone but my dragons.

"Nothing. I don't want you to call me anything." I was sure that my eyes were on fire, but the guy leaned in as if he was wanted, as if he was breathing in my heat like it was a drug.

Ugh, judging by the way his eyes were glossing over, that was exactly what he was doing. I quickly pushed my hand behind the door, I would need the counterweight anyway if he was going to push his way in. Something he looked hungry enough to do.

"You don't mean that, birdy." His voice was all lust and it was enraging me and pulling at my Phoenix, lunging me back into bipolar hell.

"I do, asshole," I snapped, thank god his smile faltered. Score one for the team. "What are you doing here?"

And just like that, the smile was back, looking even more greasy than before. If there was a vat of 'evil grease' somewhere I was sure this guy had stuck his head in it.

"I wanted to check on you, to see if you needed company. I know new places can be scary." Well that was awfully loaded, and the way his eyes darted over my shoulder and into the room was making me uncomfortable. He better not be looking at that wardrobe.

And the wardrobe better not be looking back.

"Aren't you going to invite me in?" He asked after I didn't respond, his palm flat against the door as if he was going to push it open. But he didn't put any weight behind it, it was just a hand and a bit of grey skin. Like he was dead. Because he probably is, I reminded myself. The death of his skin matched the death in his eyes as he leaned forward. Expecting. Hungry.

Sick.

"No." Simple, blunt, and stabbed him right in the heart. Yeah, I totally smiled. Two points for the team.

I closed the door, driving my point home as his shocked expression peered through the closing gap.

"No?"

"No. I've lived alone for a while. I doubt there is anything in here that can scare me." Yep. Lying like a pro. Take that demon.

Unfortunately, I don't think he believed me. That greasy smile was pulling at the corner of his lips again, the creepy look spreading as he pressed his cheek against the ridge of the door.

I fought the need to step back and instead pressed against the door harder, forcing his lips together until he looked like a duck. A duck with swollen lips and a passion for grey lipstick. He yelped in pain, I laughed like a loon and quickly shut the now vacated door before he could stop me.

"Goodnight." I said as the door snapped shut. I was so focused on not saying his name that I neglected to remember that it probably wasn't night, and I really wasn't tired. Especially with demon wardrobe behind me.

"Well, if you need me. Call out to me. I'll be here in a jiffy." His voice was muffled, but I heard him perfectly, every single word playing into the dread of what Jarron had said earlier. Holy freaking demon.

First order of business, cover the haunted wooden wardrobe. I turned away, rushing away to grab the sheet and threw it as well as I could over the carving, making sure not to look at those creepy empty eyes. Which, of course meant that I was getting an eyeful of all the leafy forest. At least it was my leafy forest.

None of that was normal, thank god that the sheet swung into place as if it was meant to be there, leaving me alone with my thoughts and no wardrobe based escape.

Okay, so I am being stalked by a demon, watched by a wardrobe, all while being trapped in a mountain.

The only other way I could get us out of here was with the magic that brought us here. And ninety percent of the knowledge on how to use my fart rockets and feather travel or whatever it was, was locked inside of me. I couldn't put it off any longer.

I lay down on the bed, and closed my eyes, ready to open Pandora's Box.

"Please don't let there be any sex scenes with a demon."

10

DRAKE

When they had flown over the Atlantic Ocean to reach Rydaim less than twenty four hours ago, Drake had experienced the sensation of flying for the first time in decades.

Flying over oceans had never been his favorite, but the smell of the ocean had filled him, it had drenched him, and the cold wind of clouds and stratosphere had wiped any former dislike away. It was as close as he could ever get to flying again.

And then he and Zoe had slid into an underground cavern so drenched with magic that his own soul was desperate to burst out of him and experience it.

His father was still alive, however, so his dragon must remain trapped inside, even if it wasn't cursed to die a slow death.

A slow death didn't seem so terrible right then, as he experienced the sensation of flying for the second time.

This was better than it had been before. This was nearly perfect.

He would even tolerate the pressure of his sister's claws

in his shoulders to get this close to the world that had been torn from him.

Zoe's rose colored claws dug into his arms, one piercing against his underarm and sending both pain and warm fluid down his side in a way that he was beginning to think wasn't caused by sweat. Not that it mattered either way, he had no intention of getting down from here. He had survived a bit of blood before and he wasn't about to let that stop this flight.

There wasn't a drop of the salty heat of the ocean. There wasn't a hint of the poisoned air of the city. This was a world of soot and flame, bathed in the stale air of a million dragon fires. Everything rippled with the memory of flame, the blackened city below him whispered with the sounds of wings. With a deep inhale, and a gaze to the dark buildings below he could almost feel his wings. He could nearly feel the scales of his dragon as the creature pushed to take over, and his soul burst to life in a flight that was truly, wonderfully, his.

Zoe's dragon growled in a low rumble above him, the creature pulling away the sheet of his bliss like a magician with a magic trick. Scales recoiled, the memory of wings was gone, and it was just the two of them on a slow descent.

Zoe spiraled, circling lower and lower toward the dark streets and buildings that seemed to be shaking more than normal. Perhaps he had misjudged exactly how much blood he was losing and exactly how long he had until he passed out.

His body was weak. His vision tumbled around in his head as his stomach spun like a broken washing machine. Whether he was ready or not, whether he could support his weight or not, his sneakers snapped against the ground as Zoe's talons released him and he went down.

Crumpling like nothing more than a baby doll, he rolled over with a groan while Zoe circled above him.

The sounds that were echoing from her dragon sounded more like a chuckle than a growl.

Not that he was surprised, he was sure he looked ridiculous. Everything ached and the river that was pouring from the gash beneath his arm was adding a new layer of injury. The world was spinning like a top now, even though he could feel his dragon work to repair the cut and stop the flow of blood before he didn't have anything left to give.

His best option was to lay here, stare at the slowly burning ceiling and wait for everything to slow down.

Too bad Zoe had other ideas.

Her dragon gave one last low growl as she landed in her transformation, kicking his leg and knocking his knees together. The impact pulled his focus away from the rippling lines of red and gold flame that were blossoming over the ceiling like flowers, like an ever growing, evermoving sun. Just looking from the bouquet of fire to the smirk of his sister was turning the black and grey world into a demonic carousel. The bright of Zoe's red sweater against the ebony world wasn't really helping the effect. The two of them were probably the only sparks of color in this city.

"You okay there little baby dragon?" Zoe asked, kicking his shoe again.

The brilliant red of her dragon was still glowing in her eyes, the ruby fire beaming through the cat eye slits as she stared at the building that was towering over them in pillars of stone and ash.

The world had stopped spinning enough that the city was coming into focus. The stony stalagmites that had burst from the bottom of the cave looked as ashy and coarse from down here, but they were no longer indiscernible shapes of grey and black. They were high rises with walls of windows and gargoyles and intricately carved entry ways. They were shops with monochrome overhangs as names carved in a language that he had never seen before tried to peek through the layers of ash. And it was that gargantuan temple looking building behind him, the towers cutting into the ceiling like a needle, each carved spire and buttress so intricate that even from down here he could see the line of stone fire dance beside the trail of onyx roses.

"Beautiful," his gasp was more of a croak, and earned him another kick and a frustrated eye roll from his sister.

"Get your ass up, Drake, you can finish healing once we get in there." Her fingers were already smoking in warning and Drake scuttled to his feet. Well, he tried. The spinning world sent him right back down to his hands and knees.

First a little Fae ignites a revolution and now they had been sucked to a city in the center of the earth. Zoe was already charging full steam ahead toward the massive cathedral. She was looking for answers probably. There was no way in hell he could see Zoe praying.

Drake and his brothers had all been blessed with gifts, all of them full of some kind of darkness and a specialty at taking or destroying life. But Zoe had none. No gift. No way to damn and control. Even though she was the first born, the true heir to the throne. She was bare of Dragon power. Well, unless you counted her impatient strong will. Irritating, and nowhere near a gift that could end or save a life with a look. It certainly gave her the power to know how to get things done, however.

Drake shook his head and tried again to stand up the rest of the way, which was the dumbest thing he could have done with the way the world was spinning. He had experienced a concussion before, and this wasn't much different. It was, however, tremendously more irritating.

The spirals of grey got a whole lot worse as his vision equalized and the oppressive fountain in the square came into focus.

Intricately carved stone wound through the dim light of the city, leaving towering stone dragons to stare at him, the water of their flame having dried up long ago and left them with nothing but a gasp of dust. A Fae girl stood in the center, covered in a black stone dress, surrounded by three dragons. All of them were intertwined, bodies and scales and claws pressed against her until it was hard to tell one from the other.

Killian had told him about this fountain, about how it used to stand in the middle of the square before his father had replaced it. Or, at last that's what his brother had said. Drake had no memory of it, but he had been so young when the Fae's enslavement had happened.

How could he?

Seeing it here, hidden in some bizarre underground city, was miracle enough.

Except, this couldn't be the same fountain. But it didn't matter. It wasn't the similarities in stories that was knocking him back on his ass.

It was the girl.

The Fae girl with her dragons, carved into black stone that glittered in a weird soft light that almost made it seem real. All of that glittering reality was nothing so much as the eyes of the girl. They sparkled with such an intensity that it was almost as if she was seeing him.

Past him. Into him. And then she smiled.

She smiled and Drake backed up against the rough ground, everything spinning again.

Okay, maybe he had lost more blood than he thought. Either that or he had hit his head pretty hard on landing.

"Zoe!" He called, the shake in his voice echoing off the stone fountain and buildings until it sounded like there was eight of him, each replica peering through the alleys and windows of the square.

"What is it?" Each word lost intensity as she turned and caught sight of the fountain, the glittering eyes, and the shadow of smoke that was forcing its way past the blackened teeth of the dragon closest to him.

"What the fuck?" Zoe charged past him, taking two steps closer to the intricate fountain and thankfully blocking the glimmering eyes of the Fae girl from view.

He didn't like how fountain girl was looking at him, if she was looking at him. Or that she was leaning closer.

As if old dried up stone fountains could do any of that.

He had already proved that shaking his head was a bad choice, but he did it anyway. Thankfully this time it didn't hurt as much, but it certainly didn't dislodge whatever madness this city was giving him, either.

The glimmering eyes of the woman were still digging into him when Zoe stepped to the side, right up to the fountain.

He really didn't like her getting that close, and if he could move he probably would have pulled her away.

"It's so similar to the old one in Rydaim," she whispered, lifting her hand toward the closest dragon, the one that he could have sworn had begun dripping smoke from his jaw.

"No don't!" Drake called out right as her hand cupped the nose of the beast.

She jumped, but her hand didn't move. She turned, her eyes red and fiery as she faced him and scowled.

Drake jerked forward, ready to stop the stone hand of

the Fae from wrapping around hers or from the jaws of the stone beast from clamping down.

But nothing happened.

The stone didn't break, the girl didn't blink, the ceiling didn't fall in and the silent city didn't collapse. It was just the two of them, standing before a fountain. Staring at each other, Zoe's irritation sliding into concern.

Concern that was probably due, considering he was seeing statues move and expecting the sky to fall in.

The exasperated sigh he let escape was something he picked up from the climbers, his body sliding back to lay against the silt stones that made up the courtyard. The smooth pavers as black as everything else. He was so covered with dust he probably looked like a spot that someone had scrubbed too clean.

"Seeing as you are going at tad bit out of your mind, you should let your dragon heal you, Drake. I really don't want to carry you into that church just to leave you there." She chuckled to herself, moving from one dragon to the other in his peripheral vision. "It's uncanny. How close they look. I used to have names for them all when I was a toddler. I want to say this one was Fire Nose."

"You would name a dragon 'Fire Nose'." Drake tried to force the laugh, but it didn't come and he was left staring at Zoe's fire as it continued to consume the ceiling. Ribbons of her flame trailed through the dark high above, the fire dancing like the tail of a kite. Trails of the dragon's sun.

"I was five. And they looked so much nicer than the dragons that were training me. I used to imagine that they would come alive at night and whisk me away to someplace magical."

"You lived in an underground city full of dragons and wished for something more magical?"

"Yes," she snickered in a sound that wasn't quite like her. "Like a mountain top with fairies, or... I dunno... something like this."

Drake laughed then. This place may not be any more amazing than where they had come from, but laying on his back, watching the fire dance, certainly gave it more magic than the otherwise terrifyingly dark underground cavern.

"Sometimes I was certain I had seen the lady blink--"

Drake jumped, jerking toward her, his dragon ready to jump out of his skin. Scales pressed against his spine as he sat on the cold floor, trying to control his breath as his sister traced the jaw of the woman, the woman who was looking right at him.

Glittering eyes, a slight smile, and his dragon was screaming, a deep rumble echoing over the stone as he felt his spine lengthen as though something was pulling the beast out of him.

Pulling him right into her.

To the damn Fae.

What was this place? They needed to get out of here, to escape whatever was about to happen.

To escape her.

"Why did you want to go to the cathedral?" The words burst through the rattle in his bones as he pushed his spine back together, pulling himself to his feet as he backed away from the fountain.

Everything was spinning again and he was more stumbling than walking, but it didn't matter. He would drag himself towards the high carved doors of the onyx cathedral, if he had to. Towards sanctuary.

"Huh?" Zoe asked from behind him, her voice more distanced than the few feet of the courtyard should have made it.

The courtyard that was still pulling at his dragon, pulling his wings from his spine.

"The cathedral. You said you wanted to go inside of it. Why?"

Stepping away from the pull in his spine took more work than he expected, but he pried himself away. Fighting against the pull.

"Oh!" Thankfully the single sound seemed closer. "Someone doesn't build a city like this for fun. This city is obviously abandoned. I want to find out why. This was the largest church I found when I flew over, it's sure to have some kind of records."

Or at least some safety from the fountain.

It felt foolish to be afraid of a fountain. To be afraid of some stone dragons and a weird looking girl. But Zoe was right, this place was abandoned. As much as he didn't want to blame whatever had happened here on a stupid fountain, he was still going to get away from it as fast as he could. The second Zoe stepped beside him, he grabbed her hand and dragged her through the massive door.

He was sure the stone dragons were right behind them.

11

CALLAY

Rydaim had fared better than the Forgotten and their tunnels in the collapse.

And no, that didn't mean that the gaudiness of the glittering diamond roads were magically able to hold things up. That meant that they had more standing buildings and the roof hadn't collapsed as much as I had hoped. Which also meant that the goddamned eye was still peering down on all the dragons and their slaves that were bitching about having to clean up their mansions.

It would be a great addition to have that monstrous stained glass monstrosity crack open and shower down over them, Ceres and his posse exposed in some kind of embarrassing position. Like boudoir photography with a clown. Too bad I didn't see that happening, even though there was already a crack down the middle of the garish propaganda. Just like Ceres's old wrinkled ass.

"Will you move? I'm tired of being cooped up in here!" Speaking of asses. Fallon's irritated whine echoed over the stone of the shallow opening into the alley, or what was left of the alley, her fingers poking hard into my back in her attempt to get me to step aside.

It only made me want to wedge my ass between the tiny opening a bit better and dig my heels in. I had regretted dragging her along on this adventure the moment I had said it, and she had made me regret it even more from the moment we set out. BFUYDCYB or not, she was irritating as hell.

I had insisted that we leave immediately, because Dragons busy cleaning up and recovering from being attacked by a Phoenix were going to be easier to infiltrate. Protecting those diamond roads were vital.

Fallon had seemed to think she needed to find a shower or take a nap or something, like she was a goddamned beauty queen. Then, not only did she insist on using her shed magic to guide us through the underground maze that the tunnel collapse had created, but she complained every time said tunnel collapse led us to another dead end. And by complain I mean whined like a child who has been told they can't have ice cream for dessert.

It only made me want to eat ice cream in front of her. Which was why I was now spreading my hips and planting my feet against the edge of stone in an attempt to trap her in the cave. Take that, shed magic.

"Will you wait a fucking minute?" I snapped, pressing my heels harder into the stone edges of the tunnel. Perfect, since I think she was now trying to get me to move with her shed magic. That or my left hip was growing warm on its own.

I shoved her back and tried to tune out the barrage of complaints that were now echoing behind me. Seriously, could this bitch shut up? How was I supposed to make sure it was safe to emerge from the barely concealed tunnel with her yapping on about how she 'doesn't deserve to be treated like this'?

If I didn't need to keep the tunnel a secret I could step to the side and let her tumble out like a boob in a string bikini. Let her face the consequences of that. Fire to the face, probably.

Okay, maybe it wasn't such a bad idea. Watching her melt into goo like some wicked witch would be spectacular. Unfortunately, no one was in the rubble of the alley. So no face melting. Didn't mean she couldn't boob up the joint.

I shifted my feet as she whined and leaned against my back to try to push me aside.

"I don't understand--" I side stepped the second her palm pressed harder, leaving the opening free for her to fall through in spectacular fashion.

She looked like a baby bird being thrown from the nest. Her arms flailed, she shrieked, and nearly fell face first into one of the big boulders that had fallen into the alley from the surrounding buildings.

Sure, it was dangerous to have her yell so loud when we were so far into dragon and vampire territory, but it was worth it. BFUYDCYB Forever!

"Oh my gosh! Are you okay?" I tried not to laugh, really I did, but it didn't work. Didn't help that she looked at me with what I was sure she thought was a bitchin' bitch face.

Still looked like a toddler freaking out about ice cream.

"Sorry, Fallon." I was still laughing, but I extended my hand anyway, sign of a best friend and all. Her scowl deepened. Oh god, all she needed was the pouty lip.

I was laughing my head off now. Plan BFUYDCYB was so not working.

Maybe I could move to plan C and convince a dragon to

burn her ass to the ground while we were up here. That could work too.

"Sorry for laughing or sorry for hurling me into a dragon infested city?"

Neither. "Both."

I shook my hand in continued offering, but she ignored it, pulling herself to stand and wiping dust and gravel or whatever her flail into the alley had coated her with. Not that it mattered. We were both still coated in dust and dirt from the collapse.

"Well, you are lucky that no one saw that." Am I, Fallon? Am I really? "That could have ended badly."

Unable to disguise my laugh, I instead gave her a nod and walked down the destroyed alley toward the house that had been mine for nearly two hundred years. Judging by the cursing, stumbling, and complaining that was following after me, my shadow was still hot on my tail. Not that I really cared anymore, my mind was focused on what was left of the vile and derelict alley.

About half of the houses in Rydaim were damaged in one way or another, a few of them missing chunks of roofs or windows that allowed spots of light to infect the shadows. I had an inkling that much of the city looked like this now, one step away from collapse.

But none as bad as the one that was now looming over us.

The entire top floor of Killian's house was gone, the alley and streets around it littered with rubble, bits of expensive mahogany furniture, and scraps of fabric that I hoped Killian never saw. I doubt seeing the remains of his precious suits torn through the streets would end well.

Good thing what I needed was in the game room on the main floor. The house seemed stable enough that we could get in, grab it, and do a quick walk through of the city without causing too much notice. Easy peasey. If only my bestie would shut up.

"I need you to show me how to get up *there*," she said with a glance to the freaky eye as she stepped beside me, folding her arms over her chest. "Not take me on a walk of remembrance to the Prince's house. I've been here, remember."

I will not punch her in the face. I will not punch her in the face. I will not punch her in the face. Instead, I gave her a grin and threw my arm over her shoulder. Best friends forever, bitch.

"True, but you haven't been inside the house, and there is something that I need in there. Something that *you* need in there." My eagerness was affecting my magic and pulling it through the air in a wave of flowing hair and flashing eyes.

"You've been spelunking, right?" I asked as I tried to lift the door so as to give us more space. It didn't budge.

"No."

"Great. Think of it like that." I was on autopilot and well aware that my response made no sense. I was too busy trying to see into the dark on the other side of the door. I didn't sense any vampires, and I didn't see any vampires, but that didn't mean there weren't any vampires there. From what I could tell, all of my wards were still in place so I was sure it was safe, but in a city crawling with this much evil I wasn't going to charge into dark hallways.

"Excuse me. I said I hadn't gone spelunking." Fallon slipped on rubble as she stepped closer, presumably to snap or complain about the fact that I wasn't listening. I moved to the side on the off chance that she would hurl herself into the dark, but no such luck.

"And I said to think of it like that. I don't care how you

do it. Hold your breath or something. Just don't run into the bats." She opened her mouth to retort against my nonsense reply, but I ducked under the remains of the door and plunged myself into the house, leaving her sputtering in confusion, and me snickering like a mad man.

I had no idea if this is how you made friends, but it was sure entertaining. Like prodding a human. But better, because she knew my magic was better than hers.

Stupid shed magic.

I lit the lamp in the game room the second I entered. The low hum of the electric light in the windowless room the only safe and memorable thing here. It didn't provide much light all the way in the kitchen. Just a buzzing noise and more shadows stretching over the once beautiful marble. I was sure it was nothing but broken glass now. It glittered from the cracked counter tops and crunched into the broken tile on the floor with every step.

"Wow. This guy was swanky." I couldn't tell if she was being serious or not, so I continued in my quest to the game room, listening to the crunch of glass and tile. I had really liked that tile too.

"Did it always look like this? Or is this part of the *spelunking*?"

"It always looked like this," I said as brightly as I could, leaving behind the tile and glass for the fractured wood of the hall and stairwell. The hardwood floors had lifted and splintered in the impact of the blast, making the hall look like the pretzel sticks at the bottom of the bag.

"Killian preferred the dystopian look."

"And the penile look, apparently."

I jumped, slipped on the pretzel floor and clung to the pieces of a destroyed wall in an attempt to stay upright, but this time it was my turn to go down. I guess the mention of male genitalia sent me into a spread eagle sprawl in more ways than one.

"Or is this one yours?" Fallon stepped over me, looking down to where I lay and waving what looked like a multicolored flag above my head. It didn't take much to recognize the yellows and reds of my favorite medieval cat, the phallic member lovingly clamped in its jaw.

"Give me that," I snapped, grabbing what was left of the priceless painting and shoving it in my pocket, leaving Fallon to scowl at me with those beady little eyes of hers, folding her arms like she was some judgmental mother. All she needed was to tap her toe and set out some bizarre assumption that would send any teenager into a tirade.

"You kinky for Dragons, Callay?" And there it was.

"And what if I am? You gonna rip my wings from my body or whatever it is you seem to think you can do with Dragons?" I didn't even try to wiggle my way out from underneath her, I could blast her away from me like she was being ejected from a cannon. Besides, she thinks that she had me pinned or something. Whatever.

"I'm glad one of those sheep has a brain enough to know I was blowing smoke."

Holy fuck.

Did that just happen? No freaking way.

Fallon stood above me, smiling like some kind of deranged teen. I half expected her to produce and brandish a knife with the way she was rubbing her thumb and forefinger together, sending out little sparks. Sparks that didn't look quite as much like shed magic as they had a moment before.

Forget the holy fuck. This was a holy shit, and I had a feeling that I got myself in a bit of a tricky situation. Damn it all, I should have listened to the Unicorn. I needed to back my way out of this as quick as possible and get an upper hand. Lying flat on my back and looking up the flared nostrils of a traitor was not getting me off to a great start.

And here I was thinking we were going to be besties.

"You do realize I am not a sheep, right?" I was clearly deflecting, but I was going to need all of the misdirection I could muster as I tried to wiggle my way out from under her.

Something that I was already failing at. I hadn't moved more than an inch before she caught me and decided to sit on me like I was a pillow.

Please, come pop a squat on my sternum, all are welcome.

"I'm glad it was you, too. You smell like her, so I'm not surprised." She pressed her bony ass into my chest more, the double impact of bony ass and pretzel floor feeling like a torture chamber against my bones. "Although you smelled different than when I first met you."

"I smell like a sheep?" Yep, still deflecting, although I wasn't sure why. It's not like I could move anywhere, her ass vice was doing a good job of trapping me.

"No." She bounced against me, pressing me into the floor. I wondered how big of a collapse I would trigger if I threw her into the ceiling.

Probably a pretty big one. Fine by me. It could crush her and then I could use my last unicorn hair to get out of here for good. Well, if that wouldn't piss off said Unicorn. Okay, on to plan B. D? I had lost track.

"You smell like the goddesses. You have touched quite a few, haven't you?" She leaned over me, the weight of her tailbone lifting as she dragged her finger down the side of my face. It would have been the perfect opportunity to throw her over my head like I was in an epic karate movie.

Sucks for me, I was frozen beneath her, no fighting, no moving. I had stopped breathing. Fallon's smile stretched.

"Goddesses?"

"Yes. I can name the one, but the other..." She paused, her finger pressing into my jaw like she was trying to press the button that would answer her question.

But I was beyond lost at this point.

I only knew of one person that could qualify as some kind of goddess and she was irritating as hell, beautiful beyond reason, and so full of herself she could make glass shatter. Definitely a goddess.

Fucking Unicorn.

I shouldn't be surprised that Fallon knew about Xi, seeing as Xi clearly knew about Fallon, but my jaw dropped nonetheless. Partially because it seemed that Unicorns had a smell that I couldn't detect, and partially because she had said goddesses, as in plural, as in two. Unless Xi had an identical twin that was taking me on an adventure I had no idea who she was talking about.

Or what. Because again, Goddesses.

"What are you on about. I haven't--" That was all I got out before the echo of crunching glass poured through the kitchen toward us, before Fallon's smile spread into a grin worthy of a demented cat, and the air turned to ice.

I knew what was happening a minute before it did. Although I didn't expect Fallon to look quite so excited about it, or for the voice that slithered with as much ice as the air to be quite so familiar.

"I must say Fallon, I was surprised to get your message, but I didn't think you would be giving me a gift quite this good for our reunion."

"Parris?" My choking acknowledgement was met with

laughter from both parties, the icy man with his ridiculous blond floppy hair appearing above me.

The man smiled with that same greasy grin that had gotten me into so much trouble all of those years ago and leaned down beside Fallon, his hands trailing up my sides.

The ice of his fingers bled through the fabric of my shirt, sparking over the skin like icicles jabbing into my ribs. I refused to show any emotion at the touch. Well, besides a glare. I wasn't sure they saw that with the way they were looking at each other. Fallon was leaning right into his fucking arms, her ugly ass lips pressing against his ugly ass face.

There might have been a tongue involved, which made the fact that his fingers were still trailing over my ribs even worse.

Ew. So much ew.

"I take it you know each other?" I asked as loudly as possible, shifting my weight between the two even though that outlet of escape was closed.

I needed to get as much information as possible, throw these two into the supporting stone wall to my left and use the unicorn hair to get out of here. I would deal with the repercussions of that later. It's not like she couldn't yank another one of those beauties off her pretty little head.

"Friends with benefits maybe?" I continued to prod them, if only to get them to stop trying to lick the back of the other person's throat. "Friends without benefits? Friends with non-matching genitalia who enjoy licking throats?"

They didn't laugh, or glare, but they did pull away. Their lips smacking as they turned to me with equal levels of hate.

"Okay, seriously, how do you know each other? High school?" I was still wiggling, trying to free one hand enough that I could lift my palm to the bony bitch's ass and send her flying.

What is it with vapid women and blood suckers? You would think they would realize how dangerous they are, but no, they flock to them like baby birds.

"Fallon and I go way back," Parris said, pulling his focus away from the woman who was now twisting her fingers in his hair. "Her master gifted us both with our abilities and we worked to overthrow the sirens that created him. That created you if I am not mistaken."

"The Unicorn." The words were out before I could bite my tongue and lock them away. At least I was right in one thing that had happened over the last few minutes.

So much for not acting surprised. If I had been standing I was sure my jaw would hit the floor. Instead it kind of flopped around as I tried to work through everything, trying to gauge exactly how much I was supposed to know.

Xi created Mattia, and Mattia created both of them. So, Mattia created Parris. Or was it more that he created vampires? I had no idea, and I wasn't about to ask. Not with the smile that the vampire was giving me. The look was all ice and malice.

"How long have you known?" My voice shook, but so did my torso, the two now so absorbed in what they were saying that I was able to free one on my hands enough to point at them.

All I needed was the right moment and I would elevator them straight into the wall.

"Forever." Parris smiled until his teeth gleamed. "I wanted to see what the child birthed from the power of goddess given light would do when mixed with my own. That's all I want, to know what the powers of the goddesses can create, and how they can work for me. You were a part of that, and now we can go retrieve Lilly and take down the last of them."

"Last of who?"

"The beings who created this world. And we are going to start with that blasted Phoenix."

12

JARRON

All of the pictures of the walls rattled with the slam of the door, the little girl who was sitting on the couch watching TV giving a tiny little yelp. It was the only sign she had given that she was actually a child since we had arrived. A little yelp, and then she was back to staring at the television.

Or, that's what Jarron would have to assume. He wasn't going to turn toward the slam of the door and give into the hissy fit that their captor was throwing. Henry was breathing with all the rage of a hormonal female, stepping too hard, and clicking the beakers and vials on his table as though he was trying to break them. If he wanted to talk, all he had to do was ask, not that Jarron would respond. The guy was getting on his nerves.

Lilly had dragged him out of Elliot's room so he could stare at the guy tinker with that head. If the demon hadn't left with a smile on his face a minute ago Jarron would probably still be forced to watch him extract who-knows-what from the thing, and prattle on about some time in Russia a few years ago...

Jarron wasn't about to willingly subject himself to that again. Besides, the guy's quick exit had given him an opportunity to inspect this part of the cave, not that there was any way out, or that the pictures were any less freaky. In fact, he was starting to question if the head was really the worst thing here.

Seeing Ellie in differing positions of scandal with this guy was enraging his dragon in levels that would normally be considered dangerous. In this situation they would be helpful. Should be. He wasn't sure what his fire would do to a demon, but seeing as the girl was immune he didn't have high hopes.

Speaking of demons.

Despite leaving looking like he was going to win the lottery, his temper tantrum was in full force now, the guy having moved onto grumbling and talking to himself. The rate of clinking glass was hitting a frequency that anyone else might think the guy was playing a xylophone.

Jarron exaggerated his movement as he bent over to inspect another image, thankfully there was no Ellie in this one. Just Lilly, smiling as she held the head of a bird. There clearly wasn't going to be anything normal here.

More clinking and another exaggerated sigh pulled from somewhere behind him before there was a rustle, a whisper, and silence. Well, silence in that the demon's spastic fit vanished. The rumble of the quick foreign language on the television making the whole room feel like the inside of a hive. It wasn't often Jarron found a language he didn't know, but this one had stumped him. Japanese maybe? He wasn't sure. The words were too quick, the scenes flashing by so fast that he couldn't make anything out.

Almost as if she was watching it on fast forward.

Turning away from the picture of Lilly and her headless

bird, Jarron realized that was exactly what it was. The show was playing at double speed, flashing the colors over the dark, and very empty room.

"Where did he go?" Jarron really hoped that was enough to get an answer. He really didn't want to say, or even think, the guy's name. Lilly didn't even move. She sat cross legged on the couch, wearing yet another poufy dress, watching the cartoon as if she had been glued there.

Okay, thing number two that made it clear she was still a kid.

"Hey Lilly," Jarron said louder, causing her to jump and turn with a scowl on her face. "Where did he go?"

Jarron gestured to the mini-lab like a woman in a silk dress on a game show, hoping the motion was enough. He would go as far as acting out the guys temper tantrum if he had to in order to avoid his name. Thankfully Lilly caught on, wrinkling her nose as she looked at the lab before shrugging and turning back to her program.

"He probably went to his room. He does that." Her voice was deadpan next to the quick Japanese.

Jarron's dragon was lifting against the rumble of her response as if he was afraid of it, smoke biting against the back of his throat in preparation to attack. Of course, his dragon had been doing that from the moment Elliot had run into him in the cave, so it may not even be the noise.

It was possibly the girl.

"Is that why he was so frustrated?" Jarron was careful not to let smoke or ash escape from between his teeth at the question. "He seemed really upset."

Lilly turned slowly, the flashing television lights reflecting over the room that he could have sworn was growing darker. Not that that was possible, there were no windows in the place, and the electric bulbs that were buzzing through the kitchen and living space were still glowing, pressing their yellow light against kitchen counters and grey stone walls.

"He does that." She repeated, speaking each word individually, her eyes narrowing into Jarron until the grey sparks made him sure she was seeing something else. He didn't need to see the slight lift of her hair to know she was using her magic. He could smell it in the air. He could see it ripple around her, and it was very clearly Fae.

Well, if the demon had in fact gone to his room, he would have to make the most of the situation. Not that he had another choice. Every time he got close to either door Lilly would stare him down. Finding an escape route was not going to happen.

"Does he do that a lot?" Jarron asked as he vaulted himself over the back of the couch Lilly sat on.

The large brown thing separated the living room from the kitchen and thankfully put the lab and all floating objects in jars behind his back. Lilly gave him a look, her eyes narrowing toward him even though she didn't turn away from the screen.

"Does he throw little fits and storm off to his room, I mean," Jarron kept his tone light as he leaned against the armrest of the couch, throwing his feet up as he lounged back. Lilly still didn't turn, although she did give his feet that were now right next to her a bit of a stare.

"For a second there I thought he had sprung a leak, sighing like that. Is that why he went to his room? To fix a leak?" This time Jarron got a look that wasn't quite as narrow, harsh, or ready to rip off heads.

She almost looked as if she was ready to laugh. That was of course, if she knew how. He was about to find out.

"Pssst..." Jarron made the sound of a leaky tire while

sagging against the couch in an over dramatic display that the kid in her couldn't ignore, and she laughed.

Well, she tried to anyway. Jarron was right, the kid had no idea how to laugh, and the sound that came out was a weird exaggerated thing that he was sure she had picked up from her television programs.

"Ha! Ha! Ha!" She threw her head back, hand on belly, as the rough sounds bounced off the stone in a ricochet that almost made it sound like a tinkling bell. If the bell was a gong clanged by a ghost.

"That's funny," she said as deadpan as before, making him question if he had imagined the last few minutes. "You're funny."

She nodded once and went back to her show as if nothing had happened. So much for trying to break the cement wall off the kid. She had given him nothing more than a crack before she turned to the still flashing screen.

What in the world had the demon done to this kid?

"He doesn't like it when he doesn't get his way." She said after a moment, her voice more lively than it was before. A bit, but not by much. It didn't miss Jarron's notice that she hadn't used his name either. "Your girl must be stubborn."

Or that she had referred to Ellie as *his* girl.

"She drives me crazy sometimes, too." Jarron said, lounging back against the arm rest and closing his eyes as much as he dared, he wasn't willing to lose visual of the girl. "Mates are supposed to do that."

"Are they?" She gave him another sidelong glance, her interest clear. "I wouldn't know."

She tried to return to her television program, but it didn't hold her focus anymore and she kept looking at him, the eagerness on her face growing brighter even as he was sure the room was growing darker.

"Well yes, you are a Fae aren't you."

"I already told you that." Disgust leaked into her voice and she turned away, all perceived interest in the conversation vanishing.

Darn it. He would have to be more careful. The hatred toward her mother's kind, or what he assumed was her mother, was deeper than he had assumed. The trickiness of getting this girl to trust him was growing.

"Yes, and that her power was like an infection." He couldn't force anymore negativity toward the Fae into his voice.

"An abomination," she corrected, still not turning to him. "She wasn't fit to raise me."

"So you know her?" He should have thought about that question more carefully, the girl's hair began to lift, her eyes sparking dangerously as she turned back to him, a vein in her jaw beginning to pulse.

Creepy. He had never seen so much hatred in a child before. Jarron should be a bit more scared of her, given the look that was burning through him, but she was looking at him.

It was still a step in the right direction.

"Why would I want to meet... to meet... *that*." Rage dripped from every word, the long flowing strands of her hair picking up, ruffling the ribbon and lace on her dress into the invisible breeze of her magic.

Jarron's dragon was snarling in his chest, the sound pulling through the room so quietly that he doubted the girl could hear it over the TV. Which was good, he didn't need to launch himself in a war with her, and he didn't need her knowing how scared he was.

His dragon wasn't even filling his mouth with ash anymore. It was fire that was burning his tongue and tapping against the back of his teeth in a desperate need of escape.

Foolish dragon, hadn't it learned anything from before? This girl was immune, his powerful flames were useless to her. Besides, even if she could burn he wasn't interested.

He was going to save this girl.

Jarron swallowed down his flame, burning his throat and giving himself instant heartburn that raged in the most human ways.

"Because it is part of you," Jarron said as casually as he could, curling his legs into him as he sat up on the couch. "Because it is her magic that causes your hair to do that. That pulls all the power from the air and the earth to give you so much strength."

The movement of Lilly's magic, as her dress and the long strands of her hair picked up, a tiny smile playing around the corner of her mouth. The spark in her eyes glittered in the dark of the room. He was sure that this time it wasn't just the reflection of the 'super-flower-magic-power' transition that was happening on the television.

Perhaps Jarron would get lucky and that is all that it would take to break the dangerous wall that made up this kid. Jarron gave her a smile, the toothy grin the only one he really knew how to give when he was in situations like these. Hopefully any residual smoke from the now extinguished flame didn't seep between his teeth. He expected a giggle, perhaps another question about the Fae, maybe even a query as to if he knew her mother.

Instead, he got a deep scowl and a spark of Fae magic so dark he was sure he could feel his own magic seep out of his skin and drain away.

What in the world? The dark look rattled his bones and he gasped, collapsing back against the couch as his dragon growled in a sound that was closer to a scream. The sound lifted above the cartoon, and the kid very clearly heard it, but all she did was smile.

"That magic comes from my father," She seemed determined to believe it herself. "Her power only makes me weak."

It was back to being an impossible task. At least he was no longer feeling like his life force was being sucked from his body, although he was starting to wonder when someone had turned off the lights. He could see them blazing but it was as though the light couldn't get through. That might be a side effect of whatever she had done to him, however.

He would have to log that away under freaky things the nightmare child could do, not that he needed any more reason to be a tad bit afraid of her.

Even his dragon was trembling. Which is why what he was about to do was nothing short of bullheaded, shit-faced foolishness.

"I believe you," he said with a shrug that had too much shake in it. "If I was you, I would want to find out everything I could, though. Sometimes you can't trust those closest to you."

"Like you, because you are the closest to me right now." She leaned closer, and for a minute she didn't look like a little girl at all. She looked like something that had crawled out of hell to end him. "And I sure can't trust you."

"Sure you can." She smiled at the warble in his voice and pushed herself closer, each jerk of her limbs pulled through the air, the lights flickering around them as the lamps burned and the TV shut off with a snap.

Okay, so this was clearly a worse idea than Jarron had thought. His dragon was screaming, scales pushing against his skin and wings against his spine, but no change was coming no matter how much he wanted it to happen. It was as if the ability was being pulled out of him.

"You do taste good though. You aren't going to last long anyway. I doubt Henry would be upset if I took you first."

"That's quite enough of that." Henry snapped as the lights returned to a raging brightness that burned against Jarron's skull. Perhaps he hadn't been imagining the dim of the lights, right then he wasn't sure he had ever seen anything this bright before.

He blinked once and she was gone, the hungry malice in her eyes drained back to silver as she sat, staring at TV as if nothing had happened.

"Sorry, Henry," She whispered, not even turning to the shadowed man who stepped up to the couch, staring over the two of them like a disappointed parent.

"I expect more of you." She nodded at the scold, the same ice that Jarron had felt so often over the last few minutes tracing up his spine.

The man had appeared out of nowhere, with no more than a mention of his name. Jarron hadn't needed confirmation, but he got it anyway.

"Sorry, Henry," she said again, still not turning from the TV. She did jump when he hit the back of the couch, however. She may not have turned, but Jarron did, his already terrified dragon moving into a bristle.

"It's late, why don't we all head to bed. Why don't I show you to your room, Jarron?" It was not a question, and Henry clearly wasn't expecting an answer, he was already walking from the inset door that led to the faux-maze.

"I should probably go to Elliot." There was no way he was getting a squeaks worth of power into his voice, not with the callous darkness that was seeping off Henry.

"Elliana doesn't need you. She has requested privacy."

Ah, his fit of before made sense now. Ellie needed Jarron, she didn't need the demon, and knowing her she had said as much. He would have to save that smile for later, when he could hold her in his arms and kiss her again. It wouldn't go amiss if the dark monster could be present for that. That would be a goal for another day.

Henry smiled, holding the door open for Jarron and Lilly who skipped towards it and straight to her own room. Jarron hurried after them, he may not want to be locked into his own stone prison, but he wasn't going to miss a chance to discover where the girl went. There had to be a way out, and she was the closest thing he had to figuring that out right now.

By the time he reached them however, she was gone. It was him and the demon, the monster smiling as he led him down the hall in silence.

"This will be you," Henry said as he opened a door directly across from where he thought Ellie was. The hallway was disorienting enough that he wasn't sure. His heart was pulling that direction, and that was the only compass he needed.

Jarron gave him a nod and stepped into the room, ready to close the door and escape the disaster of the day, focus on the plan for tomorrow. But Henry's dark eyed stare dug into him, holding the door open and blocking any plans for escape.

"Call if you need," he whispered, the chill of his breath unnatural, even in the cold of the cave. "Either I or my daughter will come to help you. And in the future I would advise you not to push her too far. She is liable to lose control."

The door closed with a snap leaving Jarron alone in a

room with one faintly glowing candle near the bed and a head full of questions. *Daughter.*

She had said otherwise, however, and he had a feeling that finding the truth to that could easily drive a lead nail in his plans.

If she was the daughter of a Fae and a demon they were screwed. He didn't need the Iron maiden in the corner to tell him that.

But thanks to the demon of the house, it was there anyway.

Jarron clearly wouldn't be getting any sleep tonight.

13

KILLIAN

THE WIND POUNDED AGAINST THE SHUTTERED WINDOW AS Killian was dragged over the hard wooden floor, watching the speck of black from where it was hiding until the leg of the bed covered it and Killian was heaved onto the overly hard mattress. Odd. Seeing as no one touched him. He hadn't felt anything but air as he fell into the bed, Mattia standing on the other side of the room staring demurely at the scene.

Mattia said nothing as he went back to the table, drinking from his glass and lighting sugar cube after sugar cube ablaze.

Killian could do nothing but watch. Restrained in the bed by nothing, mind consumed by the same black smoke from before. It moved through him, eating through the universe that the black speck had shown him. Eating through the memory of the woman with the smile, and the spark of red that he was sure was flame, and the name that Mattia had used.

He couldn't remember that name anymore, that may have been the first to go. Even though he could feel the importance of the each and every thing, he clung to the tiny black speck of darkness as if it was a lifeline. As if it was a key to escaping this place, and whatever the smoke was.

The bit of black mixed with the smoke, it danced with the sound of the wind. It kissed against the clink of Mattia's glass and it drifted away as Killian did, into a different black, a different abyss. Sleep took the last of everything with it and left a fuzzy world and a fear of something left under the bed when he awoke.

The room was dark. Mattia was sleeping in the chair beside the window, his hand curled against the pane as if he had tried to open it and thought better of it, which was good as there seemed to be a storm outside.

The pane of glass was rattling against the wind, although the shake was half-hearted, like something on the other side was keeping it from moving.

Snow.

The room was insulated in warmth, the fire blazing with strips of red and white that cast shadows on the walls. The walls he could have sworn were covered with ice.

Everything had been. The rattling of the window and the howl of wind had clearly haunted his dreams.

Dreams that were so real when he first woke, but the longer he lay in the hard bed watching the fire flicker and melt the few flakes that had managed to find their way down the flue the more they faded into puffs of light and shadow.

That seemed familiar too, but that was more to do with the snow.

So much snow. If it had filled his dreams so well, he didn't want to think about how much of the stuff had piled outside. Or how long they would be trapped in this room.

This room.

It was familiar. It didn't make sense as to why though, he hadn't been here before. But he had. He had lived here. He had dreamed of here. But it was wrong. So wrong.

So dangerous. Dangerous. He needed to get out of here.

Heat rippled from him as he threw the blanket off, the rough cotton falling away to a room that was nearly as warm as he was. The floor, however, was a different story. The chill of the ancient wood ripped up the veins in his legs like a seam, sending a shiver over his spine that immediately had him searching for socks.

Socks and perhaps clothes. If he was right about the snow he would need more than the thin cotton pants he was wearing. There weren't any boots or coats hanging anywhere, and the large chest near where Mattia snored was open and full of dozens of empty bottles. The only other place that could hold clothing was the large dresser to the side of the bed, the dark mahogany of the wood shimmering with golden lines in the fire light.

Something about the dark wood called to him, same as the dream. The color was beautiful, and seeing it glimmer was stirring a warmth through him, like a love he had lost or a place he had forgotten.

Even the drawers slid in a grind that was familiar, if not a little loud. He started at the bottom, hopeful that socks would be stored close to his feet, but it was only another drawer of bottles, rattling loudly as it opened. The others were full of an assortment of clothes, from button up shirts to slacks, but none of which looked to have belonged to him.

It was odd that the cotton pants he wore were so small, and now he was understanding why. Nothing here was his size. Even the socks he found in the top most drawer appeared to be too small. His feet were large and wide and the socks would never give enough stretch.

Placing the socks back in the drawer with a shrug, Killian moved to the other side, and to a stack of cotton pants similar to what he was wearing. Looking at these, it was becoming evident that it was a miracle that his current pants fit at all. Everything was too small, by several sizes.

Nothing was his, it all belonged to the much smaller man behind him. There had to be something here that was his. He was here after all and it wasn't like he appeared out of nowhere.

He froze, hands hovering over the carefully folded pants, and the bit of singed fabric in the back of the drawer. The scent of smoke, forest, and something unfamiliar was assaulting. The aroma pressed against chest and mind and ignited that same spark of warmth that was spreading over his skin. It was as though he had been set on fire. Same as last night when he saw those things on the table.

That had been part of the dream too, though. When the ice had covered the room, when the world had swallowed him whole.

Now, that he remembered. That he knew.

Killian nearly slammed the dresser shut in fear, his panic drifting toward the shadows that were lurking under the bed and the secret that was concealed there.

A secret he needed.

"You are up earlier than I expected," Mattia mumbled from behind him, the icy lines shaking through Killian as though he had stepped in a pool of ice. He had to check to make sure he hadn't, who knew what had sneaked in from the storm. Or what remained after last night? After ice had drifted everywhere in his dream. Or was it reality? He wasn't sure anymore, and the shadow under the bed was whispering something else entirely.

"I was cold." Why did he lie? He had no need to lie. But

yet it came out, and he found himself looking between the bed and the bit of burned material, trying to decide which to save.

Or why he needed to hide either from the little man.

"What are you looking for?" The scrape of Mattia's chair pulled against Killian's spine as the little magician stood, his feet dragging over the wood.

"Socks." This time he was honest, although his eyes were still dragging between bed and drawer. The sound of Mattia's steps grew closer, the touch of his master's hand against his back a warm weight that swirled through his mind like a fog.

A thick black fog.

"And what did you find?" Mattia whispered right in his ear, his touch a chill as it moved over his shoulder and drew a line over his chest, tugging at the neck of the thin cotton button up he wore.

His heart warmed, but it didn't feel like the heat of joy and interest that it had before. The heat was angry, if heat could be angry. But this one definitely was. It was furious, and Killian's head snapped up at the heat, at the anger, to look at Mattia's hooded eyes as they peered around the lines of muscle that made up his neck and shoulder. Mattia's fingers picked at the collar of his shirt, peeling it back and revealed the dark lines of a tattoo Killian didn't recognize.

Perhaps the lines on his skin were where the heat was coming from. Seeing them was causing everything to boil

Black feathers, heavy blots of ink, and the soft touch of a woman with a smile just as soft. With eyes that play. Not like the deep grey of Mattia's.

"What did you find, darling?" Mattia asked again, the name pulling at him as the heat grew angrier, and he grabbed at the frayed bit of fabric, pulling it out of the dresser with a flourish. He expected the girl with the smile to follow after it like she was holding onto the tail of a kite. Like the smell of smoke that was filling his head, she was connected to the fabric somehow. She was connected to him.

Somehow... the confusing blur of black smoke was already swallowing the thought away.

"Ah yes," Mattia said, abandoning his adventure with Killian's collar as he snatched the scrap of fabric out of the air, stepping around Killian to hold it between them. Much as he had with the glittering square of cloth yesterday.

With the black and the ice. Killian shook his head, the lines between reality and dream where muddling together.

Perhaps it was the same. If he could hold onto the thought longer than perhaps he could find out.

If he could hold the fabric maybe he would know.

"What are they?" Killian asked, eagerly reaching for the charred bits of cloth, but Mattia pulled it away, leaving him with nothing more than smudges of ash on the tips of his fingers.

"They are from when I found you." Mattia stroked the shards of fabric as though they were precious, lifting them to his nose and inhaling with the sound of a gasp that twisted uncomfortably in the air.

The powerful man smiled as though he too could smell the hint of whatever was underneath. As if he loved it.

The thought wound with the heat, pressing against Killian's spine in a familiarity of a stab.

The fabric was inches away, but he couldn't smell more than a bit of smoke. He held out his hand, his fingers tugging on the fabric in a hope to pry it free, to lift it to his nose.

"Do you smell it?" Mattia asked as he lifted the fabric to

Killian. Although, he did not release his hold from the scraps, even against Killian's desperation.

If anything, the man held on tighter, letting Killian take little more than an inhale before he stepped back, towards the table that was still littered with the remains of Mattia's last absinthe binge.

Killian's mind may be muddled, but he remembered that clearly. The sound of the glass, the smell of burning sugar. It mixed with the ice and the specks of black and the beady eyes of a bird until everything was confused again.

There seemed to be enough of the green liquid for another glass, because Mattia instantly began to mix one, the fabric still in his hands as he nodded toward the toppled chair on the other side. The chair Killian had sat in last night.

"What is it?" Killian asked the familiar question, carefully lifting the chair and placing it on the floor. The wood creaked and gave way, so much that Killian wasn't sure it would hold his weight. He didn't have another choice, however, Mattia was already sitting in the other, much larger chair, sipping on his absinthe, holding the fabric against his chest.

"It is the scent of power, Killian," Mattia answered, the words pushing Killian into the chair with a heavy grind of wood. Luckily, the chair held.

"It's the scent of *your* power."

If Killian could have collapsed further into his chair he would have. Instead, he leaned over the table, bumping against the thing with a jolt as he tried to piece a million questions together in his even foggier mind.

"Let me ask you something, Killian," Mattia said before Killian could find any words, setting the fabric on the table between them, in a motion that was eerily similar to something else.

Something dark.

But light.

Something recent.

It was all muddled again.

He tried to pull at the thought, like a string on a sweater, but before he could even grasp the moment completely it was smothered in the darkness. Leaving him to jerk and stare at the strip of shadow underneath the bed, at the horrors that he was sure were there.

And at something that was drawing him into it.

"Have I told you about my sister?" Mattia asked, pulling Killian from one confusion into another.

He wanted to say yes, the question seemed familiar, but he couldn't think of anything about a sister. Perhaps she was the woman with the eager eyes.

Killian had no interest in sharing her however, so he shook his head. Mattia's eager eyes lighting up.

"Good. Good." He picked char off the fabric, rubbing it between his fingers like it was flint and tinder. Instead of smudging his fingers, however, it rubbed away and sprinkled back down to the fabric in bits of black.

He resisted the urge to look under the bed.

"Have you ever heard of the City of Soot?" Mattia asked after a moment, content that his fingers were clean and went back to his absinthe.

Killian shook his head, the name of whatever he was speaking about was as confusing as everything else. He was becoming desperate for something to make sense, for something to be real and not a flash of something that couldn't be placed.

Perhaps if he could touch the cloth he could smell it one last time...

"The City of Soot is where the first of your kind lived."

"My kind? What is my kind?" He didn't know he had a kind, or that he had anything outside this room. If he did he couldn't remember it, not that it wasn't stopping him from trying.

"Not yet, I think. Right now I want to tell you of my sister and the beast who tricked us," Mattia said, pulling the fabric away from Killian, letting it leave a bit of ash behind. Killian would have been glad to touch even that, but Mattia batted his hand away and placed a tray of cheese and bread on top of the smears of black.

Where the dish had come from was as confusing as everything else, but this one he wouldn't dwell on. He was too hungry to care about anything but cheese anymore.

"The City of Soot is burrowed inside of the mountain, far below the sun where everything is always warm, and the sky always burns, creating an endless shower of soot. Hence the name." Mattia wanted a response, but wasn't going to get one with the mouth full of cheese that sat across from him.

"It was created by five great dragons and was a refuge for shifters and magic--"

"Magic?" Killian asked through the cheese, his eyes darting to the strip of black under the bed that was still pulling at him.

"Yes, Killian, you remember that of your master, don't you?"

"My master?" Cheese and bread spread over the table in Killian's confusion, but this time the shock was short lived.

Distorted thoughts moved through Killian's mind, pulling at a memory of Mattia speaking with a shopkeeper and a blue sky. Killian sitting with Mattia on the bed, Mattia's hand on his knee as he showed him a trick.

As Mattia showed him many tricks.

Yes, his master. His master was a warlock, this one he knew.

"My master." He gave a nod this time and Mattia smiled, snapping his finger and letting the lights spark as the plate of bread and cheese vanished.

His hunger was too rampant to care for the trick, however, he wanted the food back.

"Magic," Mattia snapped again, the plate returning and Killian grabbed a few extra bits of cheese and bread lest he do the trick again.

"Your master was created in the City of Soot, Killian." Mattia had returned to picking at the charred fabric with one hand, the tip of his finger on the other dragging the rim of his now empty glass. "My family was brought there as slaves when we were very young, kidnapped by a night broker who supplied the city with servants and other necessities. A man by the name of Parris."

Mattia paused. Killian stopped chewing at the look in Mattia's eyes. Dark and malicious, like hate was swallowing the world. Hate that was sweeping over Killian in that same whirling heat that was digging against his tattoo. Before the heat had felt like both a comforting weight and an angry torrent. This time, however, it was afraid.

Perhaps this was how *his kind* expressed emotion, with some weird flame that burned from the inside out. The thought seemed possible considering that tiny tendrils of smoke were drifting from his nostrils.

At least he thought that was what he saw, he jerked away from the grey smoke and it vanished so quickly it may not have been there at all.

"I was a child when Parris came into our caravan with his clan. They burned the men alive and ravaged everything else. Any food, any livestock, any woman that he deemed valuable went with him. All of the children were gathered and placed in the backs of our own wagons with the livestock. We were dragged away from our homes, and the rain, and the sea, and taken deep underground."

Mattia's voice had pulled away, the black in his eyes hardening like stone as he continued to drag his finger over the edge of the glass, leaving a line of black behind. Glittering, dark, everything.

The window rattled as though a boulder had pressed against it and Killian jumped, his heart pounding against his bones. Even with all the tension that was in the air, he was glad when Mattia jumped right back into his story.

"We were sold, we were beaten, our lives fell apart, and all because of a foolish mortal who valued gold above life. I made him pay in the end."

"What did you do?" Killian asked, his words muffled behind bits of cheese and bread.

Mattia stopped tracing the edge of the glass, the black line he was leaving behind trailing down the side like ink made from smoke, thin streaks that twisted over the glass in a dance.

"I took his life and replaced it with something far worse," Mattia snapped his fingers then, and the black ink from the glass soared through the air, right back to his fingers where it seeped behind his nails.

Magic in repeat. Magic made all the more terrifying with what Mattia was saying.

"My sister and I escaped the City of Soot. We found the pool at the center of magic and begged the creature there for the means to take our revenge. The creature cannot just give power however, she can only give magic within balance. Light and dark. Good and bad."

He was back to picking at the fabric, letting bits of ash fall from it in little piles of black that glittered against the table. What Killian wouldn't give to touch it, to feel the ash, to smell the secrets that it held.

It was a funny thought, but his fingers were already pulling forward, skittering over the table toward the ash.

"She wanted something in exchange for that power," Mattia continued as he pulled the fabric back, sliding the bits of char over the table again. "I sold my sister's soul to the monster for it. For revenge. For power. I don't regret it. But the creature didn't give me light, she gave that to my sister. The monster who controls magic damned me, and so I damned the mortal. And I damned all the beings of light she has created. And I will damn her as well. That's why you are here, darling."

Killian had been staring at the fabric, letting Mattia's words rattle like the wind against the window, hoping that either words or smells would shake something loose.

"Why?" The question didn't feel quite right. Even with the muddled confusion that made up his mind there was more that he wanted to ask.

"My life was left behind, replaced by a darkness and a city that smelled of little more than ash. That smelled like you."

Mattia grabbed the knot of fabric, holding it up to Killian and letting him take a true inhale for the first time.

The smell of ash and smoke was a wonderful buzz that warmed through him, it was familiar and powerful and he wanted to bathe himself in it. It was the scent of whatever was just underneath however, that nearly sent him off his chair.

Mischievous eyes, a wide smile and a flash of hair so red it could have been flame flashed in his mind. He had seen them minutes before and the second they returned, the heat in his chest exploded, a sound like a scream filling his mind before it was all gone, replaced by a tiny spec of black in shadow.

"You have magic in you Killian, but it is not controlled by the monster. It is controlled by another. Centuries ago I stole the horn of the beast. Years before that I stole the ash of her counterpart, of the good that rivals the bad of the monster who stole my sister. That is what you are smelling, that is what is warming in your chest and pulling at your memory."

"Memory." The word was right. The images of red hair, and the touch of her skin, and the taste of her lips came right behind, assaulting him before the black smoke swallowed them whole and he was left heaving, grasping at straws of the memory of a woman that was playing with his insides, setting fire to his soul, and everything else.

"Elliot."

"Yes. I will let you keep your memory of her once I have trained you. Once you are ready to help me."

"What do you want me to do?" Killian's voice ripped out of him in a growl, the sound feeling normal, everything about him feeling normal.

The confusion that had consumed him was still pouring through his mind, but something about the name, something about the red flame in his memory was breaking him out. Bit by bit.

"You are strong, Killian. Strong enough to fight against me. Strong enough to kill them all. I have been close to killing her once, and with you I will be able to bring them both together. To defeat the dark and light and hold all the power inside of me."

Mattia placed his hand over the fabric, leaning himself closer to Killian as the scent of death nearly overtook the smoke that Killian was still gladly inhaling. It was nauseating, it swirled in his head alongside the black smoke until all Killian could see was the coiled smile of the man across from him.

His master.

"There will be no Unicorns and there will be no Phoenixes when I am done. When *we* are done. There will only be power. What say you, darling? Will you help?"

Darkness pressed against everything, it dug into Killian until there wasn't anything else but the dangerous look in his master's eyes, and the heat that was consuming him. Killian didn't want to agree, but he found himself doing so anyway.

He only gave one slight nod of agreement before the charred fabric began to smoke, and the entire wad burst into flames.

Mattia jerked away, his smile faltering as he leaned against his chair and the dark that had consumed the room faded into the sound of the wind and the crackling of fire.

"This is going to be harder than I thought," Mattia's voice was hard. Killian might have even said it was scared if he had been paying attention.

But he was watching the bits of black that fell from his hands, watching it cling to him as something else had the night before.

The horn.

The speck.

This time he froze, he didn't look under the bed, something inside of him was roaring to hide it. To steal it. To wait.

Something inside of him was roaring to life.

14

DRAKE

Cold air rushed over them as Drake pulled Zoe into the massive temple.

In his haste to escape the haunted statue he was amazed that he hadn't used his gift on her. It had been close, his dragon was still rumbling in fear, something that was growing as the door slammed shut behind them, closing them into a black abyss.

A glittering black abyss.

Walls had never glittered as much as they did here, the high carved pillars and buttresses and what he was sure was a mural extending over him in towers of textured darkness. Darkness that swallowed the bits of light and reflected them right back like magic and fire light. Impossible seeing as there was no light. Even the ripples of fire that were moving over the roof of the cave far above were dampened here, although you could see the shadow of the kite's tail through the ash coated windows.

Even those, dirty as they were, glimmered with a light that didn't exist. Bits of colors seeped through in patches, making Drake wonder if they had been murals of stained glass at some point in their history. The bits of red, yellow, and green pulled through the ashen walls in rays of color, shimmering through the dusty air and landing on the pillars that appeared to be carved like vines of flora and of flame. A patch of yellow light spread over the floor, showing a detail of latticed crosses that judging by the shadows that swirled through the floor was everywhere.

It was a beautifully haunting tunnel of obsidian, from the gargoyles that lined the buttresses, to the oppressive structure that stood in the shadows at the far end of the hall.

This place and its statues. At least this one didn't appear to be moving, which was better seeing as it almost appeared to be a cross between an elephant and a lion. He wasn't going to look at it either way.

He was starting to feel as if they should run from this place altogether. He had been running from Ceres and his monster for years, and whatever this city was hiding seemed a million times worse.

"What was that about?" Zoe snapped, pulling her arm away from where Drake had a death grip against her forearm. Luckily she was wearing a sweatshirt or it might have left a mark.

"The fountain..." Getting any more out than that was impossible. His dragon was back to growling, as if the creature was baring its teeth at the stone beasts, warning whatever was out there not to follow them inside.

The thought sent a shiver over his spine and he earned himself another look from his sister, her eyebrow perked.

"Drake. Are you okay?" Simple question, lined with way more concern than he would like to admit. What was it about older sisters always acting like the overbearing guardian? He was already weak enough in this situation, trapped in a weird underground city, unable to fly out in case of emergency. Being afraid of a fountain was the icing on the cake that he had no interest in eating.

He shook his head, "There is something off about this place, Zo. Something dark."

"Well, considering the whole thing is made of ash and coal compacted together that's a given."

"No." He tried really hard not to snap, but his dragon was already so agitated that it burst out that way anyway, a tiny bit of flame and smoke accompanying the word. "I mean dark, as if the whole place is haunted."

He couldn't help it, he looked toward the door, the black slab the only part of the place that wasn't glittering. That really wasn't helping him to feel better.

"You have clearly been spending too much time around mortals," Zoe said with a laugh, her steps echoing through the enormous space. Each step rumbled through the air, sending new lines of sparkle through the walls, as if the ebony was reacting to her steps like a stone against water.

Water full of stars.

"Well, that's fun." Zoe said, stomping her foot twice and sending two more ripples of glitter around them.

"Considering we don't know what that is or why it is happening, don't you think it would be wise if we stepped a little gentler?" Drake tried to demonstrate, but it didn't matter. Every step he took to where Zoe stood sent specks of white from him, the two of them turning the inside of the dark church into a constellation of stars.

Stars that glimmered and danced and appeared to press past the walls and into a nothing that Drake wasn't quite sure he had ever seen before. They were standing in the center of the universe, swallowed by a sea of stars.

"I don't think it matters," Zoe whispered as the sea

drenched the walls, pushing them away and swallowing them in black. "We are already screwed."

The world was gone, it was only a universe. Only everything. So much for finding safety in the cathedral.

Leaving the fountain was clearly the worst choice he had made since he had been here. Being stared at by a phantom carved into stone was clearly favorable to whatever mess they had found themselves in.

Stars were circling around them, pulling past them as though they were being hurled through space, pulled toward some bright light that had appeared in the distance, the speck of green right where he had seen that massive statue. The thing had gone, swallowed by the stars, and if they were moving he would be concerned about lunging himself head first into it like a fledgling dragon, but he could still clearly feel his feet. Planted against the slate floor.

They weren't moving anywhere.

"I don't know what you are talking about," Drake and his dragon said with a snap, pounding his left foot into the ground. His socked foot slipped against his sandals and the stars skittered away like ants from water.

The universe fell away as quickly as it had come, leaving them standing in the same colossal space.

"There is no screwing here."

"Thank god for that. I'm sure that's against the law, and gross. Mostly gross." Zoe gave him a look before bursting into laughter, ruffling his hair and walking toward a large basin that stood in the center of the room. Thankfully, there were no ripples of stars this time.

"Sick. I really didn't need that thought in my head." His stomach was already twisting in nerves, and now thanks to Zoe's filthy mind, threatened to pull what little was left in his stomach from the hotel the other day out. Thankfully he could easily replace those images with thoughts of Elliot.

Elliot.

Thinking about her was sending those nervous coils into overdrive. He had no idea where she was. Clearly, she could take care of herself, but being stuck in this underground city wasn't going to get him any closer to helping or finding her.

A coup and a massacre were brewing overhead, and Elliot had vanished. His dragon was agitated, although that might have been because the closer he got to the looming shape at the end of the chapel, the more it came into focus.

He still wasn't able to quite make it out through the dark, although the nose was very clearly that of a woman. Everything else was still too dark, too far away. Thank god it wasn't staring at him. Although, it was odd that Zoe didn't seem to notice the thing at all. She was staring at the basin so intently that she might as well have been pulled there.

The muscles through Drake's back wound together as he stared at the basin. His dragon pulled him forward as some power on the other side of the door continued to pull him back, tugging at his wings as though they were more than sinews of magic tucked against his spine.

"What is it?" Drake asked, forcing himself to a stop before he got too close, not quite ready to see what Zoe was staring at, what she was leaning over with a look of shock on her face.

She didn't respond. She leaned closer, her knuckles growing white as she clutched the basin's edge, standing on the tips of her toes, desperate to get closer to the chest high bowl. He took one step toward her and nearly jumped back.

Zoe was crying, the fiery red of her dragon's tears dripping over her cheeks like tiny specs of blood. What the fuck was going on? Zoe didn't cry. Zoe didn't show emotion.

She had two settings: badass bitch and badass bitch with a temper. This fell into neither of these.

"Zoe? Answer me!"

This could be the first time he was seeing her cry.

The scarlet of her dragon's tears shimmered against the almond of her skin before they fell into the deep stone basin with a splash of color that made it clear she was seeing something. That something was pulling her in. Drake's muscles wound tighter, holding him in place even as the pull of the basin grew. He needed to look inside the intricately carved basin.

He needed to see what secrets it held. To perhaps understand the secrets of the city, or the universe, or both.

He took a step forward, the pull in his spine attempting to yank him back, but it was too late. Zoe lifted herself onto her tiptoes, and the massive stone creature before him shifted.

It should have been enough to pull him away, to snap him out of whatever spell he was in, but he was already lost in the color that flicked through the bottom of the basin. Lost in the memory that was replaying inside of him so strongly that he wasn't quite sure if it was a memory at all.

"Alain," Zoe's sob followed him into dust, into the smell of water and waste as he tumbled through the floor of the abandoned building he had been exploring in Rydaim. Right into the tiny city of Fae that was hidden in the tunnels beneath. All of their faces turned to him. Gayl's was the first he saw, the first he recognized.

Years, no decades had passed since this moment, but right then it was new. It was as it was then. Gayl's inquisitive green eyes, the spark of the smile that Drake had been sure he had fallen in love with right then, her hand that reached to pull him out of the rubble without question. He was clearly a dragon of some regality, if only judged by his clothes. They knew he was a prince given the upturned noses of the adults. But Gayl didn't care.

Gayl helped him up. The two of them smiled as they carved out her cave, laughing in the deep tunnels of the cave when Zoe was trying to find him. She was his first and only friend. She had vanished in the attempted coup of a decade before, they never even found her body. And here she was.

Real.

Soft.

Warm.

Something felt dirty for thinking that way. But he had always felt that way about her, it didn't make sense why he should suddenly feel different. She looked as she always did. It was as it always was.

"You are looking at me like I am a pillow again," Gayl said with a laugh, grabbing the tiny rock she had been using to scrape against the stone and make her cave deeper.

Drake had a much easier time of it, having partially transformed his hand and used the long talons of his dragon to slice through stone like melted cream.

"Maybe I am thinking of using you as a pillow. This is tiring work." He exaggerated a sigh, throwing his still human hand over his forehead and earning himself an eye roll and a chuckle from the girl with the strawberry blonde curls.

"So says the mutant. Lean on the rock, Drake. I'm busy." She stuck her tongue out at him, dignified for the girl who he could have sworn turned twenty sometime last week. Not like they knew for sure, Fae didn't keep track of birth years. But they had been the same age when he had fallen through the roof, and he was reaching the mids of his twenties, so she couldn't be that far behind. They were both mostly immortal anyway, so it's not like it mattered.

Although the work that his father had put the Fae through had changed that. He had seen the camps his entire life. Watched the training they had to endure before they came to serve the dragons. Although, the older he got the less he supposed it to be for training and not for the breaking of spirit.

Gayl still had spirit, she also had long gangly scars down her forearms where the magic was cut out of her. The raised red skin looked even worse because it hadn't healed properly. What he wouldn't give to run his finger over them and wipe them away, to be brave enough to use his gift and stop this madness.

They didn't deserve this.

"Stop staring, Drake," Gayl said, her low mumble echoing through their tiny cave like thunder and pulling his focus. She wasn't even looking at him. "I think it too. What if? What if I didn't live here? What if I could escape? What if I had magic and could blast these walls to bits? But what ifs get us nowhere."

"That's not always true--"

"Let me ask you a question," she interrupted with a snap. "If you have all the power in the world, all the strength and no regret. What would you do?"

She still wasn't looking at him, what he wouldn't give to see the spark of joy in her eyes when he answered. He didn't even have to think about this one.

"Save you all. Defeat my father and end this nonsense." His mouth had suddenly gone dry. She was turning to face him, but instead of the green and hazel of her eyes it was yellow slits of a cat, it was a face he hardly recognized.

The pulse of his heart racketed against his ribs, the thunder rolling through him as the body that once was Gayl slinked through the cave toward him, and the last of his answer fell away, just like the dark of the memory.

Drake pulled himself from the basin with a gasp, his lungs burning for air as though he had been drowning in water, or memories. Or both. His chest ached as he heaved, as his focus drifted back to the cave and to his sister who thankfully wasn't trapped in whatever trick they had encountered.

Instead, she stood straight, looking into the dark end of the chapel that housed the enormous statue. Except it didn't appear so dark anymore. And the immense shape didn't seem quite so stone.

Brilliant yellow and orange light flooded the long hall from the dais at the end, it bathed the room and glimmered in every crevice of the ash covered room, it gleamed from the perfect stone carvings and reflected from the colorful windows that lined the hall of ash and soot. It was beautiful, and it would have felt safe if the tension and pain that coiled through Drake's muscles wasn't ready to rebound.

"Drake?" Zoe stared at him with a tear stained face, eyes gleaming with a red so bright he was sure he had never seen its double. "Drake. Can you see her, too?"

She turned back to the flood of color, stepping toward it as though she couldn't help it.

The same pull was yanking at Drake, but in his fear he couldn't move, he could scarcely draw breath.

"Zoe, Drake. Come to me."

If the color wasn't enough to pull Drake's focus, the sound of her voice was. It was filled with a low growl, a high purr, and a seductive hiss that forced him to turn, forced him to follow their instructions.

Faintly, he wondered if this is what being forced to

follow the silver tongue of his dragon felt like, this longing, this lack of control.

The moment he came face to face with the beast that had been looming at the end of the hall, however, that all left.

He didn't care what his silver tongue felt like. He didn't care why he was turning. All that mattered was the beautiful creature that was towering over them.

Half lion, half woman. A woman so beautiful that he had never known her equal.

Which was fitting seeing as she no longer was.

"A Sphinx." He gasped. The creature nodded, her paws kneading the stone floor. He might as well have been knocked back onto his ass in shock.

He had thought a Phoenix was a fabled shifter that didn't exist. But this massive creature was even more impossible, and as real. Real enough to purr and stare at him with the cat like eyes he had seen in his memory, their intense stare digging into him from where she towered over them, larger than his dragon.

"This can't be happening," his muscles were coiling as if he was expecting a fight, but his dragon was calm, its roar a rumble as it cowered to the beast before them.

"Drake and Zoe, you have proven to me that you are brave enough to set foot in this city, that you hold the intelligence to be in my presence, that you have the heart to be beside a god. Now, you must prove that you have the wit to face the darkness of the world."

The sphinx smiled, if you could call the tiny twitch of her lips that. Not that Drake could look anywhere but at the oversized cat shaped eyes.

"I am the Sphinx. I guard the City of Soot and sit beside the gods of this world. I am their equal. I am their warrior and sit before the information that will place you on your path. Answer my riddle and you will be allowed this knowledge. Fail and you will be turned to stone and soot and dwell among the damned that still exist within these walls."

"Ah, shit," Zoe hissed, the Sphinx's warning enough to break the trance that she was under. Well, so much for any place in the city being safe.

"Are you ready for my riddle?" The sphinx said in that same voice, although it didn't seem near as alluring as it had before.

Regret at having come in here was at an all-time high. In fact, Drake was regretting leaving the mob of Forgotten.

They could have taken the Forgotten.

This was going to be a crap shoot.

This was not going to end well, but he found himself nodding anyway.

They didn't have much of a choice anyway. That coy little smile was turning the corners of her lips again, the huge lions tail circling around her and sending a cloud of ash into the air. He had missed the tail before, not that it mattered, the claws were enough as they dragged through deep grooves of stone with the sound of a broken lawn mower. But a million times worse.

"I will make you scream with glee." The sphinx began without warning, sending them both jumping and Zoe narrowing her eyes in concentration.

"I will make you cry and beg in death. I create the grey in a mother's hair, and the frown in the friend who is best. I make the intelligent wilt in mute stupidity, and the fowl rise in genius. I turn water brown and the sky red. I wilt. I cry. I walk on five sets of fingers. Can you answer what I am?"

"Double shit."

15

ELLIOT

THERE WASN'T A SEX SCENE WITH A DEMON, THANK GOD, BUT there were far too many 'other' things for me to get anywhere close to a restful sleep.

First, it was me standing before the same mirror I had seen before, drinking from that same vial as before. But wearing different clothes. In a different time. Maybe I liked to drink things before a mirror. Maybe it was tonic to make my boobs grow, but seeing as there was no sign of that, it was out.

Then there was something involving a woman that looked a little too perfect to be real, and a man who was equally as perfect and seemed to be made up of both height and muscle that would rival Killian's.

He would have fit in the 'perfect bucket' alongside the ethereal woman if his eyebrows didn't look like what you would see on an owl. Maybe he was an owl. Well, an owl shifter, not that I knew that was a thing. That would be a pretty lame shifter. I mean, as their mate you would have an endless supply of mice. But that doesn't seem like a good draw.

Darling, I love you. Here is a partially digested mouse head.

I didn't get a chance to ask either way. Both he and the girl were wiped from my mind without a word as I rolled over, the mattress sagging underneath me as I was treated to more scenes with that damn knife.

Silver inlay, a ruby in the hilt, a blade that I was sure would be all sharp and gleaming and shit... well, if it wasn't covered with demonic black blood.

It was always the same knife. Although the scenery changed from seasides, to dark alleys, to massive glittering ballrooms; it was all just one blood stained knife fight. Me stabbing, demon boyfriend cackling as tar poured from his face. The scene shifted so often that I was starting to believe past me enjoyed stabbing demon boy too much, not that I blamed her.

He was creepy as fuck and clearly deserved to be stabbed.

Past me liked stabbing. I would be happy to rip his head off or something. The guy was a freak, and a demon.

A freaky demon. Didn't make it any better, especially when you add the whole haunted cabinet full of men's bloody clothes into the mix. Bloody clothes. Heads in jar.

We had clearly walked into one of those horror movies with the guy that likes to rip off limbs and mind fuck his victims.

Yep, I rolled over again, this time putting my back and a few layers of worn blankets between the massive wardrobe and the sheets that had too much movement for standing in a breezeless room.

Between the haunted cabinet of death and destruction and these damn memories, sleep was impossible. And I needed sleep. Thinking straight was going to be vital to getting us out of here and I wasn't one hundred percent sure

I would be able to find a steaming cup of black coffee in this place. Or that I would trust it. Coffee was starting to look too much like black blood mixed with the grease that lined the top of the head jar.

Thanks half-asleep brain, that wasn't an image I needed.

Damn. I was going to hurl.

Time to force all of this mess right out of my mind.

Luckily, I knew which sweaty handsomeness I could use to replace it.

No demons allowed.

The perfect antidote came too easily. Tangled limbs, sweaty chests, and wandering hands replaced the haunted entourage as though it had been waiting on the side lines. For a split second I worried I was being treated to the damn demon sex scene anyway, but then I saw the tattoo.

The long stretch of dark black ink that stretched over his chest, following the lines of those damn pecs that I was fighting with the need to lick. To taste the sweat that was dripping over his skin, the same way that it had in the bathroom.

Screw it. It was a fantasy and I could lick what I want.

I was so going to trace those black lines with my tongue. Lick them like they were the best treat in the world. Coffee and black licorice, yum.

The rumbling moan of his dragon mixed with the joyful purr of my Phoenix, filling my mind as more hands wandered and more lips crashed together. My heart may be screaming in agony, reminding me that Killian was not here, that he had flown away. But my hormones were on their own journey of sexual awakening that I could have sworn pulled me right to sleep.

"You're quite the saucy little minx, aren't you?"

Well, maybe not quite.

I knew that bitch's voice much more than I would have liked to admit. She was really not welcome in this daydream. Again. This was the second one of these perfectly tangled moments she had barged in on.

And she could barge her way back out.

"Back out Dabria," I grumbled, clutching at Killian's hip bones as another pair of hands began to wind their way around me, these ones rough and calloused from years of rocks climbing. God, he was strong. "I'm uninviting you from this party, bitch."

You think she would have learned from her last journey into my subconscious. You know the one where I burned the shit out of her.

Plus, now she knew what I was. I didn't have to hold back. I could torture her all I wanted in here.

I could burn those braids off her head and turn her into Britney during her 2007 breakdown. It would be a glorious look for her.

Hold up. I changed my mind. Dabria was more than welcome to join this party. Well, maybe not *this* party, but a limb burning soul crushing party in which I could happily torture her.

Just like that, the tangling arms and legs and lips and everything else vanished, leaving me in the same long ass cave that she loved so much.

"Do you really want to fight me?" I taunted, my loud echoes bouncing over the stone and mixing with some other voice

"You can't bite girl. You couldn't even do more than hide and whimper as the roof to the restaurant came down."

The restaurant? Wow. Someone could hold a grudge. You would think that after I bitch slapped her and Parris in Rydaim she would have found something else to cling to.

Well, maybe not. My naked ass had taken two of the princes right out from under her.

I whipped around to her, letting my braid swing behind me in the hopes of whipping her across the face.

But she wasn't even there. Just the cave, and a bit of a shadow in the distance that kinda looked like her. Well her, unless there was some other gorgeously bitchy dragon who had purple hair and a passion for thigh high pleather boots.

Doubtful. There was only one ice dragon I knew that was that fake.

You think a dragon could spring for real leather. But no, those gaudy boots were shiny enough they could have been vinyl.

"The roof of the restaurant? Don't you mean the roof of your fucking cave. Did one of those big ol' boulders land on your pretty little head and knock you back a couple days?" It felt good to let all that residual teenage angst fly and give her a proverbial slap upside the head. Even my Phoenix was dancing in glee, her feathers ruffling against my heart in some kind of celebratory dance that I would have joined if I wasn't trying to posture this bitch.

Not that it was working, every step I took closer to her she seemed to step away as much, her ugly boots still facing the other direction.

Damn it! Look at me! I finally get to taunt her and her brain is broken and she is talking to the wall.

"Yes, because he's been so great at protecting those around him. His own brother..." She was mocking, laughing, certain, and saying something that had nothing to do with what I had said.

"Huh?"

That dance that was ruffling against my heart picked up, but instead of prancing around in victory, it was in confusion and fear. The beautiful beast of my soul was ready to attack her, to rush away and save Jarron.

Jarron?

But Jarron was here, in the next room, or so I assumed seeing as we were trapped in a demon's house maze. Seemed fitting with Dabria trapped in the mindfuckery of a few days ago.

"Jarron will not burn. We will not let him..." My own voice echoed through my head, over the rocks of the cave and blended with the snarl of the phoenix. The sound rumbled in my chest, mixing with the echo of days before.

Well, this shit got weird.

I had wanted to sleep. But I was perfectly happy with having inappropriate dreams of Killian and his perfectly curved ass in my hands.

Having flashback dreams of Dabria being stuck in my head was not on the menu.

"Why do you care?" Dabria snapped, the shadow of her jerking forward as I assumed she tried to posture wherever I was a few days ago. Instead, she kind of looked like a child trying to catch a doughnut off a string. So weird.

You would think if I was going to have flashback dreams I would be treated to her ugly mug bobbing in front of me, same as before. Not that this was bad. She looked ridiculous either way, I guess.

"Killian has chosen you as his mate. Your heart belongs to him... not to Jarron. You should be happy we are ending him, giving you a clear path to your own crown."

She sounded even more psychotic on this side of everything that had happened. Seeing her hanging on Ceres and Parris at the fountain in Rydaim was a pretty clear sign she was more than a crown seeking whore than I could ever be.

Damn, she had played her cards well.

I guess if I was going to be stuck in the repeating tunnel of a nightmare I could at least make the most of it.

"I already have my crown. All of them. Their hands are all over me and everything. Killian even has a tattoo of me on his chest. I licked it, Dabria. My tongue even touched his nipple." My prod drowned out whatever I had said a few days ago, drowning us in noise and the snarl of Dabria's dragon.

Maybe the beast had heard me, even if the woman hadn't. Or, I guess dream dragon. It wasn't like I was really traveling back to Dabria's dream infestation, although the air was growing too cold, and my phoenix was boiling too hot.

I took another step toward the flailing Dabria, and this time she didn't move away from me, the blurred edges of her came into focus as she stepped up to the shadow that I was sure was supposed to be me.

I was all red and white and blurred. From here, I kind of resembled a burning pillowcase. No wonder she was intimidated by me.

I would be furious if the super hot guy that I fell in love with left me for a burning pillowcase.

At least I was a sexy burning pillowcase.

"If the life of someone I cared about was in danger I would be caring a whole lot. I wouldn't be having fantasies of someone else's love in a hotel room halfway across the world." She snarled, the growl of my Phoenix swallowing whatever cool comeback I had been able to come up with a few days ago. I was pretty sure it wasn't as cool as what I wanted to say now.

"I would rather be having fantasies of that than you in

that jacket. You look like you were swallowed by a rubber snake."

I let the words fly, laughing at myself until Dabria turned. The dark purple of her eyes flashed with the flame of her dragon, confusion igniting as she looked into me. The cool me wearing this historical nighty-underwear combo, not the pillowcase me. Her lips curled in understanding as pillowcase me slammed into her and sent her tumbling back.

Her legs flailed like a cat who didn't know how to land on its legs, sending her into a ball of purple braids, flailing limbs and ugly pleather boots.

Pillowcase me, and bad ass Phoenix me, laughed at the display. It was as good watching it from this direction. Maybe even better, seeing her legs go up over her head like that. God, I wish dreams had cameras. I never wanted a cell phone before, but now I had found a good use for it. I would watch that over and over again.

Priceless.

Well, it was better until she stood up, and turned back to badass Phoenix me, jumping to her feet and staring with purple eyes that were too intense for some dream replay.

"You bitch!" Her snap rang through the cave as it had the other night, but the purple eyed monster that was staring at me hadn't been the one to say it.

Her lips didn't even move.

She smiled, her ugly heels tapping as she stepped closer.

"Well, isn't this interesting. Two of you. How did you get here?" The snarls of her anger were nearly drowned by her confusion. She was trying to hide it, but even through the sparks of hatred in her eyes I could see it. Fear.

Fear that was quickly smothering me, like I had been jumped by the burning pillowcase.

The bristling heat and excitement of my phoenix was feeling too bipolar for my liking. She was ready to burn Dabria's ass to the ground, her fire all pissed. As it was a few days ago.

I was frozen like some alien that walked into an episode of the Twilight Zone.

Well, the Twilight Zone with a drug addiction.

Here I was thinking I was dreaming up a nightmare replay, and now I was being stared at by the ice queen, in a tunnel that was glowing blue, with this bitch trying to dig through my brain.

Like I was here.

Like it was really happening. Again.

Because my life hadn't gotten weird enough.

Teleportation with two of my mates? Check.

Meeting my former, possibly murderous mate? Check.

Weird, equally as murderous memory flashes? Check.

Haunted wardrobe hallucinations? Check.

Time traveling dreams? Yeah, let's add that too while we are at it.

Not possible.

"You mean, here in this dream?" I prodded as fear, anger, and excitement blended in a cocktail that I wasn't quite sure was coming from the me of right now. "I really wanted to see those ugly boots again, I suppose. Seeing as I didn't get a good enough look when I beat your ass in Rydaim the other night."

"Rydaim?" Whatever facade she had been trying to hold onto slipped away as the echoes of my old screams rang through the cave, echoing over the stone and dripping from the fire that was pouring through the air and devouring her. Devouring everything.

"No! Shit! No!"

That scream I joined in on. Pillowcase me shrieked and lunged, I yelled and lifted my suddenly fire blasting hands toward Dabria who was frozen in the crossfire. Shrieking and waving her hands in the air as she tried to block or extinguish the fire that was now coming from both sides. Fire that was streaking red and gold over everything, not just Dabria. Although she had turned into a mighty fine pillar of fire.

"I will find you, Elliot! I will find all of you!" She screamed through the flames that were swallowing her, still batting and waving at them as if that would help.

It would have looked ridiculous if it wasn't so horrifying, if I couldn't see the flesh begin to melt off her skull.

Holy fuck!

I knew I could burn a dragon but this was a horrifyingly melty disaster. I already had images of heads in jars. This was so much worse.

Dabria gave one last shriek, the fiery mass of what was once an ice dragon taking a flying lunge at me. I couldn't even step away from the bomb of smoke and flames. I was frozen in dumbfounded shock as she jumped toward me only to fall to the ground in a sparkling shower of ash, leaving nothing but a pile of grey and some partially melted pleather boots.

"Sick," I hissed as I stepped forward, kicking the boots to the side and sending a shower of the former dragon through the black air.

The cave around us had vanished, leaving the bits of her to stick in the black like stars. Beautiful twinkling stars.

"Are you quite done pretending to forget yet?" I jumped at the voice, at the figure of a little girl who was stepping through the black, sending the stars swaying as though they were attached to a curtain and she had been hiding behind it the whole time.

What the fuck was up with that? Yes, I totally jumped back. I mean, the weird time traveling dream and haunted cabinets had clearly done me in. I was not adding hallucinations of yet another little girl to my list of fucked up weirdness.

"Xi? What the fuck are you doing here?" I would have watched my language, but the last time I saw her she was sniffing a pool of blood and acting nothing like the little girl she appeared to be.

I'm pretty sure I swore and farted fire, too. At least this time I wasn't ass rocketing up the joint.

"You drank the potion, El. You chose to drink the Kool-Aid, so now it is time to come back. You've played this game long enough." She was sure, confident, and not making a drop of sense.

"Wanna try that again in English?" I prodded, perking my eyebrow at her as I tapped my foot. Okay, so I was in a saucy mood.

And she clearly wasn't taking it too well.

"Stop fucking off," Xi snapped. So, I had clearly judged my not swearing around a kid thing accurately. "Get your head on straight, open the damn door, and get out of there!"

She snarled at me, took one step closer and slapped me across the face so hard that I could feel the heat of the hit against my cheek as my eyes fluttered open to the pitch black of my room and the two looming masses of white.

The sheets that covered the wardrobe and whatever the hell the other one was rustling as if there was a breeze.

Calling to me.

No, not calling to me. Just being generally freaky. There was clearly a breeze on the other side of the room. Like an air conditioning vent or something, cuz that made sense. I refused to admit that I had lost it enough to think that the dark looming shapes were calling to me; that the way the sheets were moving, revealing the hinge of a wardrobe door, and a clawed foot I was sure I had seen before wasn't meant for me.

I clearly needed to go back to sleep.

Too bad rolling over sent me sprawling onto the floor with a sound that was as hollow as spaghetti against a tile floor. Except the tile floor was cold stone and the spaghetti was me.

"Ow."

16

ELLIOT

NOTHING WAS COMFORTABLE ABOUT THIS. I WAS TANGLED IN A cocoon of fabric, my feet pinned together, my knees spread apart and my ass wagging in the air in such a way that I really wished my weird underwear didn't have that old-school butt-flap thing, that had of course opened, if only to complete the embarrassing display.

The tangles of sheet was partially covering the face smashing that had occurred when I had compacted against the stone floor. My cheek was pressed into my eye, my nose flattened against the uneven floor as something warm and wet and probably blood drizzled out of it.

Everything hurt, and not because I had hit the floor with the force of a rhinoceros.

I was pretty sure my body was attempting to rip itself apart. I had felt this ache before, the morning after my Phoenix had bonded herself to my three dragons, and then I had become little more than a bed slug. Bones and muscles and veins splintering and breaking and turning me into mush.

Since then, at least one of the boys had been careful to

be near me when I would wake. It hadn't been a bulletproof system; Killian and Jarron had been away and I had been left with weird aches and gnawing holes most of the time.

With Jarron locked away in another room, however, and Killian and Drake lost somewhere in the world, I was officially reverted back to bed slug status. Well more like slug pretzel snake.

I was stuck, forced to relive the weird dream thing that had startled me into this awkward position.

Dream was giving it too much credit. I was starting to think that this room was doing weird things to me.

Like making me think I could time travel.

Nuts. I was nuts.

Although not as nuts as the kid that was apparently stalking my dreams as well. Although I had a feeling her nonsense might actually help. *Open the door.* Sure kid, whatever you say.

I mean, that was already the plan. Escape the demon that clearly had some unsavory plans for me. Well, unless we stabbed each other first.

I really ought to stop blinking. I was getting tired of seeing that damn knife dripping with demon blood.

An icy chill wrapped around my achy muscles and I shivered. Great, even that hurt.

Okay, step one, de-pretzel and cover my ass before someone walked in. If only because that someone would probably be a demon.

Fighting through the pain, I heaved and groaned in an attempt to stand. Instead, I flopped over slamming my hip into stone, my butt ramming against the wall. Okay, so that didn't quite work. My feet were still tangled, and now I was wedged between bed and wall in a genuine pretzel slug, forced to stare into the dark under the bed that my heart was telling me Killian was hiding in.

Because that made sense. He had been there the last time I had woken up from Dabria's interference, but he wasn't under the bed.

He was beside me, he was touching my face.

This was turning into a mess. I really needed to get my ass out of this pretzel and track Jarron down. One less ache would be really nice right about now.

Who cares if my bones were trying to splinter inside of me as I forced myself onto my hands and knees, I was going to track him down.

"I'm going to walk out of here like a badass." I was confident, cool, and landed right back on my face when my muscles gave out and my attempt to stand sent the pretzel slug back to her humble beginnings.

"Shit."

Okay. Let's reconvene. Walking out of here wasn't going to work, which meant my only other option was to crawl. Well, and I guess roll out of here, but I don't think I was ready to resort myself to that yet. I was going to force my stubborn ass to crawl out of here if it killed me, and it might.

Keeping every single "Oh my god" and "What in the fucking hell is wrong with me?" locked inside, I pushed myself forward, hitting the door after what I was sure was hours.

My fingers throbbed as I lifted them to the thankfully unlocked knob, pulling the lever and letting the heavy stone slab swing open. I had half expected the door to still be locked, and I wasn't one hundred percent convinced that the door being unlocked was a good thing.

When there are demons running loose in an underground maze, unlocked doors only meant one thing.

Death.

The hall stretched forever in either direction, which in my agonized and clearly deluded state was probably a million doors.

A million identical doors.

I really should have thought this through.

"Mother fucker," I snarled, pushing myself against the stone wall and sagging against it. At least I had been able to ditch the tangled sheet.

Haunted demon doll had said that Jarron's door was right next to mine, but the first one I tried was locked and I was pretty sure the second door was a mile or so away. As much as I was trying to focus on aches, or heart strings, or whatever super dragon mating power I had, I couldn't figure it out.

"Fucking Jarron. Come here now. I need you." I was forceful, growling like I was the demon. It had worked before, but this time I might as well have been talking to a stone wall.

Oh wait, I was.

Swearing and agitation clearly did not turn on the heart strings. It did however, prompt what I was sure was glass breaking from two doors down.

From the door that was flashing yellow and black light from under the crack under the door.

On. Off. On. Off.

Yeah, I remembered what happened the last time I had followed a mysterious blinking light and as much as I would like to hightail it back to my room, or run to Jarron, I had no idea where Jarron was. I had a feeling that whoever was on the other side of that blinking light, however, did. Going back to my room would do me no good. Unless I was also going to roll myself back to my shower and live the rest of my life as grout.

God damn it. I was a badass circus babe and I was sitting on the floor contemplating a future as a bit of shower grout. This was so not going to stand.

I was.

I was going to stand.

"Pull yourself out of it," I scolded myself, Phoenix ruffling in my chest in what was clearly indignant agreement.

Good. We were on the same side.

Agony ripped through my bones as I pulled myself up, veins swelling until it felt as if each one was a line of electricity, sparking through muscles and organs and making me feel like Frankenstein. Or Frankenstein's monster. I had no clue which one. I had never read the book, so I didn't care about the difference, all I knew was that I was stiff, uncomfortable, and exerting far too many grunts to truly be thought of as human.

Staying close to the wall in case my legs decided to give out from underneath me, I made my way to the door. The light flickered underneath it as whispers of breaking glass echoed over the stone.

I nearly turned back. I probably should have.

When I pushed the door open it was not to my sexy dragons, or to some super-secret escape tunnel, but to the living area. Flickering light illuminated the couch, the white tiled kitchen, and a large black shape that was hovering behind the singed table. The massive thing was a smear of smoke and feathers.

I had clearly walked into a horror movie. I gasped, the sound acting like a switch that plunged everything into darkness.

Every muscle was tight, my breaths coming in sharp

little gasps as I tried to process what I had seen. I couldn't have seen that, could I? It looked like a monster.

No, that tiny little voice in the back of my mind hissed. *It looked like a demon.*

Holy fucking shit! What had I walked in on?

Jarron's prediction was pounding against my chest with all the strength of a jack rabbit, the fear pulsing to join it in a tempo that was sending my phoenix into a frenzy. An obviously needy and grabby frenzy. The emotions didn't make any sense, the fear was pulling at every single muscle, my mind screaming at me to run, while my heart and my phoenix were screaming at me to rush into the dark.

The monster. The demon. The smoke.

I was really not ready to admit that whatever I had seen was not a figment of my imagination. A horrifying terror of my imagination.

Like everything else in this damn cave.

The fear multiplied with the abhorrent panic that was heating and swelling in both heart and abdomen, and I, like the fool I was, stepped into the room. Well, I more like stumbled into the dark, barely able to grab the wall before I fell face first to the ground.

Again.

At least there was a plush carpet here and not the rough stone of the hallway, but I wasn't really sure that that would make much of a difference.

"Fucking shit." My profanity was swallowed by the rug, and the low rumble that was echoing over air and through stone.

Double fucking shit.

Trying to restrain a groan, I pushed myself over, forcing myself to stand. Well, to lean against the couch in something that resembled an epic fighting stance.

Yep, I'm an idiot.

What did I think was going to happen? A fist fight with a shadow that I was fairly certain was staring at me from the corner. Either that or shadows had learned how to breath in the last few minutes.

"Hello?" I called into the dim space, the light over the oven beginning to flicker again. My voice shook as much as my hands as I clung to the couch, slowly guiding myself closer to the dark, to the faint clinking of glass that was echoing to me. "Is anybody there?"

No one but a breathing shadow, Elliot. Pull yourself together.

Yeah, I knew I was being ridiculous. Here I was in the room that contained the only escape to our freedom, and I am worried that the shadows are going to hear me. Shaking my head, I hustled my way over to the door, careful to palm the wall and not the hundreds of equally as creepy photographs of me that lined the room.

I kept my eyes on the door, my fingers trailing over ridges and decorative framing as I tried to find a hinge, a gap, or even a keyhole. I wasn't finding anything other than cold stone under my fingertips and I doubt that looking at the door in the bright fluorescent light would help. The guy had pushed the key for the door into the tip of his finger.

That was still creepy enough to make my stomach twist, never mind the fact that I would need the key to open the door. Finding the key hole was like working backwards. That technique may have worked for Mary Lennox, but the key to her garden wasn't stuck inside of a fucking demon.

"Fucking Henry," I growled to myself, realizing too late what I had done. What the one rule that Jarron had given me had been. I broke that way too fast.

"Fuck."

My fingers curled against the cold stone of the door as I turned toward the low growl that was billowing from the kitchen and the shadow I had been pretending didn't exist. The shadow heaved as dark smoky feathers swelled through the kitchen like liquid smoke. Billows of black shifted hauntingly as the light began to flicker, the smoke swallowing the blasts of light as it congregated before the table in a shape that was too man-shaped for it be a coincidence.

I guess I needed to add demon summoning to my resume. I was so fucking screwed.

"Well, well, I think that can be arranged. The fucking part I mean." Even in the haunting flicker of light the slime in his grin ran up my spine like poison.

"Not the demon part?" I taunted as the light gave one last blast and plunged us back into shadow. "Because I'm pretty sure you have the demon part down pat."

I was doing my best to stand up straight, which was turning out to be nearly impossible. The bones in my spine were clearly attempting to meld on into each other and return to their true form. I was fighting against the cringes and the pain, but it was all shining right through with the way he was smiling.

"I'm not a demon."

Wait what? The shock of that might as well have been a dead weight against my chest. I collapsed against the wall with the impact, leaving the non-demon to smile and nod his head with a click of his tongue.

"Yes, you are. Jarron--" I said with a grunt, trying to push myself back up to something that resembled standing a bit more. I got about half way before I collapsed back against the wall, although this time my legs gave way and I slid down the slick surface like buttered bread. The sound of my skin sliding against stone wasn't really helping that imagery.

"Oh, my darling girl," Henry's slick British accent cut through the air as he stepped around the kitchen table toward me. Dark shadows swirled through the dark like he had a cape of smoke. "Jarron is a fool and you are better off without him. He has clearly not been around you enough to know what truly awaits him. What I truly am."

"And what are you if not a demon? A bastard?" I may not be able to stand up straight, but I was sure as hell going to give him the best glare I could muster and slap him with as many words as possible.

"Not quite." He stepped closer, pressing his hand above my hand as he crouched before me, his free hand tracing over the air above my shoulder as if he was scared to touch me.

Maybe he thought I was going to burn him. It was a good assumption. My phoenix was already boiling in her bipolar need-want-hate triangle that this guy brought out in her. It wouldn't take much to bring all that to the surface and send him and his tail of black smoke tumbling through the air.

Well, it wouldn't if my veins weren't still threatening to explode. Goddammit, where was Jarron when I needed him?

"Then what? A cloud of ass gas?" I smiled, he scowled, the black smoke that filtered around him lifting up, smothering the color in his eyes until there was nothing but darkness looking through them.

"You know what I am, Elliana." He leaned closer. "Why are you still playing this game? Why haven't you let the memories return?"

My muscles were already wound in tight painful coils,

but his choice of words sent the pain rippling into agony as they rolled over my back. As my heart beat a little faster and my Phoenix began to scream.

"I'm not playing any game." I said it loud enough that maybe he and freaking Xi would hear too, wherever she was hiding.

He didn't get the message.

"Come out and play little girl, daddy misses you."

"Gross." I snarled. Just when I think this guy can't get any creepier. "You can't call me that either."

"Daddy can call his little girl whatever he wants. You know this." His voice was a hiss, the low tones sending the lights into a demonic flicker as he leaned closer, his free hand trailing over the air of my arm, my shoulder, my breast, my neck, and finally my cheek. His fingers flicked in the air as though he was touching me, the quick movement sending a weird electric chill of his touch through the air toward me.

Touching me, but not really. Maybe he was scared I would break his fingers if he touched me. Good call, because that was exactly what was going to happen.

I tried to shift away, but the pain that was rolling over me had pretty much glued me to the wall.

I was one with the wall, now.

"Say it," he whispered, his voice a low moan that was too familiar. That I had heard too many times before. I didn't need the flash of memory that came with the blink. The feeling of his touch was already permeating through me, my bones were already melting underneath him. I saw it anyway, the exact thing I had been dreading.

Demon sex scene.

I practically forced my eyes open. There were too many

limbs, and too much sweat, and one damn sexy ass that I suddenly found myself wanting to grab.

No!

No ass grabbing, Elliot. Especially that ass. Because it wasn't a fine ass. It was a saggy old demon ass.

Shit stained saggy demon ass.

Thinking that wasn't doing anything to banish the thoughts.

"Say what?" Why the fuck was my voice shaking? I was so not okay with this. He, however, was giving me another greasy smile, obviously overly okay with this.

I tried to shift away, to avoid his touch, but my body still wouldn't obey. If anything it was trying to take me in the other direction. Toward him.

Fine. I could use this.

"Say it." He hissed again, his voice that same murky rumble and I pushed my way forward, lunging myself forehead first, right into him.

It didn't work out quite as well as I had planned. Yes, my forehead made contact with his. But his forehead appeared to be made of iron. You think I would have remembered that from the whole punching episode of the day before. But no, I hit against his iron head with the force of a pendulum. A pendulum when faced with a solid wall of steel. I fell to the floor with a gasp and shriek, a splitting headache adding to the pains that were already ripping through my mate-deprived body.

That was a terrible choice.

"Damn it! Fucking bitch!" Henry screamed as I writhed on the floor, I really looked like a slug now thanks to the beige Victorian underwear. "What the hell was that?"

"You deserved it," I said through the moans of agony that

were still ripping through my throat. Henry only swore more and knelt beside me, bending to look at me.

The bright red skin on his forehead was a good addition to his dumb ruggedly handsome demon face.

No, not handsome. As ugly as his shit stained ass.

"Demon bastard." Yes, I was moaning in pain. As much as I tried to put a snap in my voice, it came out like a weird grumble.

"Aw, come on baby. What happened to being fucked by a demon."

"Go to hell." That time I put a good snarl behind the words, even though I was still stuck on the ground, the British man hovering over me.

"Fun fact, baby. I've never been there. Been to the other place, though. I didn't like that one so much. That's why I came here." I froze. He smiled and started doing that same thing with his hands, letting his fingers flutter against the air above my face, sending those electric sparks into my skin.

"Ha! You expect me to believe you are an angel?" I was still trying to shift away, but my curiosity was getting the better of me. I was frozen beneath him. Frozen beneath that damn smile and the smoke that was billowing behind him in a shape that was too much like wings.

"No, no. Maybe once, but I left that behind. For you. After all, it takes someone who has walked with the gods to dwell with a goddess."

He seemed too sure of himself for the nonsense that he spewed.

"What the fuck are you on about?" I really didn't like the way the muscles in my back were tensing, the way my phoenix was pressing against my heart and igniting my skin in a million spots of gooseflesh.

"I will tell you everything when you say it, Elliana."

"Say what?" I snarled, trying to shift away from him. He wasn't holding me down, but with the agony that was roaring through bones and veins I couldn't manage more than an inch or two.

"Please."

"Please?" Ultimate regret. I clearly didn't think that response through and had walked right into his trap, only to be welcomed by the greasy smile of the not-demon.

"Perfect." His hand fell against my skin, sending a lightning bolt of electricity through me and taking away every last one of my body aches.

I was so not okay with this.

17

KILLIAN

Mattia kissed Killian on the cheek before he left, his lips cold and lifeless against the burning heat of Killian's skin, against the monster that was roaring inside.

He had let the roar build since he had felt it a few hours before, the rumble accompanying the heat that was everywhere. It drifted with the black that he was sure had come from Mattia, the muddled mess of heat and dark raging louder as they fought for space.

And now that Mattia was gone they were screaming.

He had only minutes. The bathroom was down the stairs, he could already hear the little man's steps thunder down the old wooden staircase. Too fast for someone who trusted Killian to be safe alone in this room.

The black smoke in Killian's mind was a fog, it drifted over his vision and through his mind like a wall that if it wasn't for the low burn in his chest he wouldn't have been able to bat it away. Instead, he fought against it, turning from the door and dropping to his stomach, as he had before.

Or, he thought he had. He still wasn't sure if the images that were assaulting him were real or not, but this was the only time he would get to check.

The darkness was screaming that the shadows under the bed were dangerous, that they would stretch out and devour him. Laid out on his stomach as he was, listening for the squeak of a hinge or the heavy pound of feet against the stair, that danger was growing. His mind screamed to close his eyes, to run away from the shadows and whatever was hiding there, but the heat in him wouldn't let him. The burning was pressing at his throat and filling his mind with flame.

Enough that he could think clearly, that he could taste ash on his tongue.

Killian's eyes snapped open to the dark, to the layer of dust that was covering the wooden floor, and the spark of the world that was nestled amongst the dust bunnies.

A speck of light that was like an ignition switch to the flames that were burning through him. For a second, everything was clear. And that little spot of black glowed brighter than before, glints of color reflecting off the ebony surface as if it was sucking the color into it. As if it was calling for him.

A bang of a door echoed through the walls, the floorboards rattling as someone began to run up the steps. There wasn't any time. If he was going to do something, he needed to do it now.

The speck of nothing rattled against the pulsing steps of Mattia's return, the bead wobbling against the dust as Killian reached for it, as his muscles flexed and he lodged himself under the bed to reach the bit. Or to try, but it was out of reach, shaking under the pressure of the steps as they grew closer. Another jerk and a stretch and he was almost there, the steps in the hallway now as it shook and rolled right into his fingers.

Like it wanted to be there.

The bit was so small that he wouldn't have known he was holding it if a prickling heat didn't move over his skin, spreading from the bit of light and dark that Killian was staring at. The hinges of the door creaked open and those pounding footsteps found their way inside.

"Killian?" Mattia's voice was half panic, a line of anger hidden under the surface that sent that burning flame lapping over his tongue.

Hearing Mattia was doing weird things to him. Fire was dripping through his mind with images of the girl, of fabric, and the taste of her. His mind cowered in both fear and power, the emotions battling against each other until the prickle of energy on his finger filtered everything away as though the world was being pushed through a sieve.

The world.

That's what was on the tip of his finger. The world, his world. Memories. Life. He was one step away from losing it. Losing everything to the man who had entered the room.

"Killian, what are you doing?" Mattia asked, his voice harder that time. The single pound of his shoe against the floor as he stepped closer rippled through the floorboards. They ripped against his bones in energy and fear that was ready to explode.

Killian did the first thing that came to mind, he placed the glistening piece of the world on his tongue.

Colors sparked through his vision, colors he had never seen before and never knew existed blossoming through his mind as Mattia began to choke and sputter behind him. The sound was so garbled that the man sounded possessed. Or rather, like a record run backwards. No, like the world run backwards. A world that was spinning behind the color, that was opening up like an endless abyss and swallowing his mind and soul.

He lay there, listening to Mattia move in reverse, stepping down the hall and back to the bathroom, his mind bursting at the seams of the nothing that was filling him. Everything was too large, it was too big; he was beginning to feel like he would explode with it.

The steps were gone, the world was spinning, the heat was growing and the roar of a dragon burst from his throat, fire ripping from his jaw and devouring the last of the smoke that had trapped him.

Smoke from a Warlock.

Fire from a Dragon.

A Dragon that was bursting through his skin, pulled out of him by the expansive nothing.

He remembered everything. Every day that had passed locked in a dream. Everything about Elliot and where she was, Zoe and Drake, and the rest.

It all snapped back into place with a speed and force that might as well have been a slap.

He needed to get out of here. *Here* seemed to have changed drastically from where he was a second ago, however.

The rattling window filled the air, the warmth of the hearth burned the bottoms of his bare feet. He was still in the room, still under the bed, but everything else had changed, including himself.

His dragon stood, proud as it always was, on the sandy beach of a place as far away from the Himalayas as you could get. There was no snow, there was no warlock, and nothing about it was familiar. Except for the little girl.

She, he had seen before.

"Well shit," Xi, at least he thought that was her name, was the little girl from the circus he had accidentally destroyed. He had only met her a handful of times before, and he didn't quite remember her looking as irate as she did now, but it was definitely her.

Well, the *her* that this hallucination had brought anyway.

"You're not hallucinating, and that is not my name. I am not going to tell you my real name, however. Your soul is already threatening to splinter with the power you have swallowed. Hearing that would destroy you altogether."

Killian, or rather Killian's dragon, growled, heat spreading over the black scales as he towered over the little girl. Little girl, who wasn't so little.

None of this was making sense. His dragon was massive, easily the size of a well-appointed house. But this girl stood before him, standing over him as though they were the same size. Or as though his dragon was little bigger than a giant dog.

"You are inside of my soul, Killian. You swallowed a bit of me and now my magic is inside of you. The world is inside of you and unless I fix it the world will swallow you whole."

He would have been more impressed with having swallowed the world, or that the world was going to swallow him, if it wasn't very clear that the girl was reading his mind. Killian recoiled, the tail of his dragon hitting hard against the sand in warning, the impact of it sending a wall of sand and diamonds through the air, each little piece sparkling in a million colors before it fell back to the ground, back to the beach. A normal beach, but that didn't seem to be the case anymore.

The more he looked, the more everything sparkled. The more the colors rippled and swallowed his mind with everything that was threatening to explode out of it.

"Look away, Killian. I am creating this place so that the magic you swallowed does not absorb you. Keep your eyes on me alone and focus on the man inside the beast. I am reading your mind, but if we wish to fix this, I will need to speak to you. Look at me, focus on the calm. Focus on a memory of the man that houses your beast."

Killian's dragon growled in frustration, he had never liked to play second fiddle, but Killian pushed past his annoyances, focusing on the child even though his mind wished to look everywhere else, at every spark of color. The shimmering green leaves, the rainbow of sand, the flame of the sun as it prepared to set.

The color was like Elliot's hair. Like Elliot when she shifted and her whole body was bathed in brilliant flame. Just the memory of her and he felt his dragon fall away, leaving him standing before the little girl who was now the size a little girl should be.

Just a child and a man clad in his favorite suit. The silk and linen against his skin was a heaven that he hadn't been sure he would find again, and certainly felt better than the too-small cotton of another man's pajamas.

The thought had his dragon bristling again, but the creature stayed contained inside, only a low rumbling growl escaping from his chest. The sound moved away from him in a wave, running over the beach in a line of sparkle. As though someone had dipped their hand in glitter. Or like the glimmer that lined Elliot's skin after a shift, when she stood in her lines of nude--

"I can still hear you, you know." She interrupted with a knowing gleam in her eyes that wasn't quite fit for a child.

Perhaps because she wasn't a child. And because this wasn't a beach. He could still hear the crackle of flames and smell the dust that lived under the bed. Nothing was real, what it was, however, was causing a pain in his temple to grow, the same expansive nothing to press against his skull. Pressing against him until he was sure he was going to explode.

Like the colors that were glimmering through the sand.

"I told you not to look, Killian," Xi whispered, taking a step forward and pulling his focus, although that may be because the sand beneath her feet was erupting in rainbows again. Painful rainbows that were ripping apart his skull.

Okay, he wasn't going to look.

"What are you?" He asked, careful to keep his focus on the girl. She was all business, so much so that she didn't look like a child at all. Just a tiny adult with too much worry furrowed in her brow.

"You know what I am, Killian. If you haven't pieced it together by now, you will soon. Wasting our time with an answer will only end your life sooner."

"A simple response would have... what do you mean end my life?" As he said it, color drifted through the sky behind her, the blue erupting with a spectrum that he couldn't avoid, and with one glance was quickly working to split his head in two.

"You have swallowed a piece of my soul, Killian. You swallowed the magic that came first." Her voice low as she leaned forward, sending the long sheet of black hair over her shoulder like a flow of water. It sparkled as much, and he tried to keep his focus from it, but the color was everywhere. He couldn't avoid the sparkling world. He couldn't avoid the pain that came with it. "I will answer all your questions, but first we must save you."

"Well, whatever you are going to do, do it fast," Killian growled, planting his wide palms against both eyes, blocking out the light and pressing against his skull. As if the pressure would stop the pain, as if it would hold him together.

"It isn't as simple as that. You may choose to die instead of follow this path."

"Why would I choose to die?" Killian pried the palms of his hands away from his eyes, taking a glance at the girl who didn't seem to be glittering quite as much, although that might have been because the darkness in her eyes had sucked it all away. They had sucked everything away.

He couldn't look past them, which was fine seeing as they were the only things that weren't prying his bones apart.

"To save you I will have to change your soul. Change your life. I will have to give you magic so that you can hold the power you swallowed, so that it will bind to your soul. For some, death is easier than that choice. For some, they would rather walk away than doom another."

His hands fell back the rest of the way, dropping to his sides as the pain annihilated him.

"This is magic? Like the Fae?" He had seen so much of the Fae magic before that it made sense, the sparkle, the way everything was warm.

"I gave the Fae their magic eons before the cities were built underground. Their magic comes from me,

"Is that what will heal me? This light? I have seen Callay's magic--"

"Callay's magic is something different, though she may

not know it. She is not Fae." Xi stepped closer, the dark in her eyes flashing again and sending facets over him, but that may be the sparks of light in the water behind him. Just the reflection of the light was splitting his head in two. "Her magic is light. There is too much darkness in you for me to grant you light. I can only give you the darkness that you swallowed, but the light must go to someone. There must always be balance. The light in the world has not sought me out for a century. If you wish to live, if you wish to take the power you have swallowed, you must give me a name, Killian. A name of light. You must doom someone to your fate in order to save yourself. That in itself will be your first act of villainy."

The last word pressed against his heart with as much pain as the pressure that was building in his skull. Between the pain and the riddles that the kid was talking in, Killian wasn't understanding much. But that last word... that last word he understood.

"You are going to turn me into a villain?"

"No." She stepped closer, blocking the light until there was only her almond shaped eyes, narrowing at him making her look like more of a villain than he ever thought he could be. "That choice will inevitably be up to you. The magic of darkness does not always equal evil. The darkness of your dragon cannot hold the magic of true light. To save you, that magic has to go to another and you must accept the magic of the darkness into your heart. A light, and a dark. Always equal."

"A good and a bad," Killian interrupted, pressing his palm against his head again, trying to hold back the pain and the pressure.

The skin felt damp and slick underneath his touch, but

he refused to pull the hand away, to know if the damp was sweat or blood. With the pain that was ripping against him there was a high possibility it could be both.

"Just like Mattia said."

"Yes," Xi said with a nod, her hair swinging and shimmering again. "You are remembering what he told you. I was the one to give him and his sister their powers, back when they were locked inside the city."

Everything was bursting, his skull was splintering into pieces and even though he was an immortal, for the first time death was certain. Pain didn't matter right then; the city was part of the story that he remembered.

"The Unicorn." Blood or sweat no longer mattered. Killian's hand fell away in shock, leaving a line of red to trickle down his nose.

The Unicorn was fabled, revered, and hunted by the mortals for centuries.

When Mattia had told him this story before, he hadn't realized how impossible it was. The Unicorn wasn't something real. It wasn't something anyone had seen.

No wonder the world was opening up around him.

"Yes," Xi said with another nod of her head, and another rainbow of color flashing over her hair, although this time the color seemed to stick. Fitting. "But you are running out of time, Killian. I can tell you everything, but only after your life is saved. You are too important to lose, but this choice must be yours."

"What do you mean I am too important?" She only gave him a look at his question, her eyes narrowing as she pressed her lips into a tight line.

"I need an answer, Killian." He clearly wasn't going to get his answer.

The world had turned to nothing but color and agony. It drenched him, same as the blood that was dripping over his body. The heavy scarlet poured out of him in dozens of rivers. He wanted nothing more than to die, to leave this pain and wander through the vast skies that awaited a dragon after death.

But he couldn't.

He couldn't because in the color was life, in the glimmering world was her smile, and in the sparkling sunset that was slowly ripping him apart was a future that he wasn't quite ready to leave.

He wasn't quite ready to give up.

"I need an answer Killian." Her voice echoed through the pain, his eyes burning as he looked at the colors, as he looked at her.

He could do little more than nod in agreement.

"Then I will need a soul. I will need the name of a dragon whose soul is good and pure and that will be tied to yours in ways that even you cannot fathom. Give me a name of a shifter that is meant to do good in this world."

Elliot's face was clear in his mind, her smile was dragging him through the pain, but it was not her name that drew against him. It was not her name that was assaulting his mind.

"Zoe. My sister. She deserves light." He was barely able to gasp the words past the pain. The second he did, the pain that was splitting through his body left and he fell to his knees, heaving against the sand that was rippling with a million facets of colors.

So many colors that he braced for the pain. Instead of the pain of impending explosion, however, his vision opened up, his mind lifted and everything became clear.

Beauty, a wisp of power, and the black expanse of the universe was everywhere. He knew it. He understood it.

He held it.

The whole world, it was burning inside of him, right beside his dragon.

Hot sand rained over his fingers as he stared at the glittering nothing, his fingers running through it and sending a million new colors trickling behind.

"It is done." Even her voice felt filled with color, it shimmered as everything continued to pulse and grow, every cell in his body sparking with color.

"You are part of the world now; the deep magic is intertwined with your soul. What you do with it now is up to you."

Killian lifted his head, colors sparkling around him until the whole world looked like magic, but none more than the woman who now stood before him.

The girl had gone, replaced by a woman of such color and elegance that even though she stood, nude and bare, he could find no flaw. Even if there had been a need to search. He already knew of her perfection, of her regality. From the point in her toe, to the multicolored curls of her hair. He and his dragon were already bowing down to her, both of them finally recognizing her for what she truly was.

"The Unicorn."

"Killian," she whispered with a voice that swallowed all light, the sound both hollow and vibrant. "You have taken a power into you that can change the world. You hold the power of the Unicorn inside of you. But you have already come in contact with a goddess, though you may not have known it."

"The Phoenix." He knew the answer without prompting,

the whispered answer coming to him as if he had known it all along.

"The Unicorn. The Phoenix. The Griffon. The Sphinx. We rule the corners of the world and have formed it for centuries. My sister was torn from us when our city was burned to the ground, when I created a man who became a devil. The one who has you captured, and the one you must escape from before he steals what I have put inside of you."

As she spoke, the world around them glimmered with the last light of a crystal sun as it set. The darker the Unicorn's eyes grew, the more that darkness swelled over the world, the more the wind in the shimmering trees began to sway, pulling at the long loose curls of his hair.

The wind whipped at him, buzzing against the scales of the creature inside of him as the aroma of dust and fire traveled in the breeze, as the sound of wind rattling shutters, as the faint sound of a footfall on a stair beat against his heart.

"Mattia." The growl of his dragon rumbled, the warmth he had felt through Mattia's bind making sense. All of the warnings of his dragon burst through in a fear that he only now understood.

"You must escape him, Killian. What I have placed inside of you will help." The rainbow facets in her hair glistened.

"How can I use it if I don't even know what it is? Tell me what you have done to me. Tell me what is coming." Killian's voice was near a demand, even though he was attempting to keep his tone even.

The frustration and fear of his dragon was mixing with the pride in his head in ways that the graceful woman did not seem pleased with. Her eyes darkened, her smile spread in a dark line that made Killian step back.

"I will answer all your questions once you are free of him."

The wind that was bursting through the trees cracked through the bows and broke a few palm fronds off with such force that he could see the anger in them. Although, whether this world and this anger came from him or the powerful beast before him, he was beginning to question.

It didn't much matter to him, either way. He was letting that rage run free.

"You said you would answer..."

"Soon." She cut him off with a snap, her dark eyes flashing with red and golds that he had only seen once before, in his brother. He knew what came after with him. He had faced it enough that he was not afraid to face it with her.

"Don't be a fool, Killian. You cannot best me. You can best him, however," she said as the wind that whipped through the crystal palms of their imaginary beach came to a stop, replaced by the sounds of a hinge and the sigh of a monster. "You are almost out of time. Ours is already gone."

He opened his mouth to protest, to yell, to scream, and demand all the things that were due him as the son of the king. As the holder of whatever magic spell she had given him.

Not even a sound escaped before the shimmering world fell away, replaced by a nest of dust bunnies and a hard wood floor that held as much of the glittering world as before.

"Killian," Mattia said from behind him, everything about it was the same as before. Except the laugh that had lined the single word before was filled with more dread than he had sensed in his confusion of before.

The bed hit against Killian's back as he shifted his

weight, the movement sending all the dust flying, filling the world with stars.

"Killian what are you doing?" The laugh was gone from Mattia's voice, the worry and fear replacing what before had been humor and coy.

He sounded the same as he did the night he awoke from his fall. The spell was broken, and he had only minutes to disguise it, to deceive the man so he could plan his escape.

The Unicorn reeked of everything but trust. For this, however, he would trust her. He needed to get back to Elliot.

"Darling, answer me." Hatred bled off Killian's captor, the same black smoke he had felt seep through his mind crawling across the floor, swirling against the dust and lifting it around him until he was covered.

He was out of time.

Drake's silver tongue would be perfect in a time like this. Killian would have to make do. Good thing he had been lying for years.

"I thought I saw something," he mumbled trying to keep his voice in the low slur that he assumed had come with the warlock's spell.

Warlock.

The word held more familiarity and danger than it had before, danger that was stepping closer.

"What did you see?" More hatred. More danger.

Killian shifted his weight, wiggling backwards out from under the bed, his hands dragging through ash and smoke in search of anything he could have seen. Charred fabric, a bottle of absinthe.

The moment that he thought it, his hand filled with the cold bottle, green liquid sloshing inside.

Holy shit.

He had conjured a bottle with a thought. But if he could

do that, what could someone with hundreds of years of experience do?

Danger was everywhere.

"This." Killian sloshed the bottle behind him, trying to keep whatever power was still rumbling inside of him locked away, right beside his dragon who was desperate to roar and destroy Mattia.

Killian already knew the warlock was immune from his fire, that path was already closed.

"Ahhh." The bottle slipped from his fingers as Mattia grabbed it, stepping back and allowing Killian the space he needed to shimmy free.

Dust fell from his hair as the curls fell over his face, blocking his vision as he pulled himself to his feet. Thankfully the room didn't spin and fill with smoke the same as it had before.

"Well, that explains the bottle, but how about the suit?"

The darkness had filled Mattia's voice, filled his eyes as Killian looked from him to the expensive linen suit that he wore, the same as he had on the beach with the Unicorn.

"God!" Killian yelled, jumping back in shock and fear at the expensive cut of cloth.

The shock was real.

A bottle was small, possible. But this suit was the exact cut of one of his favorites, one he was sure had fallen to fire in ash when Elliot had destroyed his home.

He spun on the spot, expecting the beautiful goddess to be behind him, but it was only an old bed with mussed sheets.

His dragon threatened a growl in his chest, the fire of its anger drenching his throat. He couldn't be sure if Mattia had heard, but the man laughed anyway, the low chuckling following him to the table and to the clink of glass and spoon.

"It appears that my magic has begun to take hold. Come here, darling, let me show you how to use what I have placed inside of you."

Killian froze.

Mattia didn't know. Perhaps he still had a chance.

18

ZOE

SO MUCH OF MY LIFE HAD BEEN SPENT DAYDREAMING OF finding some secret magic in the world, away from the nonsense that my father had created. I didn't even care if it was with the humans. I wanted proof that magic and good, and kindness was real. I would dream of Fae princesses and tiny fairies. I would draw the fabled Unicorns and Sphinxes and imagine how good and kind they were.

Then I met one.

And I was forced to listen to the grind of her claws against the stone as she sharpened them, reminding us of the death that waited us if we answered her damn riddle incorrectly. I had taken one fleeting moment to contemplate shifting, grabbing Drake in my talons and breaking through the grimy stained glass windows in an escape.

The moment she had finished her foolish riddle, however, it was as though my powerful dragon had been hit with a tranquilizer dart. I could even feel the useless thing snoring against my chest. So that escape route was closed, as was the door, that seemed to have vanished.

Not that we could make it there before the lion-woman

would pounce on us and swallow us with one giant gulp. That was if we didn't get cut to pieces with one swipe of her now razor sharp claws.

Which she was still sharpening. I cringed as she ran them against the massive grooves in the stone again, her giant yellow cat-eyes unblinkingly focused on us.

Well, on me, Drake looked as though he had fallen asleep. If it wasn't for the flutter of his lips as he recited the riddle over and over to himself, I would think he had chosen to sleep through this mess. At least he could tune out that infernal grinding. I couldn't think past it, and it was taking everything in me not to jump to my feet, yell at the creature to knock it off, spit fire at her disturbingly perfect face, and promptly get eaten before I could make any attempt to leave.

The last time I had felt this hopeless hadn't ended well either.

I pushed myself from the onyx pillar that I had been leaning against and crawled over to Drake, who was laying out like he was sunbathing. The thing hadn't given us a time limit, but I doubted she would let us go on forever. The quicker we could figure this out the better.

"I will make you scream with glee. I will make you cry and beg in death. I create the grey in a mother's hair, and the frown in the friend who is best. I make the intelligent wilt in mute stupidity, and the fowl rise in genius. I turn water brown and the sky red. I wilt. I cry. I walk on five sets of fingers."

Drake was repeating it like a song, the words tumbling one over the other as he tapped his toes, his ridiculous socked sandals covered in so much grime that I couldn't tell when the sock ended and the sandal began. Socks. Maybe it had something to do with socks. Except I didn't see socks turning the sky red.

God, this was hopeless.

"Any luck?" I whispered as I lie down beside him, careful not to disrupt whatever rhythm he had created for his song. "Do you have an answer?"

He opened one eye to peer at me in a glare he had had since he was tiny. Yes, because me interrupting his incessant repetition was going to stop him from finding the answer. He shook his head and closed his eyes, going back to his sing-song.

The grinding of the Sphinx's claws picked up and I cringed against the nails on a chalkboard sound that was reverberating off the onyx walls. Maybe the beast wasn't going to eat us, maybe she was going to melt our brains with that infernal sound. It was the only countdown we needed.

"I know a way you can speed this up, baby brother." And the glare was back, although this time the honey brown of his eye was swallowed in flame. It was an empty threat and he knew it. I smiled and stared up at the ceiling. "You could ask her."

"You know I am not going to do that."

"Why is it when our life is on the line you always decide to be honorable. You already killed me once, Drake." I was playing dirty, pushing every single button of his insecurities that I could. And I didn't feel a tad bit bad about it. This was a much more imminent situation than the torture and death that we had faced before, all it would take was one word...

"No."

"Drake, don't be ridiculous." I turned to him, my own fire blazing as the sound of claws against stone picked up. I had a feeling that the invisible countdown that we had been subjected to was winding down.

"I said no." His eyes were open, although he still wasn't staring at me. "It's just a riddle. We can solve a riddle."

"And what if..."

"No!" He cut me off with a snap, the echo of his shout rattling the windows and bringing the scraping of claws to a stop. A low purr was left behind as the beast gently rose to its feet, everything rattling as she began to paw her way toward us.

Oh shit. Oh fucking shit.

The glare my brother was giving me was full of all the blame and frustration I would expect from him. As if this was my fault, if he would use his silver tongue when it mattered then we wouldn't be in this situation. We could have been ruling Rydaim for the last ten years.

"Don't you dare blame this on me," I snarled as I pushed myself to sitting, the low rumble of the cat's purr practically on top of us now.

If I wasn't mistaken the monster was hungry. And we had no answer.

"Little humans," she said with a voice that was swallowed by her purr. "Is that your answer?"

"Now would be a really good time to do that thing," I hissed between my forced smile, looking right into the sphinx's hungry yellow eyes. I already knew he was shaking his head. No matter.

If she tried to eat us, I would fight her. I may not be able to save my useless brother, but at this point that wasn't much of a loss.

"Can we hear the riddle again?" Drake asked confidently, pushing himself to stand before the sphinx until it was just him and the massive head of the monster, her eyes nearly as big as him. Her jaw big enough for both of us.

And Drake didn't even flinch. Maybe he was going to prove himself useful after all.

"I will make you scream with glee." The woman said as the tail of the beast twitched, as her claws curled in preparation of a pounce. "I will make you cry and beg in death. I create the grey in a mother's hair, and the frown in the friend who is best. I make the intelligent wilt in mute stupidity, and the fowl rise in genius. I turn water brown and the sky red. I wilt. I cry. I walk on five sets of fingers. Can you answer what I am?"

"No." Drake spoke without hesitation, with all the bull-headed confidence of a punk kid who had sentenced us both to death. "No is our answer."

"You idiot! What the fuck do you--"

"Correct."

My tirade was silenced as ice and heat rushed over my body and my dragon burst back to life. The beast snarling mad at having been restrained. Not that I blamed her, I was snarling mad at my brother for whatever that stunt was. I was going to throttle him, wipe that smug ass smile off his face.

"What the fuck was that?"

"The answer." He was still smiling, the punk giving me a goddamned wink before he walked over to the dais that the Sphinx had returned to, her massive paws kneading the stone as if that would make it more comfortable.

Oh, he really needed a good old fashioned smack.

"The last line of the riddle is 'Can you answer what I am?'," Drake said as I caught up to him, still staring at the Sphinx that had finally settled against the cold stone floor. "So our answer is no. We cannot answer what the creature in the riddle is."

"And how long did you know that?" My snarling dragon

was dripping from my words now. I was barely able to control the liquid flame and ash that was coating my tongue from making an appearance.

"I'm surprised you didn't."

What I wouldn't give to smack the smile off his face, but the sphinx was looking at us with its electric yellow eyes, emanating a purr that was becoming as bad as the grating of nails and stone. Screw it. Frightening mythical creature or not, I smacked Drake upside the head.

"Ow!" He pouted, rubbing the back of his head as though I had tried to take it off. As if I had hit him hard enough to do so. Some things never change between us.

"You have wise souls," The sphinx interrupted our scowling match with a gentle laugh, her tail flicking as though a fly had landed on it. I would hate to see the size of that fly. "Curious, and kind."

Why did I suddenly feel like I was being scolded by mother when I was small? I was even shifting in my shoes.

"What knowledge do you seek? I will answer a question from each of you." The question, coming from a massive Sphinx was too loaded. I had a feeling that we could ask her anything and hear the answer.

But only one. There was too much I wanted to know, that I needed answered. Every question and curiosity rampaged through my mind, overriding the reason I had come into this damn building in the first place and leaving me sputtering with my mouth hung open like a child drooling over ice cream.

I refuse to accept the possibility that I was drooling. My brain may have completely shut down, but I was still too dignified for that.

"What is this place, this city? What happened to it?" Thank God Drake was able to keep his head on straight.

"That is two questions, child?" The sphinx lowered her head to her paws, looking Drake right in the eye as the dark slits of warning pulsed and narrowed at my brother. My brother who was stepping right up to the creature. Facing a beast who had vowed to eat us minutes before.

Freaking Drake, acting before he thought things through. You would think he would have enough sense not to challenge a creature who could eat him. He won't use his silver tongue on the beast, but he will challenge the monster's logic. Genius. I would forever be amazed that he wasn't already dead. I gave him a groan and grabbed his collar to pull him back, but not before he opened his trap and tried his hand at giving us another death sentence.

"They are one in the same. For the history of the city also includes the tale of its destruction." The last word was swallowed by the tug of collar against neck, the idiot tripping on his own feet as he stumbled back into me.

"If your fool headedness ends up getting us killed I will never forgive you," I snarled in his ear, letting my dragon rip from my chest in one warning growl before I released him, leaving him to stumble forward.

"Of course you won't," he whispered, straightening his sweater as he faced the sphinx again. "You'll be dead."

I don't know if the powerful beast heard Drake, but her low chuckle rattled the windows and earned me a smug look from my brother, who apparently hadn't learned anything and earned another smack upside the head.

"Accepted, young prince. Here is your answer." The purr in the sphinx's voice had left, leaving only a low rumble of something powerful and dark.

Magic, my mind whispered as the giant cat padded her way toward us, every loose stone in the long cathedral bouncing under the impact.

"This place is known to the ancients as the City of Soot. But it wasn't always known as such a dark, dreadful place. It once had life and color and was guided by the burning fire of the sky and the power of those on the ground. It was the place where the first of all magic began, buried under the dirt so as to place us all between the bowels of heaven and the sky of hell. They are the two pillars of our kind and bring equality to those with the power to rule, to the goddesses who created this world, and the dirt dwellers who live above and were graced with the gift to serve us below."

I cringed, what an elegantly disgusting way to describe slavery. Why must everything in the world rest on the backs of others. There is no power in that. There is no strength in oppression. I should have known better than to scowl at the massive beast that could end us both with one snap of her jaws, but I did anyway, earning myself a low growl that was instantly answered with a snarl and a puff of smoke of my own. Even my dragon was a fool.

Luckily, that time the cat only smiled.

"Was it the *dirt dwellers* that did this?" Drake asked, interrupting our standoff. With the way he said the words and phrased the question I could tell I wasn't alone in my assumption.

"It was only one." The feline said with a flash of her eyes. "There was one who was brought here and saw something that he desired. He sought out one of the four goddesses of this city and tricked her into giving him power. It offset the balance and she has worked for centuries to make it right, to undo the death and destruction that the dirt dweller caused. He brought the undead to our door and burned it to ash, and before the goddess of life could intervene she was whisked away by another, a demon who lusted after a power of his own. Our world was scattered, our power weakened, and centuries have been spent guarding what is left of this city. To guard it until its glory can be returned, and the four gods of this world can sit atop their thrones."

"And we thought our battle for rights and thrones was dramatic," Drake said with a chuckle. No one reciprocated.

"Young prince, you are a fool if you think the throne that could be yours has any meaning beyond a bit of tarnish. Your throne has lost its strength in the centuries since the Dragons left this realm. They built a city in mirror of the one hidden below. They vowed to protect this city from the undead who rule the night, but instead you have allowed them into your home. You have destroyed the sister of the fountain that guards the magic of this cathedral, you have blinded the sentry who protects you and I can no longer see the blood covered night demons who have infiltrated you."

"The vampires," I hissed, my mind snapping into place as I turned to her, but her cat-eyes were still tuned in on my brother, bending his back as he wilted below the jaws that were only inches from him.

"Yes, those unnatural creatures are one step away from destroying you all. One step closer to revealing the power that lies underneath the depths of this city. I can smell them on you, smell the rot and the blood. But I can smell something worse, something far more dangerous. I can smell both the magic of the man who ended our world and the goddess who betrayed us. It is dripping from you with the odor of deception and lies. Lies you would die with if I didn't see the misplaced trust in your eyes. I would end you for that alone, but your souls are pure. There is something on the horizon for you. Something that can end all of this"

She smiled, resting her chin on the soft paws of the lion as she watched us, eyes narrowed. If she was waiting for a reaction she was going to get one. I wanted to be pissed that everything in our history was filled with slavery and some self-righteous magic keepers that deemed themselves goddesses. And I would have, if she wasn't threatening to end us because we smelled like some beast who had ended them.

Of course we smelled that like that. We were in the city. Although all I smelled was the ancient odors of shifters, well and whatever foul odor lingered around that bastard girl.

Oh god. "Fallon."

Now it was Drake's turn to look absolutely confused. The Sphinx, however, was smiling, the yellow in her eyes glimmering as she began to purr, the sound was more like a growl.

I had a sickening sensation that I was on the right track. No matter which side of the story that freaking little mongrel was on, it wasn't spelling a happy ever after for the Forgotten and even the Fae in the city above. We needed to get out of here before she did something. Before Rydaim was turned as black and dead as this place.

I said nothing, I just turned, ready to bolt out and fly away. Thank god the door had made a return. I didn't need to beg the Sphinx to let me out so I could go kick some lying Fae ass.

"Zoe, the Queen of the Beasts of the Air. What question do you have of me?"

"I am not queen." I didn't stop walking.

"You always have been. The city has chosen you. It wished to give you knowledge. Ask your question."

I froze in place, every question I had before now locking itself away as I stared at her, at her smile and the knowing gleam in her eyes, a gleam that was full of more glitter than it had been a minute before. In fact, the world was full of glitter. The black smothered with a million different colors. Colors I didn't even know existed.

"How do I defeat her?" I gasped, pulling my focus from the walls, even though everything had begun to spin again. Like the universe, but without the stars. Without the vast nothing that was threatening to swallow me. "How do I save the Fae?"

The last of the question was swallowed as the spinning slammed into me, hurling me through the air and pushing me into the ground with a hollow thunk of skull against stone. I barely heard Drake's shout of alarm. I barely saw him run towards me. There was only the massive creature's smile, her tail flicking as she rose from her haunches and began to pad her way toward me, each step sending sparks into the air. Each step swallowing more of her until the beast fell away and she was only a woman, a perfectly formed woman with hair the color of savanna grass and eyes like the sun.

"I believe someone has chosen the answer to that question for you, Zoe." I wasn't sure who had spoken, the voice was so far away, everything swallowed by the nothing that was moving into me, by the beautiful woman that was standing in the middle of the nothing.

"I believe someone has given you exactly what you need to destroy them all."

19

ELLIOT

Jasper Muller.

He owned a textile company in London in about 1920. He was kind and always brought me flowers when we were courting. He smelled of dyes and bleach but always used a cologne of lavender and sage that would sometimes make my eyes water. He had bought us a large house in the middle of the city and talked about having children one day.

And now his head was in a jar.

His jaw was mostly disconnected, his once dark brown hair was bleached by whatever chemicals had been preserving him, the color of his eyes was gone. He was gone.

But I knew that would happen the second that the fallen angel I had made the mistake of bonding myself to had found me again. He had done it to all my mates. I hadn't been able to get to Jasper in time. My fallen angel boyfriend had tracked him down and lured him to an alley, cut off his head and let his hat roll over the cobbles to my feet as I arrived.

He had waited to behead him until I was moments away. Waited so I could see. Just like all the others. Every single one of my mates. Every single man who belonged to the clothes that hung blood stained in my wardrobe.

Angelic history or not, he was still a demon.

The memory hurt. In fact, I was pretty sure the memory was ripping itself out of my body and taking heart and lungs and everything else with it. But I wasn't going to show it, although I had folded my arms over my chest harder in an attempt to keep all my pain and gut wrenching fear inside and not showing on my face.

Especially with the way he kept looking at me from the other side of his science lab, his demonic eyes digging into me each time he extracted fluid from the head jar. I was pretty sure he knew that I knew, that I remembered. That I remembered every fucking thing he had done, not that I knew what to do with it. Because really all that had happened was that he had put his hand against my cheek and reminded me how much of a bastard he is, and how much of a fucking bad situation we were in.

I thought the bone key was a bad enough hurdle we had to overcome.

Turns out his fallen angel status gave him a few more tricks than I would like to admit. Like restricting some of my powers, which he had been doing since he had locked the door.

Now that I remember the basics of Traveling I couldn't do it. I could feel the buzz and the pull, but any time I tried to pull the power up it fizzled and died. Which means we needed to get out of here. At least now, thanks to my memory jog, I knew what the heart strings were, and how to follow them.

One step out of this cave and we were saved.

Which means I needed to cut off his finger. Which means I needed the knife. Apparently killing fallen angels was harder than it should be. You needed a specific kind of knife to even break their skin. They were like demonic little Supermans running around and cutting off people's' heads.

You needed an even more twisted Lex Luthor to destroy that mess. I could be that. Good thing I knew what I was looking for. I had to remember where I had hidden it.

His sweet little touch hadn't given me everything.

Didn't matter. I would figure this out.

"You don't want to crease that pretty little forehead so much, baby. You'll give yourself wrinkles." He gave me a look as he sucked fluid from the jar, something I was really upset to remember he had done many times before.

My face contorted and he winked with a hooded gleam that I was sure he thought was seductive.

Newsflash, idiot. You can't look seductive when you are sucking brain juice off my ex-boyfriend. Idiot.

"Well, aren't you quite the sexist pig," I full on snarled, letting my phoenix's instant anger roar through my words and a tiny puff of red tinged smoke drift from between my teeth.

That was a fun new trick. Even better that he seemed scared of it. I so let a bit more snarl toward him, the weird burping sounds that accompanied it were worth it for the look he was giving me.

"You would think you would be kind to me, considering I took away all of these pesky pains your weak mate has left you with." He smiled again as he dipped the syringe back in the head jar, purposefully knocking against the bit of exposed skull and sending the once beautiful head rocking. The motion dislodged an eye and my stomach flipped around for more than one reason.

Hurling was a real possibility. As much as I wanted to step back from the demon and his head jar, I pushed myself away from the back of the couch I had been leaning against and took a step closer, my stomach twisting even more. If I was going to hurl I was going to get myself within range.

"I would rather be writhing on the floor in pain than have your hands anywhere on me." I didn't think my voice had ever hit an octave so low before, that there had been so much of a threat in every single word.

The smoke was still drifting between my teeth, and the demon froze, fluid filled syringe still in hand as he turned to look at me. His eyes were as dark as they had been when the smoke of wings or death or whatever it was had flowed behind him. Now would have been the perfect time for my stomach to upend itself all over him, but the damn thing froze under the darkness of his gaze.

Holy fuck. Is he completely sure he isn't a demon? Like an actual burst from the bowels of hellfire and lava demon? Stepping closer was clearly the wrong choice.

"You wouldn't have said that a few years ago, my love," He smiled and my stomach went back to threatening vomit.

Yes, I would have said that a few years ago. But I wasn't going to let him in on that little secret, not when I still had a knife to find and a demon thing to slice apart.

Black blood assaulted my memory as Henry lifted the lid to the head jar, swirling the fluid with his syringe and sending a noxious concoction of formaldehyde, rot, and sage through the air.

And there went my stomach.

I only heaved once before my mostly empty stomach turned itself out and sent a river of bile, partially digested steak, and bright red flame out of my mouth, over the table, and dripping over the front of his dumb lumberjack shirt.

"What the bloody hell?" The British demon shrieked as he jumped away, barely escaping vomit wave two, this one mostly flame. His precious table erupted in flames in every color the second my puke-fire hit it, sending demon boy shrieking and jumping around as he tried to figure out how to put out the fire while avoiding the sick of his precious Phoenix.

Which was awesome because it kept coming. I would have loved to laugh at the dancing demonling but the smell of my own vomit was mixing badly with the head jar aroma that was now assaulting the air thanks to Henry having left the damn thing open. And with nothing in my stomach I was left with burping and heaving lines of vile dripping fire.

As awesome as this was, the burn of bile in my throat was hitting a high I wasn't sure I could survive. I think I would actually take farting fire over this.

This was awful.

Desperate to escape the smell and memories of the head jar, I turned away, sending a line of vomit fire over the room and instantly igniting couch, rug, and a few of the pictures on the wall.

Damn the acid heartburn. I couldn't even rejoice in the destruction of his damn cave, in the screams of the genius that was now dancing around behind me.

"What are you doing?" Henry screamed, his hands fluttering around me like he was trying to figure out what to do. Thank God he wasn't touching me. If he did I might turn and vomit on him again.

Actually, that wasn't a bad idea. I spun to him at the question, the weak man jumping back even though the vomit seemed to have slowed.

"I'm so sorry," I lied, wiping ash and bile off my chin. "The smell... that head... I just can't."

"Can't control yourself, Elliana! I expect better of you!"

Oh god, he was close enough I could reign vomit hell on

him, but my stomach was thankfully starting to settle. It made sense seeing as I had burned away most of his experiments, something that he was now moaning about, hands tangled in his ugly blonde hair.

"I think I need to go clean up." Or finish burning another part of this hell hole to the ground. Probably starting with my vomit covered clothes.

"Fine. Fine." He waved me away, now hovering over his experiments like the mad scientist he was.

My throat was still on fire, and my stomach was twisting even more seeing as the head had escaped the broken jar and rolled onto the floor, its dead eyes staring right into me.

"I need to get out of here." The garbled statement had more than one meaning, not that the frantic mad scientist noticed. He was now lifting the head, cradling the damn thing like it was a baby.

What the fuck was wrong with that guy.

"Go. Go." he mumbled, waving toward the hall, smoothing back the hair on the head. Oh god, it was going to come back up. "Second, no third, door on the left."

"And Jarron?" I asked automatically as I backed toward the door, doing my best to look anywhere but at the psychotic man and his head baby.

Even thinking it was causing my stomach to curdle. I needed to get the fuck out of here.

"I'll have Lilly bring him."

Bastard. I was pretty sure I could find him anyway. I high tailed it out of the still burning room before anything else happened.

Like a fiery ass cannon. I knew I could do both. Although the vomit was new.

The hallway was as long and oppressive as it had been a few hours before. Thankfully it didn't have any frightening little girls in it, which meant I was free to follow that tiny little thread that was pulling me toward the door directly across from the third door on the right. So, I guess the little demon doll was telling the truth. He was right across from me. Of course she would be honest so that I would think she was lying and then never find him.

Clever little demon doll. Not a demon. Not a cave troll. That girl I would have to figure out. Or just kill.

Probably just kill.

But first, I needed Jarron.

Too bad the door was locked.

I jiggled the lock and whispered through the door as loud as I dared, but short of summoning demon or freaky child I was at an impasse. I was also covered in vomit.

As much as I was sure Jarron would appreciate the story, I should probably take care of that first. I backed up as some very demonic screaming began echoing from the living room and plunged myself into my room, taking great care to not look at the towering white sheeted monsters pushed against the wall.

The bathroom filled with steam as fast as it did last time, the scalding hot water burning away the vomit and ash residue and wiping any smell from my mind. Too bad it couldn't wipe away the memory of the head. Of Jasper.

Of the demon lobbing off his head and laughing as it fell, coddling the deteriorated appendage as though it was his child. I shivered, closing my eyes and pressing my face into the water as my mind replayed the moment after my demented mate had killed the other, and my sobs as I held the headless corpse of a man I loved, as I placed his blood stained clothes in the wardrobe, and I smiled at the woman that was carved there.

As I spoke to her.

My eyes snapped open, scalding hot water burning my eyes as I turned toward the wardrobe in the other room.

"It can't be so easy."

Water ran in rivers over my skin as I ran from the shower, leaving the door open as the sound of water filtered into the dark bedroom. White coils of steam danced through the air as though they were luring me back to the comforting streams of water.

I didn't even turn. I stood, my naked ass dripping with water as I faced the cabinet, my hand shaking as I pulled the white sheet down.

Before, I had thought that this cave and that demon was making me lose my mind. Now, I was starting to think that I had lost it all along.

The cabinet loomed over me the same as it had before, the dark colored wood looking ever more like a mutation without the faintly flickering lamp behind me. It was only me and a lady carved into a cabinet standing in the dark. The bright white light from the bathroom poured over us like a spotlight, highlighting the curve of the carving's ass and breasts with a little bit more perfection than I could ever accomplish. Even as naked and shower wet as I was.

She wasn't looking at me. She wasn't even moving. *She*. Good lord. *She* was a carving in some old ass wood. Old wood that I had been talking to in memory. I was going to have to have myself committed after this.

"So... ummm... Hi." Yep, I was totally and completely bonkers. "So, my name is Elliot. Or Elliana. I'm not sure. It's something. Probably starts with El. I'm sure you know that. But I think I need your help. From a cabinet..."

The more I talked the more insane I sounded.

I half expected my Phoenix to laugh at me, the heat that was spreading over me was one step away from that. Or so I thought. Because the damn carving had blinked and my heart went into overdrive, my Phoenix starting to prance about like a peacock in heat.

"Oh fuck," I hissed as the hand of the carving moved, the wood shifting as she turned, her hand moving her hair back. The movement was smooth, so much smoother than you would expect for a woman carved in wood. You know, if you expected wood to move.

"Ummm okay, so I need help to find something." I was stuttering now, which was even better because the wood image of me was smiling, her hair flowing around her like she was caught in a breeze. Just like mine had been doing in that alley in Rydaim, just like it was doing now. Bright red strands that were lifting in the wind, sparkling in the glow that I was pretty sure was coming from inside of me.

"The key is inside of you," A voice that was very close to mine pulled through my mind, or through the cabinet? I wasn't sure. Her lips didn't move any more than the smile she was giving me, her hair continuing to float against the carved background of the wardrobe, her body continued to shift as she moved, pointing to the other sheet covered object in the room.

Well, shit. I had hoped to avoid uncovering that. The cabinet was weird on its own, I really didn't want to know what other freaky thing was waiting for me there. My mind was already painting a picture of the creepy demon and his naked ass carved in wood or some bizarre throne made of the bones of all my mates he had murdered.

But now I didn't have another choice.

The sheet slid off with little more than a tug, the fabric falling to the ground in a billow of dust that landed over me, making the reflection I was graced with look even more bizarre.

My own naked body all squiggled and grey and fuzzy. I brushed the dust off the smooth reflective surface, making me look a little bit less like I had walked into a carnival fun house.

There may have been a dusty ass underneath the sheet, but thankfully it was mine and not some weird ode to me carved in wood.

It was a mirror. Carved as intricately as the wardrobe. Vines and flames tangled over the side, intermingling with tiny little forest animals until it reached four figures carved into the top. A Unicorn, a Sphynx, a Griffon, and a Phoenix. All impossible creatures, except for the fact that I clearly existed. It was beautiful, and although I hadn't seen it as closely in my memory it was clearly *the* mirror that I had seen in more than a few of those memories. Memories of me drinking and talking to some weird cloaked figure... a figure that was now standing right behind me, tucked into the corner of the room.

"Holy moth balls!" I screeched as I jumped, turning around to face... the empty corner of the room.

"Okay, yeah, this is all clearly normal and I am not losing it." I grumbled to the corner as though it had personally offended me and giving the cabinet the stink eye. Carved me had gone back to her first position, however, she wasn't even watching.

Again. *She*.

Maybe Dabria wasn't the only one to get hit upside the head by some rubble.

I turned back to the mirror and jumped so much that the boob jiggle reached an all-time high. No one liked looking at their naked ass in the mirror, but seeing as I was being stalked by a cloaked mirror man, it made it even worse.

Okay, well, I'm already all in. Might as well go for broke.

"Can you help me?" I asked, my heart falling to my toes as the figure stepped closer, dropping his hood to reveal the same bushy tailed man I had seen the night before. Although his eyebrows seemed more intense, if that was possible. I wasn't even sure he could see through them, although the clear white-blue of his eyes were piercing. The color seemed fitting for an owl shifter, or whatever he was. It was just him, however, the woman from before was nowhere to be seen.

"That depends, child. Do you know who I am?" His eyes flashed as the deep roll of his voice rippled through the air, pushing into me like something familiar.

"An owl shifter?" It was the only answer I had, and the man chuckled in response, the sound as familiar as him.

I spun to face him, but there was still nothing there, nothing but a shadowed corner, swirled in the dancing ribbons of steam that were drifting from the still blasting shower.

Blinking, I turned back to the mirror, seeing a flash of the same scenario. It was the same room, the same mirror, the same wardrobe, the same hooded man holding something out to me. Although this time I was wearing a super ugly brown dress instead of standing buck naked before an old man in a mirror. I was suddenly regretting not grabbing a towel in my haste to reach the wardrobe. I would go back, but I didn't want this guy to leave.

Although I was pretty sure he wasn't staying here for the nudist colony presentation.

"I'm afraid I cannot help you." He was stern, decided, and my Phoenix pretty much lost it. Her scream burst from my chest as the smoke that usually preceded disaster began to run over my arms in waves.

Foolishly, I tried to bat it away, as if that would help. You think I would have learned by now that there was going to be no stopping whatever fire blasting I was going to do, not now that my power was unleashed. You think mirror man would have realized that, even the woman on the wardrobe had turned. But the mirror man only laughed. The low husky sound didn't sound quite so familiar now.

It sounded fucking irritating and I kinda wanted to punch the sound out of his throat.

"Oh, come on! I need to kill that guy. I need to save Jarron. I need the knife to do that. And I have a feeling you can help me." Who the fuck cared about fiery explosions? I was officially begging to a carving on a wardrobe and man in a mirror. If I ended up shooting fire darts out of my nipples it might be the most normal thing to happen in the last few minutes.

Maybe I would get lucky and scare him into helping with my laser nipple powers.

"Jarron?" The older man clicked his tongue and shook his head, his eyes digging into me before he replaced the hood and pulled his face into shadow. "You can't avoid it forever, child. You can't avoid the pain forever. We need you."

"I'm sorry, I..."

"Take this," the man interrupted, pulling something from underneath his cloak and holding it out to me. "This is the last time. The princes will help you. But the end is too close to ignore, Phoenix."

His palm was flat, a small key on the weathered skin on his hand, gleaming all gold and silver. I turned around to take it, my mind running through a million and one things that it could be, but again he still wasn't there. Just a corner and quickly dwindling steam, I guess I had used the last of the hot water again.

"Reach through," the old man said, pulling my focus back to the mirror and to the key that was on the other side. "Give it to the woman."

"Okay." I had woken up in another dimension and was now reaching through the mirror to grab the tiny silver key. I expected some rush of chill, some wall of ice or heat but instead it was the familiar pressure of gelatin air, like when I had stopped time.

The same as the first time when I fell from the silks, when I kicked Parris's butt. Whatever was on the other side of the mirror was made of the same stuff. It buzzed the same against my heart, it pulled itself into me.

"Take it." The old man said, dropping the key in my outstretched hand and stepping away.

Leaving me alone with a key and a carved woman on a wardrobe, looking at me so excitedly that I wouldn't be surprised if she burst from the doors.

"I suppose you want this," I said, holding it out to her. It would have made perfect sense for her to reach out and grab it seeing as the whole world had gone mad. Instead she moved, stepping to the side and revealing a tiny keyhole.

"This better take me to fucking Narnia," I hissed as I turned the key and let the door swing open.

No Narnia. But there was a silver knife with a ruby in the hilt, the blade already stained with black demon blood.

Somehow, this was better.

20

JARRON

WAKING UP TO THE JIGGLING OF A DOOR HANDLE WAS ONE thing, waking up to a little girl staring at him was another. Especially when the little girl was dressed in the same creepy white dress as the night before. The tiny child was a monochrome phantom at the foot of his bed, and even though the jiggle of the door handle had been what woke him, seeing her standing there sent him jumping straight into the air, howling like a child who had seen a ghost.

As far as he was concerned, there wasn't much of a difference here.

"Pathetic." She snarled, folding her arms over her chest as Jarron settled back into bed, pulling the sheets and blankets over him. He hadn't been offered much in the way of clothes, and what he had been given didn't really qualify as being warm or decent.

"What the fuck are you doing here?" Jarron snarled sleepily, fully aware that the golden fire of his dragon was shining in his eyes.

"That's no way to talk to me," Lilly snapped, shaking her head and narrowing her silver-blue eyes at him. She even gave an attempt at a smile. "Not when I have come to deliver good news."

She seemed way too chipper for the girl he talked with the night before. There was less murder in her eyes, which meant there was less trust toward her on Jarron's part.

He narrowed his eyes at her, waiting for her to continue. She only leaned against the footboard, staring at him with her arms folded over her chest, tapping her foot against the floor.

"Aren't you going to ask me what it is?" There was the hostility that he had been expecting.

"Is it Elliot?" The murder in her eyes made an even grander appearance at that, the silver slashing through the air as she glanced at the door handle. The thing was no longer jiggling, he wasn't even sure if it had been, but Lilly seemed pretty pissed about it.

"Is Elliot there?"

"No!" She hissed, hair flipping as she spun back to face him, the daggers in her stare pressing Jarron against the ornate headboard. It would be really helpful to have iron bed sheets right about now, her glare might as well be made of real daggers and he would really like more of a shield than thin cotton bed sheets.

His dragon quietly roared at that. Understandable. Neither of them really liked feeling as useless as they did in that moment.

"*Elliana*, is cleaning herself up after a rather unfortunate episode." She chuckled at some unknown joke. He jerked, his muscles flaming in pain at the subtle movement.

Oh god, everything ached. And if everything ached for him, he didn't want to know what kind of condition Elliot was in.

"Is she okay?" Jarron's thundering question cut through

the tinkling insanity of her laugh, cutting it short and sending her back into a glare. Although, it was clear she was trying to look as sweet and demure as she had when he had first seen her.

That illusion was already broken.

"She is fine. Henry has helped her."

Jarron cringed at the name, half expecting the demon to come barging into the room at the single word, perhaps that's who was jiggling the door handle. But nothing happened, nothing beyond Lilly's frightening smile making a grand return.

"Well, good." It was lies, and she clearly didn't believe them. Although, it would be really great if the kid would stop smiling at everything he said. With a look like that she was going to either swallow her face whole or devour his soul.

He wasn't interested in either.

"I brought you clothes," Lilly said, thankfully moving away from his false joy at that damn demon being anywhere near his mate. He would be more concerned if he didn't know that Ellie could take care of herself. "You can change there."

Lilly motioned to the old accordion room divider tucked beside the iron maiden and the carefully folded clothes on the bench beside.

Great. Nothing in that pile looked either attractive or comfortable, but it's not like he had another option. There wasn't a dresser in here and he highly doubted that the iron maiden held the secret to stylish and attractive clothing. He was clearly expecting too much from the cave.

"Okay, give me a few minutes--"

"I'm not leaving," she cut him off, an unsettling light rippling from her eyes. That was not a good look for a kid, not even a freaky ass kid like her. The light flashed as the silver tips of her hair lifted before she turned from him, arms still folded against her chest as she faced the door.

Like that somehow made the whole thing any better. Objections weren't going to get him anywhere. Best course of action is to bolt his ass into those clothes and hope that they fit even a little bit. He didn't want to think about where they came from, and the lumberjack was smaller than him.

Wrapping the sheet around his waist, Jarron hightailed it to the stack of clothes and the flimsy, mostly transparent barricade.

Judging by the strangely baggy boxers he was provided this wasn't going to be an enjoyable fashion day for him. His balls may enjoy a bit of breathing room, but this was approaching full on commando status.

Whatever. He quickly changed out of the shredded boxer briefs for the cartoon printed circus tent and moved to the pants. Until this moment he had assumed that society had forgotten about corduroy. He was wrong.

"Do you know my mother?"

He nearly fell into the flimsy room divider at the tiny voice in the question, the soft voice nothing like what he would have expected from the beastly girl on the other side of the room. Jarron peeked around the edge of the barrier to check, but no one else was there. Just the girl in the frilly dress staring at the door with her back to him, although she was no longer folding her arms, she was picking at the hem of her dress in obvious nerves.

Odd seeing as last night she seemed ready to crucify the woman who had given life to her.

"I think I do," he spoke loudly, still peeking around the flimsy barrier to watch her reaction. She tensed, her fingers knotting into fists around the lace. But she didn't turn, or burst into flames or start raging about bastard unfit magic.

He wasn't foolish enough to barge into this with too much hope. But this was the exact thing he had hoped for last night. He was going to dive in face first. It may come with a higher chance of being burned, or beheaded, or whatever the girl was capable of. But it would be worth it for Callay, if only to say he tried.

"She worked with me and my brother for years," he plowed on before she had a chance to respond, careful to choose his words. She may have been assigned to their household, but he knew as well as Killian did that they didn't treat her as the slave she was supposed to be. The title didn't seem to fit. "She is one of the most powerful Fae I have ever seen."

Laying it on thick wasn't going to help him in this case. Yes, Callay was kind and gentle and one of the funniest and most caring people he knew. Behind Elliot of course. But Lilly didn't care about any of that, so power it was. And Callay was the most powerful Fae he knew of, so he wasn't lying. And thankfully, Lilly didn't try to fight him or start spouting about weakness, so it was a bit of a win.

He ducked back behind the barrier and finished pulling on the pants, that while they fit, were easily the ugliest thing he had ever worn. Well, perhaps not as ugly as the shirt that had come with it, the orange and brown plaid perfectly matching the pants and featured a lapel that flared about as wide as the bell on his super swanky pants.

Great. Disco had gobbled him up and spit him out.

"If she is so powerful why hasn't she come to fight my keeper for me?" The question followed him out from behind the screen, the girl turning as he emerged, clearly trying to hide a laugh at the clown that he had become.

He didn't blame her for the laugh that burst out of her, but he had other things on his mind, like the fact that she hadn't referred to the demon by his name when the word had come so easily before.

"Your keeper is strong," Jarron was careful to keep his voice level as he slid his feet into the provided, and equally as ugly shoes. He had to find a way to answer this that didn't reveal that she was a slave with her soul bound to a cave in Italy. He doubted that would go over well. "He has kept her away. That's why she sent me to find you. That's why Elliana is with me."

Lies and half-truths. They poured from him as easily as they had for so many years, they stained the dress she wore and splashed against the shoes he was wearing as though they were nothing more than vomit. Vile word vomit. He had even used the name they had given Ellie. It stung his tongue.

The thick leather soles of his out of date shoes hit hard against the stone as he approached her, watching for any sign of disbelief or anger. There was only a gleam so strong he wasn't sure if she was going to cry or throw herself down on the ground in a fit not unlike the children do when learning to shift for the first time.

He certainly hoped that she wasn't about to do that. Even if she could. This child becoming anything larger and more dangerous would only spell death for the lot of them.

"She wants you to take me back?" She was still tugging at the hem of her dress, her hair lifting as her magic swirled around her. He wasn't sure if that was a good or a bad thing.

Best to keep charging forward, get as much out before she explodes.

"Of course. That's why we are here. Why we are facing--"

"No!" She suddenly snapped, jerking as the dark light

flashed in her eyes and the scowl replaced the momentary awe.

"No?"

"No. You can't do that. Any of that. Let's go," Lilly said abruptly, cutting him off and trying to force a bit of a hard edge into her voice and sounding too much like Callay in the process. At least she didn't explode.

"To Elliot?" He already knew the answer, but a guy could hope.

"Soon. Right now Henry needs your help with something. I guess something got destroyed and he needs help building a replacement." He expected her to smile with the haunting grin that normally accompanied her cryptic statements, but it never came. Instead she stared at him, biting her lower lip before turning and escorting him into the endless hallway of doors.

As if Lilly wasn't freaky enough, she goes off and looks at him like she is actually regretting something. Like she has a soul.

Wonderfully dangerous.

Stepping slowly behind the girl, he followed her into the hall, already trying to plan an escape. There was no way that this was going to end well.

The door across from him was pulling both him and his dragon toward her. He knew she was there, maybe there was a chance that he could grab her and they could find a way out of here. Maybe she had figured out how to do that teleportation thing. Traveling or whatever.

It was worth the risk. Before he could take one step, Lilly's tiny hand wrapped around his forearm, pulling him toward the cursing and breaking glass that was echoing from a few doors down.

"It will end badly if we don't go." There it was again, the scared little girl, looking up at him with wide eyes.

"Then let's don't go." He whispered, bending down to look at Lilly, her silver irises shaking with something that he wanted to believe was fear. "Let's get out of here. Get to your mother."

Wrong choice. Anything that he had thought was fear vanished in a flash of hatred and malice so strong it made the silver in her eyes spark scarlet.

"It's the only way out. It's your only way out," she snarled, pulling him toward the door, toward the growls of a demon and away from the place that his dragon really wanted to be.

The place he was starting to doubt he was going to see again.

Not that he wouldn't go down without a fight.

21

CALLAY

Xi had told me to keep an eye on Fallon and I was.

Technically.

I may be tied to a post in Ceres' freaking doom chamber, but I could still see her and her ugly beady eyes. She was staring at me as intently as I was staring at her. I hadn't failed yet!

Yes, my legs were tied to the post and I really couldn't move thanks to this really uncomfortable rope that was going over my shoulders and between my boobs like I was in a bad bondage shoot. Which would actually make this is a really bad situation seeing as the post I was tied to faced Ceres propaganda mural, and the three people who might as well have stepped out of the twisted visage of a Fae genocide directly behind them.

Fallon's beady eyes weren't the only ones that were trained on me.

Her stare joined by Parris and Dabria.

The two girls flanked the vampire, clinging to him like the vapid girls they were. If they weren't staring at me with glares that would be better suited on the devil they would be running their fingers through his hair. Giggling. Maybe trying to get in a little nonchalant grind in between murderous proclamations. Well, maybe Fallon on the grinding, Dabria was already there, her ass jiggling more than usual as she tried to mold herself to the vampire.

The only good part about this was the fact that Fallon and Dabria really seemed to hate each other and had hissed, glared, and ridiculed each other enough that even Parris was pissed off.

It was like watching a twisted supernatural soap opera, complete with the decrepit grandfather in the background that was drooling, possibly drunk, and would emerge from his seat long enough to yell a racist slur and pass some overly loud gas. Although, with how he was yelling I was sure that the old man had lost it.

I guess watching the kingdom you had built crumble around you could do that. Either that or Parris had finally enacted his plan. I didn't care much either way. My problems weren't with the crippled man in the corner, they were with the three right in front of me.

If only they hadn't gagged my mouth, I would be spewing insults and every other bit of nonsense at them right about now. Instead I was forced to watch the dramatic rendition of Twilight while I tried to shake off the goo that was covering my hands. That part was vital considering I was sure that stuff was what was restricting my magic.

Hopefully, the thick, cold goo wasn't something else. Because again, ropes between my boobs. Thank god I had worn a thicker sweater today.

Didn't stop Parris from staring at my fucking boobs. Dabria didn't like that and the scowl she was giving me almost made it worth it.

"Two of the four ain't bad," Parris said, finally stepping

away from where he had been whispering and hiding with the two women. Dabria following behind him like a lost dog, although I had a feeling that was more because he was getting closer to me.

I wish I could tell her that I would rather spit on Parris than kiss him, but I was still gagged and bound. I tried anyway, but Parris smiled, clearly thinking that I was trying to threaten him or something.

That part was coming.

"One will come to save you I think, and then it will be easy to draw the other out. Then we will go for the guard." Nothing that the ice man was saying made sense, but I wasn't the only one confused.

"What are you drawing out, Parry? I'm sure I can draw them out on my own. We don't need her."

Dabria was trying to look cool and powerful, while simultaneously attempting to follow the external monologue. It only made her look constipated. But more like she was constipated because she didn't know what was happening to her body.

'What is happening to my ass? Save me!

That time I laughed, earning me a scowl from all of them, and an irritating eye roll from Fallon.

"Mattia and I have been trying to lure that damn Unicorn out in the open since the last time we saw you, when we laid waste to the city, do you really think she's going to show up for one little girl?"

"I'm not little!" I snarled without thinking, the fabric swallowing all of my words and coming out something more like 'I like chicken!'

Which I did, but not in creepy bondage situations.

Dabria laughed with a weird hacking sound that echoed off the stone, but she was the only one. Parris and Fallon continued to glare, Parris stepping closer to me while Dabria tried to stifle the sound of her hacking laugh. Which made her sound like she was choking.

"Do we really have to keep her around?" Fallon went from looking at me, to Dabria. Not that she noticed.

"I've been saying that all along," Dabria's once powerful voice was now little more than a whine against the other two.

"I was talking about you. Fucking whore. When are you going to move on from the cheap screw, Parris? You can do better than this." Fallon snapped with something a little more hate filled than I would have expected from the villain squad, even with the shade they had been throwing at each other.

It only got worse. Dabria screeched, turning toward Fallon and shooting a line of her ice fire right at her mocking face. Fallon only laughed, side stepped, and transformed into a Falcon with little more than a pop, soaring to the other side of the cave and landing on Ceres' head with a caw, and a fart from the old man.

Holy shit! The beady eyes suddenly made sense. The shitty magic, however, did not. Fae were not shifters, so her cock and bull story about having been created or given Fae magic wasn't holding up. Especially when she transformed back to the stringy haired girl and shot a lick of fire at Dabria, this one not anywhere near the gross shed magic I had seen before.

"Holy! Holy Shit!" I screeched, which again, sounded like 'woolly mammoth shirt'.

Parris didn't turn to the fight that was quickly escalating behind him, he stepped closer to me, running his icy finger over the line of my jaw and down my neck as he smiled.

"She will come because this is the only being with the

magic of light that she has willingly created. One of the few that is left. Hasn't Mattia destroyed all the others?" His finger was moving under my shirt now, pricking against my collar bone and sending a shiver down my spine.

I refused to react, forcing my body to remain as still as I could as I let all the hatred I had for the disgusting vampire pour through. He wasn't going to stop trying though, his fingers were moving toward the rope, toward the exposed skin beside it. Freaking bondage.

"All but Suvi. And I guess her." Fallon said with a nod to me as she returned to Parris' side. "We've tried to reach his sister before, but she's got Suvi so closely guarded that every time we get close we lose our men. We didn't know about this one. But again, it looks like she was guarded too. Trapped in the middle of the dragons keep. Smart."

Fallon smiled at me before holding her hand out and shooting another attack of some kind from her palm and right into Dabria who was still trying to attack her, although she wasn't able to get close enough to do anything.

"Please be nice with the distraction, Fallon," Parris whispered as she stepped up behind him, the beady eyed girl still mindlessly attacking the ice dragon when she got too close. "We need her."

Fallon shrugged, "Don't see why, we have this one now."

Between Parris' roaming fingers and Fallon's intense stare I was beginning to question if I was food or some sort of sexual appetizer. Either one was not really going to work for me and I went back to working the goo off my hands.

"Callay will bring us the Unicorn, Fallon. We need Dabria to bring the other ones. She already has a connection with the Phoenix, she can bring her right to us."

"Or you can just wait for her to come kick your ass." I spoke slowly, forming every single word around the fabric that was pulling against my tongue, causing a bit of really sexy drool to drizzle over my cheek.

Fallon laughed again, throwing her head back as she leaned against Parris, clearly staking a claim as Dabria came up on the other side. If I wasn't in such an uncomfortable situation I might be able to enjoy this more. Dinner and a show.

I better not be the dinner.

"I'm sorry, beautiful, what was that?" Parris' finger pulled back up my skin, dragging over my neck and my jaw before pulling the fabric away enough that I could talk. Although now my mouth was a weird combination of wet and dry that was making it hard to form any words.

"Why do you want to destroy the Phoenix anyway? Didn't you create her? Calling her here sounds like the end to a Victorian novel, the creator's monster destroying the creator. I mean I would like to see that but--"

The gag was back in my mouth with a growl from the vampire, and an exaggerated eye roll from Fallon. I guess I should have taken the opportunity to word stab them more seriously.

"I didn't create her. I used her to create others. Just as Mattia created me."

"And me," Fallon interjected with a smile, the sugary look those two gave each other was enough to turn my stomach.

"I watched my creator kill her as the city fell. I watched her fall time and time again. Each time she remembered less and less, until I forced her to remember something different and worked with that damn keeper of hers to create an army. An army he thought he was going to control."

It was like he was talking in code and nothing about it

was making sense. And thanks to the gag I couldn't do more than mumble and nod my head, well and try to convey my undying hatred for the three of them with a bit of light in my eyes.

That one wasn't working so well.

What I wouldn't give for even a drop of power right now. It wouldn't take much to throw them against the wall.

Or even better, throw the lot of them out of the window. Ceres clearly wasn't in any shape to transform and I had been fantasizing about that fall for a while.

Back to shaking the goo off and listening to these buffoons monologue like the villains they were.

"Would you like me to kill her?" Dabria pulled their focus as I shimmied, keeping my motions limited as I whipped and dragged my hands one over the other. The gunk was almost gone now and I could feel the tiniest of sparks against my bones.

"No. But I have a better idea," Parris said giving Ceres a nod, as if he was paying attention. "I think it's best to have Callay kill them for us. Light and dark and all that nonsense."

"No!" That outburst they heard, not that it mattered.

Dabria and her pout had been thrown around the room like a rag doll, but now she was absolutely glowing.

"Well, technically, I'm going to kill them," Dabria said with her signature smile, stepping right up to me, until it was only the lavender of her eyes and the smell of ice and cold that always lived around her. "I'll just be controlling you while I do it."

If there was a time to take control of my magic, that was it. The last chance. The sparks were growing, the desperation mounting, but before I could grab hold of anything Dabria pushed her palm against my forehead and everything went cold.

22

KILLIAN

THEY HAD BEEN SITTING AT THE TABLE SO LONG THAT KILLIAN could tell where his palms were laying by the grooves in the wood grain. He could tell exactly where Mattia's spoon was hitting against the glass by the hollow tones that were filling the air. And he was fairly certain that he would never be able to wash the smell of sulfur, ash, and what reeked too much of death from his mind.

He would never want to, not with the power that was inside of him. Not with the darkness.

"Perfect!" Mattia roared with glee, taking another drink before he wiped away the tiny ash creature that was writhing on the table, cawing and shrieking like a baby bird that he had attempted to cremate with his fire. Except this one he had conjured, he had pulled it from nothing, dragged it up from an underworld that felt a bit closer than it ever had before.

With a quick wave of his hand, Mattia returned it to nothing but a fine dust that rained down to the floor. Killian stared at the ashy storm with what he hoped was impassive eyes, he was still supposed to be under Mattia's control after all. He wasn't completely convinced that Mattia hadn't already figured it out, but he was determined to drag this on as long as possible. Learn as much as he could about the magic that was now inside of him and hopefully, find his way out of this mess the moment things turned south.

He was desperate to leave now, but he couldn't best Mattia, not yet. And seeing that the first trick that the tiny Italian had taught him was severing arteries and stopping organ function with a simple thought he wasn't about to go charging out of the door. Not until he taught him a shield, and despite trying to prod the instructions in that direction, they hadn't gotten there yet.

"Those little ash Pickets are perfect for spying and poisoning enemies while they sleep. You can easily deposit them in fireplaces and lanterns and they can remain undetected for days, weeks if the place is dirty enough." Mattia rambled on as he grabbed something else from a large carpet bag that he pulled toward them.

Which, despite the incessant clinking of glass was full of more than empty absinthe bottles. Now that Killian had conjured a perfectly full one he understood why the man kept the bottles around. They were easy to refill when you can control the power from the underworld. Although, why he kept so many bottles when he would just need to refill one he had no clue. But again, the guy was always drinking, perhaps he was always drunk enough that he couldn't part with them.

Seeing as Mattia was, again, taking another large swig of the green liquid, Killian was amazed he was able to sit up straight.

"Can you conjure larger Pickets?" Killian asked, his stomach twisting as Mattia threw yet another infantile animal onto the table, this time a tiny squirrel. The thing was mostly hairless and so drowsy that it could barely stand itself up properly. It nosed around the table and flopped around in such a way that it might as well have been drugged.

"I can. If you had magic, you could call anything by speaking the true language of darkness. But you don't have the strength to do such things as your power is drawing from my own. My magic is swirling around inside of you and has taken hold enough that you can use it, but not in that way. Even if you could I wouldn't suggest you do so. The larger the Picket, the more connection they have to the underworld and the souls that live there. It's easier for them to break from your power and become sentient. You wouldn't want to release a demon in this world would you?" Mattia peered at Killian over the top of his glass, his eyebrows piercing together as his eyes flashed.

"No, Master." It wasn't the first time his look was too all knowing and Killian dropped his head, mumbling in a way that he hoped was reminiscent of his cowering servitude, watching the thick black smoke of Mattia's spell creep over the wooden floor, growing closer to him.

"Good. Because while I can end a Picket, they would run you through. But if that ever happens, it might be good to know this spell." Mattia prodded at the tiny squirrel, the poor thing whimpering and falling to the side. Definitely drugged. "Removing life from something living."

Killian perked up, his eyes wide as he turned to Mattia, almost giving himself away. He probably would have if the warlock had truly understood Killian's fascination and exhilaration over what he had said.

"Yes. Using my power, you will be able to suck the life from those around you. It takes a great amount of strength, but brings an instant death. There are only few in this world that can cast a shield by calling the ash of the underworld around their heart, so it is an easy and effective way to end a life."

Killian was clutching the sides of his flimsy chair now, his knuckles white as the black smoke continued to swirl around his ankles. No wonder the Unicorn had refused to give him the power of light. If this was a great trick of the power of dark then he had no other option than to follow this path. Killian had been able to suck life from a living soul since his dragon had first burst from his bones. It was his dragon's skill, and one he had easily mastered.

The creature was already rattling his soul in its own brand of excitement. Something that was doubled seeing as Mattia had unwittingly explained how to cast a shield. It was the last thing he needed.

"You want me to suck the life out of this little guy?" Killian was really struggling to keep his voice level now.

"Yes, similar to how one would suck juice from a straw. You must find it, grab it, and bring it into you with a tiny bit of pressure." Mattia's eyes were mad, the drunken light that always hovered around him shifting to something that was closer to greed.

He was hungry for this little guy's power too. For his soul.

"You are devouring his soul?" Killian asked, not even flinching when Mattia gave him a nod of confirmation. "If he is magic do you devour that too?"

Mattia's face fell, Killian's hands clutching the edge of the chair until he could feel the hard ridge attempt to break through his skin.

"No. I have tried, but it is not a skill I believe one can master."

But I do. Killian's dragon was growling right alongside him in excitement. *I can suck your power away, too.*

He wasn't foolish enough to try that, not until he could master that shield without Mattia knowing. Trying to suck the power and soul away from a much more skilled warlock who could do the same thing as he, would never be a wise choice.

"Now," Mattia plowed on, shuffling the wandering rodent back to the center of the table and giving him one of his half soaked sugar cubes. "This is a skill that only those with magic of the dark can harness, and one that only I have mastered. I will allow you to use my power to do this, because I feel it will come in handy with what I have planned for you."

He smiled at Killian. It was becoming harder and harder to keep his face screwed up in what he thought was a glazed over mask of servitude. He would give anything to laugh and show the fool how weak he was. Instead, he nodded and gripped the chair harder, he had a feeling he was going to break the skin soon.

Or the chair. It was amazing the flimsy thing was still holding together with the pressure.

"The two powers, light and dark, draw from the two sources: The underworld and the demons that dwell there, for the dark. The heavens and the winged monsters that call the skies home, for the light. But the goddesses can draw from either side, they are equals, which is why they are so difficult to kill. Only light can destroy dark, only dark can destroy light. Only one goddess can destroy another. I need someone of light to finish her off completely. To finish them both. That is where my falcon has gone," He faded off, his finger tracing the bit of wet that dripped off his glass to the table as he stared at the boarded up window. The sound of water and wood squeaked against the crackling of flames, mixing with the howling of wind that was still seeping through the window until the room was growing too loud.

Wind rattled louder. The squirrel cowered at the sound, as if the tiny creature knew what was hidden outside, as if it thought the wind was going to be the one to take its life and not the warlocks towering on either side of them.

Warlock. It was weird to think of himself that way. To think that the darkness of his dragon had been part of something more. More.

"What do you need of me if the falcon is bringing light?" Killian's voice shook with the question, his nerves heightening as the man smiled, as he turned from the window and the dark of the soul swirled over the floor again. Like someone had stirred the pot.

"You are going to bring her to me. You are going to bring them both to me." Mattia's smile stretched as he reached inside his bag again, but instead of producing another animal cursed for death, it was the folded square of fabric from the other night.

Killian's heart moved into a heavy tattoo of thunder in his ears as Mattia unfolded the corners of the packet, revealing the sparkling dust. He braced for the pull, for the universe to swallow him whole as it had last time.

But nothing happened, nothing but a swelling of energy and a bit of tingling that ran over his skin like ice and heat. The shiver came before he could stop it. Luckily, Mattia only laughed, nodding toward the fine black specks.

Black specks that weren't black anymore.

Before the specks had swallowed the world, and drawn all color into them. They were specks of nothing and everything. Black bits of the world. Now they gleamed with every color that he had seen on that beach and every color in between. They were a rainbow of light, a mirror of all the darkness inside of him, and all of the light around him.

"What are they?" He asked again, knowing he was a broken record, but also aware that Mattia had been wiping his memory before now. It seemed like a fitting question, and Mattia smiled at his feigned stupidity.

"They are the last bits of the magic I stole from the Unicorn. They are the last bits of the ash from the Phoenix. They will no longer come to me because I was gifted with power from the horned beast. You are not. You touched them before and awoke their souls. Your touch screamed to them that the horn still exists. Now your touch will bring them right to us. Touch the dust, Killian. Let your soul bring them right to me."

Tension wound over Killian's shoulders, it rippled over his chest and flattened his suit against his broad chest. He already knew that this would not end anywhere near where Mattia was planning. And he hadn't been able to practice that shield yet. Getting out of here was going to take a miracle.

"But the falcon has not returned with the power of light," Killian stalled aware that there was too much of his usual gruffness in his voice. "I am not ready to destroy them."

"Touch them, Killian."

Everything was screaming at him to run, to fly, to destroy this man and return to Elliot and save her. Save her from whatever this monster was planning. But before he could act, before he could move, Mattia reached across the table, grabbed his hand and forced it into the center of the fabric, the colorful specks withdrawing to the edge like polarized magnets.

"I thought so."

23

DRAKE

"How do I defeat her?" Zoe said with a shake of the head, her eyes sliding in and out of focus. "How do I slave the say?"

Clearly, that was not what she had meant to say. First, because it made no sense. Second, because stubborn as she was he couldn't see her wasting an opportunity like this.

She had practically blanked out before from trying to find a question to ask. Now, she was falling face first onto the floor.

"Zoe!" He yelled, racing to where Zoe was twitching on the floor.

White bubbles flowed from her mouth, bright red blood flowing from where her head had impacted against the carved ebony floor.

"Oh my god, Zoe!" Drake knew what to do in a critical situation when climbing, when a mortal would fall and sustain an injury. But a Dragon? Even if he had seen something happen this severe he wouldn't have any idea what to do for her.

She was freaking fine a minute ago. And now she

seemed to be having a seizure, everything shaking, more white foam flowing from her mouth as all fire left her eyes, leaving them white and staring.

"Zoe! Fucking hell!" Did he shake her? Sit her up? Touch her? Unable to decide on any course of action, he instead found himself fluttering around her like a neurotic butterfly. Waving his hands over her, he finally collapsed to his knees as the massive Sphinx came to sit before them, her eyes burning into them as her tail twitched.

"What did you do to her?" Yes, blaming a massive man-eating lioness for injuring his sister may not have been his finest moment. Luckily, she did nothing more than twitch her tail and lower her head to inspect Zoe. Licking her lips.

Like she was ready to eat her. Great. This could not get any worse.

Well, until the massive woman's face began to smile, the bright white line of perfect teeth coming into focus. Drake was preparing to jump over his still shaking sister and lunge himself between the broken woman and the set of overly sharp teeth in order to protect her. Thankfully, the Sphinx leaned back, lifting her head toward the pitch black ceiling, sniffing.

Trapped in shaking panic, he looked up, ridiculously expecting the monsters who had once attacked this place to be circling above them.

Thinking through fear had never been a strength. Even his dragon was ready to explode in his stress.

"Sister." The sphinx said with a sigh, lowering her head and collapsing into a haunch so that she looked like one of those Egyptian statues. Or rather what they had been before centuries of wind and weather had gotten to them.

"Your sister did this?" Drake asked, thoroughly confused

now. He didn't see another of the massive fabled creatures here, and he really didn't want to.

"In a way, although it was not her choice. Zoe is being given something by the choice of another."

The Sphinx was certainly living up to her reputation. She wasn't making any damn sense.

Nothing about this place was making any damn sense.

"So what non-choice is she being given?" He snapped, finally deciding to throw caution to the wind and move Zoe. It didn't seem possible that she could break her neck from such a simple fall anyway. Luckily she didn't moan or seize when he shifted her onto his lap.

But she didn't wake up either. At least the shaking and frightening flow of foam had slowed to a stop.

"What did you do to her? Did you give her something?" It was quickly becoming impossible to keep both temper and dragon in check, especially now that Zoe's eyes were losing all color, her focus drifting into nothing.

"It's a gift." This was beyond irritating, and the beast seemed to know it with how she was smiling, resting her head on her paws. She wasn't licking her lips anymore.

Not that the look in her yellow cat eyes was giving any illusion of safety.

His dragon was ready to lash out in frustration, to face the cat-woman and protect his sister.

"Okay, what gift did they give her?" Thank god his growl didn't find its way out, it was just the snarl of his own frustration. The sphinx perked up anyway.

"You have already asked the world for your answer. Ask this one of her." The sphinx rose from her haunches, nodding toward them in a solemn bow as so many of the dragons in Rydaim had done through his life, before slinking away to the shadows at the head of the cathedral.

"Hey!" Drake yelled, jerking to run after the cat, to demand an answer. He would kick, yell, and even stomp on the massive beast's paws if he had to. But he couldn't shift underneath Zoe's weight, couldn't break free from her grasp, from the white glistening opalescent fire in her eyes.

"Zoe!"

His yell was drowned out by Zoe's own shout. The shriek echoed off the glass and sent a curtain of ash towards the ground, revealing specks of color and something that may or may not have been a face on the pane of glass closest to them. It could have been a candle with the shade of red right above it.

"Zoe?" She jumped to her feet, looking around the hall as if she was searching for something. The Sphinx probably, but the massive thing had returned to stone at the head of the long hall.

"Zoe, are you okay? What happened?"

Instead of answering, she yelled again, although this sound was more of a laugh as she turned to face him, her hands outstretched as sparks of light flicked between her fingers. She had become her own personal Tesla coil. That same opaline fire was in her eyes, either power or madness swallowing her as she stared at sparks that were jumping around her.

Sparks of light. Or magic? Drake was having trouble comprehending.

"Zoe? What is going on?" His voice was shaking now, although his dragon was still perked in a protective stance that was pulling him closer to her.

She finally looked up, the sparks leaving as the flames of her eyes burned into him.

"What happened?"

"I saw her." Zoe said nothing more, she didn't explain,

she just pushed her hands to the side as though she was going to take off in flight.

A rush of wind poured from her, kicking up the dust and ash and the bits of bones that had been hiding in the corner. Swirls of dust pressed around them in their own mini tornado, wiping away the wear and destruction of the city and leaving them standing in the middle of a cathedral that looked nothing like the shadowed ruin they had walked in on.

If Drake had to guess, this was the way the cathedral had looked before the destruction the Sphinx had told them about. His sister had somehow done this. He gave her a look, his jaw sagging as he tried to understand what in the world had happened and what his sister had done. Scrubbing a thousand years of grime from a cathedral was quite the party trick.

That's what he hoped had happened. If she had somehow transported them back hundreds of years before Rydaim had been founded, he might be the one to lose it.

He was already teetering very close to that line.

It didn't help that there wasn't a Sphinx or anything else to ask. The stone feline had returned to its former glory, the perfect representation painted as intricately as the beast they had been talking with. She was built out of the same stone of the building, right up against it. Not walking. Not talking. Okay, there was no question, he was losing it.

That huge statue wasn't going anywhere.

"Okay, Zo," Drake said through the quickly growing fear that was wrapping over his chest. "I need you to tell me what in the world is going on. Because I thought I was going bonkers when I pulled you away from a moving statue, but now I am starting to think that I am too far gone to save."

"I saw her," she repeated, turning to him with a smile, the

words making even less sense seeing as she was looking at him like a love sick teenager.

It was not a look he had ever expected to see on Zoe. Ever. Even when she found her mate she had been stoically unaffectionate. Now, she looked like a mortal who had found religion for the first time. Which was not a bad thing. Just not a Zoe thing.

"I don't understand?" The question was more of a stutter than actual words, he was staring at Zoe, who was still smiling like a teenager. Except she was turning to the illuminated color that ran down the far wall.

The wall of stained glass had sent speckled lights over the floor when everything had still been covered by soot; now the four panels blazed with a million facets of color and images so perfectly created that if he didn't know they were made from glass he never would have guessed. The way they glimmered, the way they shone, you would think that they were real.

That each of the four women were real. Not that they could be. The four panels each featured a naked woman against an ethereal background, each one so perfectly formed that there was no possible way they could exist outside of these panels of glass. Even without looking, Drake could fathom a guess that they were the goddesses the Sphinx had told them about.

Even more reason for them not to be real.

A beautiful Asian woman with long curls of dark hair that shifted in colors and waves that looked more like an oil slick than a color that could exist in real life.

A dark skinned beauty with a short cropped cut and lips that pulled into a pout that anyone not bonded to the love of their life might describe as kissable.

A tanned woman with hip length hair that fell in tawny

curls, the color sparking against the gold of her cat like eyes until he was sure even in glass form that she was looking into him. As the Sphinx had.

He jerked at the recognition, glancing to the massive stone beast, but whatever had haunted the stone had gone. Left them alone with their partial insanity.

Drake whipped around to Zoe, ready to ask if it was the Sphinx she had seen. To demand to know what the beast had done to her. Instead of an answer, he was drenched in ice when he caught sight of the last panel and the partial face he had seen before.

Eyes the color of moss and sky, hair like a flame burst to life, freckles that spread over her pale skin in a million hidden smiles. He had never seen her naked, but he didn't need to see that to know it was her. To have his heart, and his dragon, recognize what he was seeing.

And the goddess that was standing right before him.

"Elliot."

24

KILLIAN

KILLIAN GRABBED THE SQUARE OF FABRIC A SECOND BEFORE Mattia did, doing his best to wrap the gingham around the specks of light and not lose too many of the precious things. He could have sworn he saw a few of the bits scatter into the black smoke that was filling the room, but it was less than if they had still been on the table.

Chairs clattered as they both stood, fabric pressing into Killian's pocket while Mattia upended the table with one blast of darkness, sending lamp and squirrel and bottle of absinthe into the opposite wall where they all converged into a screaming fireball. Paraffin oil and alcohol spread over the wall, over the dresser, over the soft hay-filled mattress and ignited with the last spark of the lantern, turning the left side of the room into an inferno.

An inferno that was spreading strangely slow thanks to whatever Mattia had done to the room to protect it from his flame. They were apt to burn before the room did. Good thing Killian was fireproof, a benefit that would have served him well, if Mattia wasn't fireproof as well.

"I take it she found you then. And you chose to curse

another?" Mattia taunted him with a low rumble of what he surely thought was a growl. The roar fell pathetically short as the growl of Killian's dragon broke free.

Flames of both the wall and the hearth picked up at the sound of the beast, as though they were being pulled to it. Weird. He had never seen that before. But he would take it if it caused Mattia to jump like that, fear burning in the darks of his eyes.

"I cursed no one," Killian said with a step to the left, Mattia countering and pulling himself closer to the still spreading flames. "I gifted light to another."

Mattia tsked before throwing his head back in a laugh, "We all think that. That's why we are gifted with darkness. There is no one who has been granted light. We are all too willing to curse another. We are all too dark already. We are all too hungry for power."

Mattia and his smug ass face. He stood before the flames, reaching back and letting his fingers wind through them, letting the red and yellow ribbons move over his palm and up his arm as if they were a pet. It was a disturbing image, or it would have been if Killian didn't know what was behind it, if he didn't see the magic brewing in Mattia's eyes. If he wasn't pulling the same strength from the flames and connecting to the underworld in the same way.

There was never a better time to master a shield. He hoped that he was controlling and manipulating the ash correctly. He wasn't going to get a second chance with this.

"That's not why I was given darkness at all," He prodded him on, still focusing on the barrier of ash he was building. "I was given darkness because there is already darkness inside of me. There is already power inside of me."

The growl of his dragon rattled the flames that covered the walls, sending bits of burning embers into the air. Ash and flame were everywhere, painting the air, surrounding them with something close to the hell that he drew his power from.

His dragon was ready to burst out of him, the massive creature pressing against his healed body, screaming to shift. For the first time in days he could shift. He needed to cripple Mattia enough that the Warlock didn't suck his life from him while he was attempting to soar through the air.

"There is already darkness inside of you, Killian. You were given darkness for darkness. We do not need to fight. We are both villains in this story; if we work together there will be no stopping us."

"I am not a villain!" Killian roared, the growl of his anger, and of his dragon, fanning the flames over the room. Waist high flames snaked over the floor, closing in on them, and smothering the last of the walls in embers.

Mattia didn't jump, he just smiled, played with the flames that were snaking over him, and threw his head back and laughed.

"Do you really think that you are not a villain?" Mattia taunted, stepping toward Killian and bringing some of the fire with him. The way the ribbons of flame moved over him was too lifelike and Killian stepped back, making sure to keep his pocket and its precious contents away from the warlock.

"Not of this story."

"Oh my dear boy, if you are not the villain in this story than you will be in another. You have always had darkness in you, you have always been a villain, perhaps your fairy tale hasn't been built yet. Why not join me while you wait around? I can teach you a few things and hopefully make your story that much more fascinating."

"There are already too many villains in this story." It was

getting harder and harder to control his beast; the creature was pressing so hard against him that he could feel the scales begin to bulge out of his shoulder blades.

"There are never too many villains, Killian. If you think a story has too many villains then you are a fool. Villains exist everywhere and often outnumber the good. They live in shadows and can even thrive in light. There is never just one villain stalking your perfect little world, and the stories that would have you believe that are lying. There are millions of villains. There are endless depths of darkness, as there are millions of stories. They often interconnect in the funnest ways. And often to my benefit."

"Perhaps I will have to be the darkness that thrives in light," Killian pushed a laugh into his voice, purposely trying to prod him while he locked the last bit of a barrier against his heart.

The wall of ash seemed too flimsy to take anything more than a sucker punch. But he didn't see any other way to build it. No going back now.

"You can try, but that path will only lead to death. You will never be strong enough, never be powerful enough." Mattia leaned in, holding the flame between them as it continued to dance, continue to wave. The face of the demon he was summoning blinked for only a second before it was gone.

Damn it. Mattia was ready to take him down and he had done nothing more than play in ash.

"The true darkness will destroy you, Killian, and the villain who rules over all the others will end you."

"Are you saying there is a super villain, Mattia?" He was still deflecting, although he was stepping away from the warlock in an attempt to pull himself closer to the flames in the blazing hearth, and the fire that had spread from it. "I am sure you fancy yourself as that. Ruling over everyone."

"Not yet. But I will. And when I rule over all the villains, then no one will be able to see the light."

"Seems like an awfully murky outlook." Now it was Killian's turn to laugh, the forced sound loud and prodding as he brought fire into his hand, as he let the magic tap into the darkness that was in him and spark a Picket. "You think you could aspire to more."

"Do not laugh, Killian. It will be your fate if you do not join me."

"Either that, or I'll be the one to end you." Killian stepped closer, watching his enemy's flames grow as the beast he was conjuring in his hand placed its flaming feet against the rough-hewn wood of the floor.

"Have it your way." Mattia snarled as the fire crackled, Mattia's conjured monster bursting to life and lunging toward Killian as a Picket burst from around the dragon, and swallowed the little fire demon that Mattia made with one gulp.

"Ha! Never underestimate a dragon," Killian shouted, bringing the fire around him as the ashen Picket he created continued to charge toward Mattia. Its rounded body rammed at the man who was only slightly taller than it. Its fiery steps burned into the floor as it screamed with smoke and fire, the flames of its hand reaching and snatching at the clothes of the suddenly terrified warlock.

"You fool!" Mattia screamed as he fought at the quickly expanding Picket. "You conjure a devil and expect me to congratulate you? You will not hold your power long."

Mattia sliced the Picket away with the black smoke that was still circling over the floor, sending the thing wailing into a puff of ash that showered over everything, drenching the fire that Killian was attempting to control and sending it dripping in useless globs of grey.

No matter, it wasn't as though Killian didn't have a lifetime supply of fire. Something that Mattia seemed to have already forgotten.

"Such a shame," Killian said with a forced laugh and opening his mouth, sending ribbons of black and green flame right toward the man.

Mattia was barely able to dodge out of the way, sending Killian's flame right into the wall behind, where it blasted a hole in the wooden slats of the inn in an explosion that rocked the already fragile structure. Wood groaned, the floor rocked and sent both of them to the side, and a few more slats of wall tumbling into the storm outside.

Wind and snow rushed around them, pushing through the now gaping wall and whipping at hair, clothes, and the fire that was everywhere. That was devouring everything.

"Seems dangerous up here," Mattia began in that same voice of before. He was clearly going to try to convince him to join the dark side again.

Killian had dealt with about enough of that. He was ready to end this, and seeing as breathing fire was out, and conjuring was still only a work in progress, he had only one other option.

He rushed the warlock and impacted against him like he was trying to move a building, slamming his shoulder into his side and thrilling himself with the sound of a few cracked ribs. Mattia screamed in pain, Killian's dragon leaping in joy as Killian sent Mattia stumbling. The warlock whimpered in pain as Killian rushed back to him.

This time, Mattia was ready for him, although he did not side step. The tiny Italian reached around, grabbing Killian and throwing him over his shoulder, right into the already upturned table. Despite Mattia being nearly half the size of the dragon, Killian hit the edge of the table with a force that cracked a few of his fragile, newly healed ribs and sent him gasping.

Killian pushed himself up with a heave, but before he could even lift his head, Mattia hit his back with an attack filled with as much flame as the room. His muscles curled together, his bones convulsed as though his dragon was being pulled from him.

So, he had underestimated the Warlock. He may not be able to do whatever Mattia had done, whatever was still burning through him. But he could fight dirty.

Rolling over and screaming on the floor, Killian waited until Mattia appeared above him with a grin before kicking up and slamming his heel right into the man's face. Mattia stumbled back and Killian jumped up, the agonizing pain starting to diffuse as he lunged at the man, sending them both into the flame engulfed wall opposite the gaping hole. Wood splintered beneath them, but it did not break. Cracks spread as Killian laid punch after punch on the little man, until he was thrown back with a blast of black. One screech escaped him before he slammed into the stone hearth, a streak of purple light ripping over him and eating away his suit.

He bat away the flames, keeping them away from the precious cargo that was still tucked into his pocket. The flames kept spreading however, heating against his skin as though it was trying to devour him.

He needed to end this.

The floor and hearth below him groaned ominously as he pushed himself to his feet, ready to charge the man who was already heading his way. The floor beneath them shifted again as Mattia was about to reach him. Killian took the opportunity, swinging his hand and knocking the unbalanced man down with a massive fist against a tiny skull.

No magic involved.

Mattia fell to the ground with a gasp, ash and embers circling through the air with the impact and showering over him. Burying him in the destruction that he had caused. A burning tomb. Seemed fitting.

Now to end it.

Killian's spine stretched as his dragon pressed against it, his footfalls heavy as he walked toward the little madman, ready to tear him limb from limb. Stop him from any plans of world conquest that he had.

He had no idea how to end a warlock. But a full dismemberment seemed fitting.

"I'll start with the head." Killian took another step. Just as the floor gave way and the fire that had consumed the entire building sent it tumbling to the ground, the limp warlock right along with it.

Killian reacted the moment the floor left his feet, his body tumbling for only a second before his dragon ripped through him and screamed into being with a roar that echoed through the swirling snow of the storm. Wings flapping in the wind and fire burning in his chest, the screams of both animal and villager pulsed in his wind. The frightened people scattered away from the carnage and rubble below him, and the man that was buried somewhere inside of it.

He had to finish this job. Leaving him with his head still attached to his body was the worst idea he could ever have.

Ready to land, his dragon instead reared up, spitting a line of black and green fire into the sky while his heart pulsed and screamed as the cry of his mate filled his mind, that tight string he had felt so often before yanking him away right toward her.

Mattia's spell had also blocked him from his mate, from the woman who was in trouble and appeared to have been for some time judging by the strength of the line that was pulling at him.

He didn't have time for this, he had to go.

Killian roared in fear and frustration as he dived back to the remains of the inn. Letting the darkness of his fire free he sucked the life of anyone left in the rubble away, letting everything else burn and bubble into nothing but ash and molten lines of iron.

It would have to do.

He gave it one more look, desperate for some sign of movement, some twist of black bone to know that he had succeeded. There was nothing and the cries that were yanking at his heart were pulling at him so violently that he knew he couldn't ignore it for long. Not without creating another victim. Not without allowing her to get hurt.

He wouldn't be the villain. Not to Elliot. Not to anyone. Not anymore.

Even though something was screaming for him to stay, he let out one more roar, one more stream of flame, and turned and soared away.

25

ELLIOT

Screams were echoing through the hall.

Screams that pulled at a thousand memories and laughed in my head beside a thousand failures. I had heard those screams days before and it didn't take much to recognize them.

It took even less for me to know what was going on.

My fingers wrapped around the dagger as I turned, stained blade in hand. The doors to the wardrobe closed on their own, the still frightening carving of myself in the wood removing the key from the lock and holding it out to me. I took it without thinking, sliding it into a tiny gap in the hilt that I didn't know was there.

Well, I did at some point. But not in this life.

In another life, with screams that were just as familiar. Screams that were doing something to me. I was going into autopilot, staring at the door and pulling a long robe out of the side of the cabinet. It was stained with blood and had a loop for the dagger inside the waistband where no one could see it. It already smelled like fire and death.

Death from the last time he had beheaded my mate.

God, this was quite the situation that we had found ourselves in. Let's hope Killian stayed away from this hellhole until I was able to finish this. One of my guys was already in danger. I didn't need to make it a multiple beheading situation.

The thought of Jarron becoming a floating head in a jar was bringing out the rage, my Phoenix was getting all screamy as my skin heated in ripples of energy that I was sure wasn't from the flames under my skin.

Heat that was tugging at my memory. At my magic.

I was ready.

I had said that past me was a stabby individual. Turns out I was as well.

I tied the robe as tight as I could before I took off out my door and down the hall to the open door that was echoing with shouts and screams, the tinkling of broken glass ripping between the shouts.

"There is no dispute, Jarron. You are imperfect. Stop fighting. I will have your head." Henry sounded so logical with his smooth British accent. I would have thought everything was normal if it wasn't for the piece of sink that went flying across the room at the end of his proclamation.

"If you think that is a silver tongue, you dapper demon, then we will have to keep fighting. With my head on my body thank you very much!" Jarron laughed and sent another piece of the sink hurtling over the room, the thing slamming into the wall and exploding like confetti. Confetti that Lilly was laughing and dancing in as though she had something to do with any of this.

She probably did. The former head of my mate was at her feet, leaned against the wall as though she was protecting it.

Everything had been ripped to shreds. The experiment

table was courtesy of me and my run in with the demon, but the couch was ripped and scorched, the television was broken to pieces, plastic and glass scattered over the rug with the dozens of photos that had been torn off the wall with such intensity that there were gaps of stone missing.

"Stop prolonging the inevitable. If you won't give me your head, then shift and I will take the beautiful head of your dragon."

"You will have nothing of ours!" Jarron yelled, his fingers intertwined above him like a club, swinging the large chunk of sink toward Henry who laughed and dodged out of the way with a wisp of smoke, leaving Jarron's fists to crash into the last uncracked bit of marble. It shattered into hundreds of pieces, the shards flying through the air alongside bursts of golden fire. Lilly giggled and prodded at one of the large bits of Jarron's liquid dragon fire that had fallen near where she stood against the wall. But Henry shrieked and dodged away from streaks of gold that were headed his way, evaporating into smoke again, only to reappear on the other side of the busted table and what he clearly thought was safety.

There was no safety when you were facing a dragon with treacherous fire who had no problem burning you to the ground. I saw his fear. Jarron saw his fear, his nostrils were already flaring with white smoke in preparation for taking the guy out.

I smiled to myself, glad I had got here in time to watch his last breath.

And then he stepped back, his bare feet dragging over the stone floor and right into a pool of golden flame that was slowly eating through the stone.

"No, no, no," He pleaded, the smoke billowing around his ankles, smothering everything so that Jarron could only see his eyes. So Jarron couldn't see the trap he was about to walk into.

"No don't!" I screamed, clutching the concealed dagger to my hip as I hurled myself over a fragment of couch and threw myself between them.

Tile, glass, and bits of countertop dug into the soft soles of my feet and I jumped again, hurling myself into the demon. We tumbled down to the ground in a pile, although thankfully my legs didn't go over my head and my robe was still in place. We wrestled in a chorus of grunts until I pinned him below me, dagger hitting against my hip bone.

I wasn't exactly sure what it was about the dagger, but my phoenix was screaming at me not to let the demon see it. Not to let him get it. I clutched the robe around me, or tried to. Henry had already grabbed my wrists and was pulling me closer to him from where I sat, straddling over his hips bones.

I could name a million awkward and terrible things that I had done in my life. Straddling a demon was definitely number one.

"Elliot!" Jarron yelled behind me as I tried to break free of the monster between my legs, but he wasn't about to let go. He was pulling me closer, and closer, and while logic said to head butt the idiot, I had already been down that path and had no interest in a repeat.

"What do you want from me demon?" I asked, leaning closer and letting my hair fall around us like a curtain. I tried to put on some kind of bedroom voice, and I was sure I sounded like a cross between Betty Boop and the bitter beer man, but he didn't seem to care.

Henry smiled with that slick grin that made my skin crawl, picking his head up enough so that he could whisper some sweet nothing to me.

"I already told you. I am not a demon." He leaned closer. His eyes were lingering more on my lips than at the bit of cleavage that was hanging over him, than what I was doing.

"And I am not a fool, Henry. I'm not playing a game."

"Until you choose--"

He didn't get to finish. Because I stabbed him in the neck.

Black blood poured over my hand in a river as he began to gurgle and sputter, shaking underneath me. You would think with all her talk about killing people with a blink that Lilly would have handled the whole thing better, but no, she screamed and covered her eyes.

I guess the violent cartoons she watches hadn't prepared her for Henry's dark black blood spilling over the shattered floor, and his lifeless body sagging below me.

Or maybe it was because I had killed the only parental figure she knew. Oh god, don't let this turn into a fighting-creepy-crazy-child scenario. I already knew I couldn't stab a kid. Plus, I didn't know what was going to happen if I did. Was it a demon knife? Was it my super special dagger made for me by a wizard in Zanzibar? I had no clue, because even though things were coming back, they were still little more than weird shards to a very broken puzzle.

"Lilly?" Jarron asked from behind me, coming around the carnage to pull the focus of the little girl.

Good, seeing as I pulled the knife from his neck and sent a fresh river of blood over the kitchen. Sick. I didn't know it would do that. I mean, I had seen it in movies, but seeing it in real life? No wonder Lilly was freaking out. My stomach was twisting in an upended threat again, which we really didn't need. Fire vomit was not going to help the situation.

I jumped off Henry's limp body and high tailed it toward what used to be a sink, stealing the blasts of water that was creating a geyser from the broken pipe to clean both knife and hands.

"Lilly. Look at me, Lilly," Jarron continued as I scrubbed the blood away, trying to wipe it from my hands but it was like tar. It wasn't going anywhere.

"Lilly. It's okay."

"It's not okay!" She shrieked with all the power of a banshee, the high pitched tone bouncing off the stone and off the inside of my skull like a broken metronome. I cringed, cursing the fact that I had ears as she continued. "You don't know what you've done! You know nothing! Everything is wrong and now we are trapped here."

Very little was making sense through the stuttered gasps of the crying child, her heaving intakes breaking up the words into nonsense. All but the last part.

I slid the still wet blade into the loop of fabric in the robe and raced back to Henry, and to that damn key in his finger.

A finger that was gone. Just like the rest of him. Unless he melted into a puddle of blood, he was gone. Escaped with the bloody footsteps that were leading away from the pool of blood, right toward the freaking wall and the black shadow that was pulsing and growing out of the stone.

"Oh fu--" My scream was drowned by air and smoke as I flew end over end, tumbling through the air and right into the massive painted picture of my Phoenix.

"No! I told you he would come back! He always comes back!" Lilly shrieked as the few remaining lights in the kitchen flickered.

The switch from the willful and obedient psychopathic child was almost as startling as the smoke that was billowing in front of me, the tendrils of black and grey twisting into a tall, lanky, red-eyed monster. He no longer looked like anything close to human. The features were distorted, the limbs too long, the eyes too red, and nothing about him resembled the haggard housewife lumberjack except for the fact that he was still wearing an ugly flannel shirt.

Lumberjack from the depths of hell.

"Shit, you're ugly. I knew you were a demon." Any chance at a verbal assault was swallowed as the bones in my spine slid back together, tendons and muscle snapping back together from where they had ripped in the impact.

Goddamnit! It was all I could do not to scream in pain. And I had thought that shifting into a massive fire bird hurt.

"I told you, I am not a demon," Demon Henry snarled, wisps of smoke bleeding from behind the fire that was burning in his eyes. He really wasn't doing much to plead his case.

"Well, stop looking like a nightmare version of yourself and I might believe you. I might even give you a kiss." I smiled sweetly, even as I was shifting my weight to check that the dagger was still there, the only kiss he was going to get was a blade cutting right across his jaw line.

I think I was understanding why past me was always cutting his face. She was trying to get to his neck. Stabbing it was clearly not enough.

You needed to take the head right off.

Sucks to be me, the blade was gone. Cast off during my non-stop flight to portrait land no doubt. Finding it without tipping him off that I had lost it was going to be tricky, especially with Jarron trying to calm Lilly down in the kitchen.

"I'm a god, you bitch." Demon, or I guess God, Henry snarled, taking a step toward me. I tried to step back but I was flush against the wall. Unless the door magically opened I was stuck. "If you would let your memories come you would know that. I fell from the sky, from the land of gods and sun, to be with you. Only with you. And you should only be with me. That's why he had to go."

He knocked his head toward where Lilly was still crying, but she stood alone, forcing out crocodile tears while Jarron had snuck up behind the God that could have only come from a world of nightmares and slammed a knife against his throat, sliding the shiny silver blade across the smoke elongated flesh.

Silver. Shiny.

Bless his heart, he had grabbed a knife from the kitchen. Close enough, I guess.

I darted forward, grabbing his left hand and pulling at the tips of the fingers until the flesh and bone of one gave way. It looked as if his fingernail was pulling away, stretching until the key landed in my palm. As if that wasn't bad enough, the sliver of bone was covered in blood. And there went my stomach again.

Must keep fire vomit down. Either that or aim it at the monster that was flailing at me to get the key, and grabbing at the dragon who was now stabbing the knife into his chest like this was some sort of horror film.

Except that it didn't look like one. There wasn't a drop of blood. Wasn't a bit of the black fluid leaking from the gash in his neck or the holes that Jarron was hacking into his chest.

No ordinary knife could kill him.

I need that knife. And finding a dagger in a room of rubble and chaos would definitely be a task I would normally give up on.

Lilly was screaming, Henry was laughing, and Jarron was yelling profanity after profanity as he continually stabbed the man who seemed to be growing in both height and bulk.

I didn't have time to solve that mess. I was on my hands and knees, pushing aside bits of fluff and glass that was cutting into my palms, reflecting light and screams and a tiny hint of red.

A glimmer of red, right at the elongated ash covered feet of whatever Henry was.

"A head for a head, eh Henry?" Jarron cackled as the smell of sulfur hit the air, the aroma flooding in a warning before his golden liquid flame spewed from him.

Oh god the knife! Obstacle course of stabby glass be damned, I crawled as quick as I could toward the dagger, grabbing the hilt and pulling it back as the first drops of Jarron's golden fire hit against the floor, burning paper and fluff and swallowing the glass into melty bits of nothing.

I may be a phoenix, but I had no interest in seeing what that stuff would do to me. I crab crawled back quicker than I ever had in warm ups, dagger in one hand, key in the other, right to the little girl who was watching dumbfounded as golden lava poured from Jarron's mouth.

It looked as though Henry was being dipped in gold. The thick lava poured over him, coating every bit of flesh, burning away clothes and bone until he smoked and sizzled.

When he had stepped in a pool of Jarron's fire before he hadn't shown even a flinch of pain. Being coated in it was clearly too much and the man had begun to melt beneath it. His screams were almost as loud as the sizzle of melting flesh as the last of him was melted to a crisp. He collapsed with a hiss, blackened flesh and limbs crumpling one over the other until he looked like a broken accordion.

An accordion that gave one last hiss like something an

old man in an armchair would let out when no one was looking. Smelled like it too.

"Is that it?" Lilly asked, her voice shaking so bad that, she almost sounded like a kid. Almost looked like one too with how she was cowering and pulling at her hair.

"No clue, but I'm going to fucking stab him for good measure." I jumped up, racing toward the blob of demon cave troll that Jarron was standing over, giving both dragon and blob a smile before I plunged the stained silver dagger into what I hoped was the neck of the thing.

It slid in easy, the ruby glinting in the flicker of light before I pulled it out, one bubble of black blood following behind.

"I think that's it," I said with a shrug, knowing full well that I could cheer and whoop and holler in our success, instead I did that thing that you see them do in movies and always think is so weird and cheesy.

I totally kissed the guy.

I jumped into his arms, even though the front of my clothes were covered in black demon blood and I was holding a special demon killing knife. I jumped him, straddled my legs on either side of him and kissed him until he moaned and clutched me against him.

God, he tasted good. Like honey and flame and everything that was beautiful in the world. Even with the goo pile next to us I had no intention to stop kissing him any time soon.

"Please tell me one of you guys have the key?" Well, until the voice behind us shook to life and pulled me right out of Jarron's arms. "I would really like to get out of here. He's had me trapped here for years. And Jarron says he knows my mom..." She faded off, her hands writhing together as she stepped up to us, glass and garbage crunching underneath her perfect baby doll shoes. Although her hair and dress didn't seem quite so perfect and bouncy as they had a bit ago.

She didn't seem so perfect and bouncy. I had seen the shadow of a little girl before, but now it was staring right at me. Her strangled sobs making me think that she might actually be a real little girl. After the last few days we had spent with this kid I wasn't about to trust it.

I pulled away from Jarron, mouth open and finger up ready to make some grand proclamation but Jarron pulled me back, tucking me underneath his massive arm like he had so many times before. I instantly shrugged away. I wasn't interested in pretending to be all weak underneath him. Not like I ever was, but I had just taken down a fucking demon-god.

I was officially proclaiming myself a bad-ass.

"Seems Lilly has been influenced by a certain fallen angel for the last few years," Jarron nodded to the pile of former man, which let off another old man fart.

"Fallen angel?" I mean, he said he wasn't a demon and was instead some kind of god. "God or angels or whatever can't look like that. That's horrifying."

"Can we please leave?" Lilly asked, writhing her hands with greater intensity. It almost looked as though she was going to rub the skin right off. "I don't want to be here."

She looked at that pile again, stepping away as one last blob of blood seeped out of the stab in the maybe-head I had given it.

I was hesitant to say we had won, but getting out of here was going to be the best option. Not that we couldn't take him if we went for a round three, but I didn't want to know what other demon creature he was hiding inside of him.

"I'm with the kid," Jarron said with a chuckle. "I'm in club get the hell out of here."

Placing the dagger in the loop of fabric in my robe, I stepped right to the door and to the tiny keyhole that swallowed the shard of bone without complaint.

Stone groaned as the hinges emerged, the doors sliding apart to the dark tunnel beyond. To freedom, and to a massive boulder of a man dressed in a suit that looked too new for what he had left in.

"Finally!" He roared as the rock slid apart. Looked like he had been trying to break in for a while, and had been through as much as we had been. We may be covered in demon blood, but he was covered in ash and some weird green substance that smelled like an alley behind a bar. He stunk like drunken ass but I didn't care, I flung myself into his arms anyway.

"Killian!" I yelled, as I collapsed into him, his arms barely catching me. "Where the fuck were you?"

"Burning a monster to the ground." He was clearly proud of himself, but I only laughed, pulling away from where I had buried myself in his hair to give him a broad grin.

"What a coincidence, so were we."

Killian smiled back, confusion burrowing in the lines of his forehead as his eyes sparked with the black that I normally only saw when he was really pissed. He must have been trying to get in for longer than I thought.

I was ready to go into the tyrannical story of our adventures and fill everyone, including Jarron, in on the cabinet and everything that had happened. But I hadn't even opened my mouth before Killian dropped me to the ground, staring open mouthed at Jarron and Lilly.

"What the fuck?" Killian asked, pressing me against him

as though he was afraid I was going to slide away. "I know we time jumped, but it hasn't been that long has it?"

"Time jumped?" I asked in confusion, but Killian wasn't looking at me. He was staring from me to Jarron to Lilly and making a connection that didn't exist.

"She isn't ours, Killian." Jarron said, prodding Lilly closer to the massive dragon. So much for looking like a little girl. She had slipped right back into creepy psychopath mode and was giving Killian a look that I was sure was meant to melt him.

"Meet Lilly. Callay's daughter."

"Holy fuck." That was from me.

I had been there the entire time, and even I didn't see that coming. Okay, yeah, psychopath or not we were totally taking her with us. If only to let her momma smack some sense into her.

I didn't know Callay very well. Hell, I didn't know she had a kid. But that I would love to see.

26

DRAKE

"WHAT IS THIS?" THE HIGH PITCHED QUESTION ECHOED around the now perfectly cleaned cathedral, leaving not a rattle of rock or a shake of dust behind. It was only Drake and his panic as he raced to the massive panel of his mate. The stained glass stretched far over his head, the figure of Elliot even more beautiful from here.

Even more like her.

His heart was screaming that it was Elliot. But it was hard to tell in stained glass form. Even if it was possible, and it was decidedly impossible that a perfect replica of his mate would appear in a cathedral in a hidden city that was destroyed thousands of years ago. Panels that very clearly displayed the four goddesses

"This can't be happening." He was fairly certain his brain was about to explode and seep out of his ears at this point. Not that Zoe noticed, she didn't even seem to be aware that Elliot was immortalized in glass, she was staring at the far panel, the one with the beautiful Asian with the oil slick hair.

"Zo, will you look at this?" Drake had to drag himself

away from Elliot's image, he didn't want to leave those eyes, the same eyes that he had been drawn to in the climbing gym so many months before.

But he needed Zoe to see.

Tugging at her arm didn't prompt Zoe to move, she just stared at the beautiful Asian, tears pulling down her cheeks. But they weren't the fiery red tears he had seen before. They were colored like an opal in the sun, gleaming as though light was beaming from inside of them. Yet another impossible thing to add to all the impossible things in this place. The tiny drops of salt water were probably reflecting the colors in the goddess' hair.

Goddesses. Again with the brain melting. Nothing had been normal since they had arrived here, and the last few minutes had been the worst. They really needed to get out of here before they lost it altogether.

"Zoe, I think we need to go." he tugged on her arm again, and thankfully this time she turned. "You're not making sense and something weird is going on."

His heart tensed the moment he had allowed his dragon into his voice and his silver laced words drifted through the air to his sister. Forcing her to follow him.

Too late now. They needed to get out of here and with the way both Zoe and the world was turning into an ice coated madness this might be the only way. He turned, expecting her to follow, but she stood in the same place, smiling.

Well crap, it didn't work. She was going to be pissed.

He braced himself, ready for some playful smack upside the head.

But she didn't do more than smile at him before turning back to the mural. To the beautiful Asian who thankfully wasn't moving. He had to double check, none of them were.

Didn't mean they were on the safe side of whatever insanity they were inhaling down here.

"Zoe, we really have to--"

"I saw her. The Unicorn. I never would have guessed, so many years." Her rambling was like listening to half a conversation, but half a conversation that was piecing together like a jigsaw in his mind.

"The Unicorn, The Griffon, The Sphinx. The..." He repeated the names of the Goddesses that the Sphinx had told him. She hadn't told them all of them, but she had told them enough. Enough that he could fill in the gaps. His heart froze against the last panel. The one he knew without a doubt. "The Phoenix."

"Yes," Zoe's answer was not helping to calm the twist of anxiety that was taking over him. "The Unicorn called me to her. She was given my name by another. Someone gave me power."

She held her hand up again, watching the little sparks of light jump between her fingertips. Drake stepped back, edging his way closer to the door. Closer to escape. He loved his sister, but if he couldn't pry her out of whatever madness was taking over and locking her in here, he didn't see another option.

He would save himself.

He had done it before, and he would regret it just as he had then. But he had to get out of here. They still had enemies to defeat in a city hundreds of feet above them.

"Who gave you power?" He asked hesitantly, taking another step back. "The Unicorn?"

Another step. He wanted to tell her that Unicorns were fabled, that they didn't exist. But one look at the panel of Elliot and he couldn't be so sure anymore. He had thought there weren't Phoenixes. On Sphinxes. Of course there were Unicorns. Of course there were Griffons.

"Yes?" Zoe asked absentmindedly, still watching the light bounce between her fingers. "No."

He took another step. She was making even less sense than she had been a minute ago. He could come back for her later. Find Elliot... Elliot. The mural glimmered, sending rays of color onto the floor beside him, covering him. Pulling him toward the painted smears of light.

"I have to go, Zoe," he whispered, his heart needing to say farewell, even though his dragon was pulling him another direction. To run.

His silent escape was foiled however, when Zoe jumped and turned to him. Tears and silly smile replaced by the hard defiance that was typically her. Well, almost her, the white fire still burned in her eyes, a light shimmer of color rolling against her skin.

"You're right. We have to go, Drake. I'm really sorry, but this might hurt."

"What might hurt?"

He was too close to her and in one step she reached him, wrapping her hand around his arms and pulling him back to her.

"What might hurt?" He shrieked again, trying to wrangle his way out of her grip. He had enough of this crazy train and his one stop ticket was going in the opposite direction.

Instead, he was sucked into a tight little tube that he couldn't breathe through, that he couldn't move through. With agony that was ripping at his bones and joints that might as well have been torn from his body all together.

It hurt. And he screamed in that pain, his scream echoing against the stone of the cathedral and then in the large hollow expanse of the Forgotten's cave. One minute he was in an underground city and the next he was screaming in utter agony, agony that had vanished as thoroughly as the black onyx city.

"What the fuck was that?" he didn't try to keep his voice down, and every Forgotten that was around them turned, pulled from their task of digging through the remains of their belongings to stare at the two with a weird array of fear, anger, and hooded excitement. One even took a step toward them until she thought better of it and stepped back.

Fallon had clearly done a number on them. Although everything seemed to be silent now, devoid of tiny irritating pixies screaming nonsense about ripping wings off dragons. A thousand feet closer to the surface everything was starting to feel a little bit less like an intoxication infused nightmare. Although his heart and his dragon were shuttering so fast that he was beginning to feel like he was strapped to one of those old vibrating hotel beds.

"I don't know if I am dreaming or going mad. One minute we are in some twisted city and the next--"

"It wasn't a dream, Drake." Zoe interrupted, those same creepy opal eyes staring into him. "Nothing was a dream."

"That really isn't helping, Zoe." He needed to sit down, but finding a suitable chair in the middle of rubble was too much of a time commitment when the world was already swirling away from him.

Instead, he sagged to the rubble strewn floor, doing his best to not curl up into the fetal position. He may be a few hundred years old, but that sounded really comfortable right about now.

"You aren't dreaming. I'll explain everything, I promise."

"Do you know everything?" After the Sphinx and the sparks on her fingers and whatever the hell she had done to him, Drake wouldn't be surprised if she did. Instead, she shook her head.

"But I will."

That was making it worse.

Saying anything in response to that was not going to help, so he closed his eyes and leaned against one of the still standing houses in hope of steadying either his breath or his pulse. Both would be preferable considering that they were both reacting against his dragon in dangerous ways. He didn't need to call his father to them right now, and shifting would be like giving the old man a map to disaster.

The murmurs of some conversation Zoe was having with one of the Forgotten sounded like mumbles against the sound of his pulse, the throbbing now so loud he could hear it in his ears. Moving statues. Sphinxes. Yes, all of that had made him feel uncomfortable. But it was seeing Elliot in the glass that had done him in. It was too impossible for him to wrap his head around.

Immortal or not, it was impossible. Besides, even if Fallon had been telling the truth and she had seen her regenerate there had been nothing about goddesses and underground cities. He needed to see Elliot, to ask her.

But she was gone. Vanished in smoke and flame if the stories were to be believed. He had no way to reach her, even if he could fly.

"This is impossible."

"What's impossible, Drake?" Drake jerked up at the response to his mumble, his heart rate hitting unsafe levels as he jumped to his feet.

Elliot and his brothers were right there.

Right there. He thought about her, and here she was. She was covered in blood, and she and Jarron were dressed as though they had done some exploring in decades long passed. But she was here. He swept her into his arms before she could take a step, before his brothers could stop him.

"Elliot! How did you get here?" He yelled right in her ear, but she didn't even cringe. She just held onto him peppering his neck in a million kisses.

"Traveling," she said between pecks against his jaw, as if that solved it. The half answer only frustrated him more.

He wasn't about to let go of the girl, but he held her at arm's length, his fingers pressing into her shoulder blades as his dragon growled, his eyes flashed, and she smiled. He was supposed to be scary, but she fucking smiled.

"You're so sexy when you are pissed," she sighed. "I missed you."

"Missed me? It's only been a few hours, Elliot." The same frustrated growl of his dragon mutated his words into a snap, and she still smiled, the color of her eyes glittering the same as they had in the window.

"Not for us!" She was still beaming. "Turns out that I pulled us back to a few days ago."

She looked to Killian, who folded his arms and gave a nod, like he was the keeper of nonsense all of a sudden. Probably for the best, with all the ridiculousness that was popping up someone needed to be responsible. The world was back to spinning again.

Killian took a step forward as though he was going to pull Elliot away from him. Wouldn't be a bad idea seeing that standing was difficult. The blood may have dropped out of his head completely, and not in the good way.

"A few days?" Saying it aloud was really not helping the whole blood to toes situation. "That's not possible."

"Turns out it is." She shrugged. How could she shrug? Nothing about this was close to a shrugging situation. "We were trapped with an old mate of mine who happened to be a demon."

"A demon?" And he was down for the count. His legs gave out, he collapsed to the ground, laying flat on his back and looking straight up at the sky and to a pair of silver eyes and white blonde hair that looked too familiar.

"Were we all dragged back in time?" He asked in a low monotone. "Because I'm sure I found Callay."

"I'm her daughter." The girl said it as if she didn't believe it herself.

"I am either losing my mind or the world has gone on its head." Drake threw his arms over his eyes, blocking everything out until he was trapped in the dark with only the sound of his heartbeat.

"Killian and I will go find Zo. See if we can track down Parris so we can finish this once and for all. Come on, kid." The silver eyes of the girl smiled before following after Jarron's voice. The cavalcade of thunderous footsteps pulling against the rubble Drake was laying on and making everything sway and spin.

Maybe he needed some water. Or a good stiff drink.

"Are you okay?" Ellie asked, her voice soft from above him. Her touch was tender as she pried his arms away and looked over him, her fingers intertwined with his as she laid by his side.

"I'm not sure. Are you a goddess?" He really hoped he wasn't imagining the tension that wound against the arm he was pressed against. As quick as it was there, it was gone, and she shrugged.

"Probably. I've had an interesting couple of days and I am starting to think anything is possible."

"I am starting to think I'm going crazy."

"You aren't going crazy," she was clearly trying to push a

laugh into her voice, but it was only making his dragon snarl more, the creature ready to burst out of his skin and hide amongst the rubble.

It was a foolish idea, but it made him feel safer somehow.

"I think I was attacked by a fountain." Saying it aloud did not make him seem any saner. Instead, he was questioning why he was scared of such ridiculousness in the first place. The accompanied groan echoed over the wood of the house beside them, and Elliot chuckled, although the sound was nowhere near mockery.

"I had a conversation with a hooded man that lives in an ancient mirror." She shifted against the rubble they were laying on to face him, her hand over his chest.

"I had to answer a Sphinx's riddle or she would eat us. I answered correctly."

"Obviously." She turned her head and gave him a smile and knocked against him, the smile fading almost immediately. "I was apparently in a forced relationship with a fallen angel-demon-thing that cut off the heads of at least seven of my former mates and would have cut off Jarron's too if I hadn't found a secret knife in a cabinet that was carved with a naked figure of me that moved."

All he could do was stare at her, neither of them smiling, neither of them really wanting to detail all that they had seen. With the look Elliot gave him and the pain that was growing in his heart, everything didn't seem quite so large anymore.

"I think you win."

"I think you're right." She smiled, the bright red flame of her fire sneaking over her eyes as her skin heated against his. He leaned forward, suddenly desperate to feel her lips against his.

To taste her.

"Okay love birds, get up," Killian said with his usual snarl, kicking against the ash covered sock and sandal of Drake's left foot. "We know where they are. And we might have a problem."

"Unless it involves going past an all you can eat buffet on the way to vampire slaying then I don't want to hear about it," Elliot mumbled, curling herself into Drake's side more.

He wrapped his arms around her, pulling her closer, desperately hoping for one more moment that he could pretend things were normal. Unfortunately, the darkness in Killian's eyes, and the shadow that was passing over his face, was very clearly not going to allow that.

"If that's the biggest problem we are facing, then count me in," Jarron grinned, bouncing up behind Killian.

Drake had always been the smaller of the three, but having those two tower over him was only making it worse. Add an elegant Zoe who was now chattering to Callay's kid and he might as well stay down here forever. A mortal among giants. The idea made him smile, which seemed to only ignite Killian's anger more.

"No buffet, dipshits. They are up in the tower room. All of them. Parris, Dabria, and that bitch who seems to think she can defeat us all." Killian paused, swallowing something that looked too much like fear. Today was getting odder by the minute. First Zoe is crying and now Killian is afraid.

This did not feel as though it would end well.

"They have Callay," Killian continued with a low growl. "And I would rather get her away from that bloodsucker before he does anything else to her."

"I call the vampire." Lilly said, snapping her fingers and replacing the frilly dress she wore with something more combat ready. Although, the leather skirt and bright red leather vest seemed a little too anime.

"This will be no place for a kid," Killian barked, helping Elliot off the ground and pulling her right into him.

It was irritating the way Drake's dragon growled in ownership, but it was also normal. Drake would happily take that normal over the battle they were going to go into.

"Okay He-man," Lilly snapped, stepping right up to the prince, even though she only reached his waist. "If you think you can keep me away, then you are dumber than you look."

The two were caught in a standoff, but Jarron only laughed, stepping between them as he had so many times with Killian himself.

"She's coming, but only because I know what she can do. And it might be fun to scare the shit out of Parris before this is all over."

Ellie, Jarron, and Lilly might be smiling, but Drake was suddenly wishing the only thing that waited for them was an all you can eat buffet. With the scowl of Killian's face, he wasn't the only one.

27

HENRY

REGROWING BONES WAS THE HARDEST PART.

The stretching and snapping of the hard tissue burned in an agony that he hadn't felt since he had first chosen to fall from the heavens. It ripped over his body and made him nothing more than a useless mass of flesh for hours, forced to watch the water from the faucet spill over the floor as he waited for the flimsy human body to return.

This time it was his own fault, really. It was clear the way that Elliana used the knife that she didn't remember how to wield it, how to end the life of a fallen angel. A demon as so many in the mortal realm prefer to call him. He wasn't sure how she had found the knife seeing as she had no idea how to use it, this version of her was more stubborn and bull headed than he had seen in a century. He had fed into that, showing her something closer to his true form so as to take control of her.

Somehow, she was able to outwit him anyway. He wasn't sure how as it hadn't happened. He would make sure that it didn't happen again.

Being so close to his true godly image had weakened

him enough that he hadn't been able to call on the shadows of the heavens to revive. And by the time he had, they had gone.

Taken everything that mattered with them and leaving him nothing but rubble.

His home was destroyed, the lab smashed to bits. The most intact of the heads of Elliana's mates turned to nothing but a bit of fluid and bone. Luckily he had something resembling a backup, and knew where he could get a brand new specimen in a few days' time.

She may have escaped, but following her would be easy. Then he would take what was his.

Heads and birds alike.

Bones and tendons snapped loudly as he pushed himself to standing, leaning against what was left of the couch and the buffet cabinet they had bought in Tibet nearly eighty years ago. At least that wasn't harmed. It was one of two things that had survived her fool headed assault, the other being the massive painting of his love.

The one he had painted when he had first seen her cut through the air from the heavens. The first of the fabled goddesses he had ever seen. It had been in that moment that he knew he needed to fall. That he needed to descend to earth and make her his. Centuries ago she was, she had relinquished her role as Goddess to be with him. She had loved him.

He still didn't know what had changed, but he was determined to get back there. To make her remember what she was and why they belonged together.

Storming out of the ruins of his home, Henry charged into the eternal hallway he had built to trap the bastard and his head. Not that it did any good. With one snap the doors pushed together like an accordion, smashing thousands of identical doors into five. Four perfectly exact, and one so expertly carved into stone that he was sure the child didn't know of its existence.

They had taken it, and he would need it back. The child belonged to no one but him. It was another thing he would have returned to him. Another thing for which they would pay for taking.

Mumbling to himself, Henry pushed through the stone door, grabbing a wooden crate and filling it with beakers, Bunsen burners, and what remained of the head he had procured before Jasper. Karl if he remembered correctly, not that he had allowed the man to stay around Elliana long enough to commit his name to memory.

It's not as if the name mattered. He needed the power she had left behind when she had mated herself to the poor bloke. She was a goddess and her mates filtered that power off her. He filtered it off them and made himself stronger. Made weapons and potions to bring Elliana back to him.

He would need them now.

With the empty house he didn't even bother to close the doors, just slipped the last of the supplies into the box and charged back into the kitchen, hoping he could find enough of his supplies to finish the procedure he had begun last week.

He didn't get more than a few steps into his home before the box fell to the floor with a clatter and the last head was as lost as the one before.

"What the fuck are you doing here?" Henry's still growing bones threatened to splinter as his arms lengthened, his weakened state pushing him right back into the offensive and into his true form.

"I could ask you the same thing," The shorter olive skinned man said, his voice laced with a deep accent. Not that Henry could hear it over the clatter of glass as the man kicked it with his shoe.

He was dressed far too nicely for a mortal in this part of the wood. The few mortals that had found their way into his cave had been dressed in mountain gear and had enough food and supplies for a month. Henry had eaten them in quick manner. The MREs would hold, after all. Human flesh, not so much.

"I live here," Henry snarled, trying to size up the man who was still wandering around his home, picking up bits of his life and kicking at what was left of Jasper's head.

"Like this? I would expect better for a fallen angel." The man gave him a low smile before continuing his excursion of the room. Henry however, froze. Not many could define his origination, let alone that quickly.

Most of the time he could define the power in his enemies, but he couldn't get a read on this guy. Other than that he shouldn't be here. Didn't matter, he would taste fine either way.

"Do you know many fallen angels?"

"No," he said with a grin, turning in place before freezing, his back stiffening as he faced the painting of Elliana's phoenix. Henry really didn't like the way the man was looking at her, hate and lust was dripping from him in a way that should strictly be reserved for him.

"The Phoenix." Awe was adding to the lust in the older man in ways that was making Henry's spine prickle. "Do you know her?"

"She's my wife." What was the harm in telling this man the truth if he was only going to eat him in a few minutes anyway?

"I take it she did this?" He didn't even gesture around him, he was only staring at the picture. Henry was one step away from destroying the thing just to stop him from looking at it with such eyes.

No one looked at his mate that way. Perhaps he wouldn't eat this man, perhaps he would use his head before he could replace it with the one he really wanted.

"Her and her boyfriend." The darkness in his laugh was too close to the surface now. "I'm preparing to leave. To make them pay for what they have done."

"Wonderful." The short man clapped his hands together, sending the room into disarray with the motion, stone and glass repairing itself as a black smoke very similar to his own stretched over the room.

Magic that Henry hadn't seen in centuries.

"You have been gifted." There was no hope in disguising the awe in his voice.

"I'm Mattia. I'm hunting the Unicorn. I believe we can help each other."

"I'm Henry. I believe we can."

Death of the Demon is Coming
Get it at a Special Pre-Order Price

Flight of the King, Book Three

Flame of the Phoenix, Book Four

Death of the Demon, Book Five

The Dragon Queen Series

Rising Flame (coming March 2019)

Books 2-4 TBA

THE OTHER WORLDS

The Through Glass Series

Book One: The Dark

Book Two: The Blue

Book Three: The Rose

Book Four: The Cut

Book Five: The Light (Coming 2019)

Book Six: The Ascended (Coming 2019)

Of River and Raynn, The Series

The Catalyst: Act One (Rereleases 2019)

The Requisite: Act Two (Coming 2019)

ABOUT THE AUTHOR

Rebecca Ethington is an internationally bestselling author with almost 700,000 books sold. Her breakout debut, The Imdalind Series was cited as "Interesting and Intense" by *USA Today's Happily Ever After Blog*.

From writing horror to romance and creating every sort of magical creature in between, Rebecca's imagination weaves vibrant worlds that transport readers into the pages of her books. Her writing has been described as fresh, original, and groundbreaking, with stories that bend genres and create fantastical worlds.

Born and raised under the lights of a stage, Rebecca has written stories by the ghost light, told them in whispers in dark corridors, and never stopped creating within the pages of a notebook.

Find me online
www.rebeccaethington.com
contact@rebeccaethington.com